PRAISE FOR

Maternity Leave

"*Maternity Leave* is the laugh-out-loud funny novel
you'll beg all your 'mommy' friends to read."
—Julia Fierro, author of *Cutting Teeth*

"Those first few days after you've popped out your brand-new baby
are epic, and author Julie Halpern depicts this roller coaster with wit,
warmth, and authenticity in her novel *Maternity Leave*. Edgy yet still
breezy, this novel flies by faster than those weeks on maternity leave.
Read it with a baby on your boob for relatable belly laughs."
—*PARENTS Magazine*

"Hilarious and perceptive."
—*Library Journal*

"It is exactly what its title suggests: the story of _____ ity
leave, of coming to grips with that all-_____ _____ning
few weeks after the arrival of _____ _____o
did not love their child's infan_____ _____.
—*New York T_____*

Maternity Leave

ALSO BY JULIE HALPERN

The F-It List

Have a Nice Day

Don't Stop Now

Into the Wild Nerd Yonder

Get Well Soon

Maternity

Leave

Julie Halpern

SQUARE
FISH

St. Martin's Press ⚓ New York

This is a work of fiction. All of the characters, organizations, and events portrayed in this novel are either products of the author's imagination or are used fictitiously.

SQUARE
FISH

An imprint of Macmillan Publishing Group, LLC
175 Fifth Avenue
New York, NY 10010
macmillan.com

Square Fish and the Square Fish logo are trademarks of Macmillan and are used by Thomas Dunne Books, an imprint of St. Martin's Press, under license from Macmillan.

Our books may be purchased in bulk for promotional, educational, or business use. Please contact your local bookseller or the Macmillan Corporate and Premium Sales Department at (800) 221-7945 ext. 5442 or by e-mail at MacmillanSpecialMarkets@macmillan.com.

The Library of Congress Cataloging-in-Publication Data is available upon request.

ISBN 978-1-250-11850-9 (paperback)   ISBN 978-1-4668-7153-3 (ebook)

Originally published in the United States by Thomas Dunne Books, an imprint of St. Martin's Press

First Square Fish Edition: 2017

Square Fish logo designed by Filomena Tuosto

1 3 5 7 9 10 8 6 4 2

For Ma

"I don't think I've seen that position before." I'm draped over the top half of an L-shaped hospital bed, kneeling spread-eagle and hugging the pillow for dear life. Every time a contraction ends, I'm so exhausted I could fall asleep. The wave begins again, and I scream to my midwife, "Here comes another one!" She presses my back, tells me to breathe, and counts down until it's over. My husband, Zach, stands beside me and tries to hold my hand for support. The bed feels sturdier than he, and the pain is so unbearable that all I can do is grunt my way through the torment while smacking Zach repeatedly in the shoulder. I can't tell if it helps relieve my agony, but something about inflicting damage to the man standing helplessly next to me while I attempt to squeeze a human life out of my vagina is comforting.

Another contraction, and the baby is still inside of me. "What the fuck is taking him so long?" I can't stop swearing and whining. This is not how I envisioned the bad-ass, warrior-woman, refusing-all-pain-meds birth I chose. It's not that I want an epidural. The thought of someone coming at me with a ginormous needle and sticking it somewhere I can't see terrifies me, as does the complete loss of control. Friends tried to sell me on the idea, claiming they could barely tell they were pushing and their births were like cocktail parties. I can't imagine not knowing what's going on down there, no matter how much pain there might be. And holy fuck is there pain. Take the most intense menstrual cramps you're ever had, multiply by seven thousand, and add in fifteen hundred cans of cabbage to gas up your stomach. Then shove a two-ton poo in there that refuses to come out, and that's essentially how I feel right now.

"I'm going to puke! I don't want to puke!" I shout. The thought of puking in public paralyzes me, and even though I'm buck naked, save for an Olivia Newton-John–style headband in a weak attempt to catch my flop sweat and a monitor belt strapped around my enormous belly, I'll still be mortified if I puke.

"It's okay if you puke. Go ahead and puke," my midwife advises me. I don't know how she stays so calm. I guess it's years of practice combined with the fact that there's no one inside of her hanging on for dear life while she does her damnedest to kick him out.

"Focus on Doogan. Here's his picture." Zach shakily shoves a photo in my face of our cat, Doogan, a sweet and fluffy half Siamese whom I'm supposed to use as a focal point during each contraction. Somehow, someone believes, focusing on Doogan will make me forget the extreme situation attempting to rip apart my body.

"Doogan's soft fur . . . Doogan's soft fur," I chant to my-self. This purportedly takes away the pain? "It's not working! It still fucking hurts!"

I swore I wouldn't end up in the traditional birthing position, opting for squatting, walking, dangling . . . Hell, I spent an hour sitting on a shelf in the hospital shower, letting the warm water wash over me as I tweaked my own nipples in order to stimu-late contractions. An hour is a hell of a long time to both en-dure the pelting of shower water and fondle oneself, so to alleviate the boredom I asked Zach to put on a Pandora station. Alas, the hospital Wi-Fi gave out, and I was stuck giving myself titty twisters to the dulcet tones of a Bob Dylan CD left in Zach's laptop. A hard rain's gonna fall indeed.

Minutes or hours later, time stretches like my belly, and I'm on my back, too tired to hang on to the bed. The midwife and nurse are camping out near my wide-open spaces when another contraction rumbles through me. They've now got me pulling my own knees toward my head while simultaneously pushing out the baby and holding my breath. It's brutal. I feel like I'm drowning. Anyone that tells you you can prepare your body for birth is a royal asshole. Unless there's a woman out there shov-ing a cantaloupe up her hooha in order to practice preenacting the art of expelling a baby's head, I don't see what I could have done to make this more pleasant.

I weighed all of my birth options the second my pregnancy test glowed positive. Should I go the Bradley route? There were too many classes involved. How about a water birth? I envisioned parts of my body shriveling to a raisinlike consistency and a bathtub never providing solace again. I considered a home birth but nixed the idea when I realized it meant I'd have to clean the house before and after. Plus, my grand old age of thirty-six puts me in the higher-risk birth category. Zach and I chose to go with a midwife at a hospital, as natural a birth as possible while still surrounded by beeping sterility. I diligently typed up a six-page birth plan, and we perfectly timed the pregnancy and birth to give me maximum maternity leave with the baby while not taking extra time off from my job as a middle school English teacher: twelve weeks until the end of the school year plus twelve weeks of summer. And voilà: Here I am, bearing down and pooping out a kid.

"Why isn't he out of me yet?" More whining. I wish someone would just pull the damn thing out. Can't somebody find a pair of barbecue tongs and yank him out by the head? Don't they do that?

Zach rounds the edge of the bed and chants next to my midwife, "We can see the head! You can do it! You're doing great!"

How am I doing great? The baby is still inside me, and now Zach can never unsee the bloody massacre of a vagina he used to covet.

I try shooing him away with my arms, but no one is looking at my top half. All eyes are on ol' Betty Sue (a nickname for my vagina that most certainly will never be used again under any sexual circumstances). Another five rounds of pushing, and I don't think I can muster the energy for another go.

"What the motherfuckin' shit hell is going on?" I groan. "Why isn't he out yet?"

I'm guessing the midwife has heard it all, but I also feel like people who use midwives and have natural births are supposed to be weeping organic tears of joy and proudly shouting womanly affirmations, not slapping together random strings of profanities that pop into her sweat-soaked brain. It's hard to feel empowered when I'm pretty sure I just took a crap on the bed. "Zach! Get away from there!" I yell as my last morsel of mystique lies somewhere on the white sheet.

"You're doing great, Annie!" he cheers, belying the look of panic and attempt at hidden disgust on his face.

"You've got this. Big push now. Come on." The midwife and nurse count me through the moment they call "crowning," which I can only assume describes my overstretched labia making a crown for my baby's massive melon.

It certainly does not make me feel royal.

Finally, that big-ass cantaloupe head busts its way out of my nether regions. Another couple of slightly less grueling pushes, and something wet and floppy slithers out of my body and immediately begins crying. I fall back onto my pillow, the pillow they told me to bring from home that is now covered in hours of sweat and gristle and that I will throw into the hospital biohazard garbage the first chance I get. Moments later, someone plops the baby onto my chest. He squints, not crying but looking extremely rumpled and confused. Bits of viscera stick to his little face. He stares at me with foggy, dark eyes. I stare back at him, wide-eyed and frozen.

"He's okay. He's here," a nurse encourages me. I don't move. "You can hold him while we sew up your tear. It's just a small one." I weakly put my arms around the being who until very recently resided inside my body, and try not to think about the fact that my midwife is sewing a rip in a part of my body that no one should be near with a needle and thread. I concentrate on the baby boy on top of me. The boy who made me nauseated for months, who made my feet look like loaves of bread, and who kept me up night after night with his incessant hiccups that caused my stomach to jump. None of that matters anymore because he is here.

My baby is here.

A human being that my husband and I created just came out of me and is now lying on my chest, really and truly, honest-to-God here, after months of waiting and years of dreaming.

And all I can think is, *What the fuck do I do now?*

1 Day Old

I met a woman once at a baby shower, not mine but one I was pregnant during, who told me that when she had her second baby the nurses asked where she wanted them to put him within her hospital room. She told them to wheel him back to the nursery and give her a sleeping pill. I wish I had the balls to do that. Instead, here I lie next to a baby in a plastic box who, while he may be sleeping, has already mastered the annoying art of mouth breathing. I've been ordered by everyone from the nurses to our mail lady to sleep when the baby sleeps, and after my recent entry into the vag Olympics, I would have thought I'd be too tired to do anything else. But it's four A.M., and on one side of me dozes my husband in a pleather Barcalounger and on the other side is the new baby I ordered whom we call Sam, and it's all rather terrifying. I can't hold him without the fear of dropping him, change his diaper without panic of breaking off his limbs, or breastfeed him without abject terror due to the horrific amount of pain it's causing me. People like to joke about babies biting boobs, yet this guy has no teeth and my nipples are going to start retracting if he doesn't figure out how to latch correctly.

What am I doing wrong? What happened to breastfeeding being this natural, instinctual ability that I share with my earliest, primitive ancestors? If I were alive thousands of years ago, I'd have to give my baby to a more accomplished Neanderthal while they threw me out of the rock cave to fend for myself. The hospital is pushing the formula angle hard. They sure don't waste any time making me feel like a failure. A lactation specialist is supposed to come to my room later today. Hopefully she'll figure this out. I hope it's a she. Are there male lactation experts? Pervs.

Lunchtime

The lactation specialist's advice is to compress my breast into a tasty, sandwichlike shape in order to get the baby to latch. Because babies are born with the innate ability to enjoy sandwiches. Then, when the baby looks good and ready, she shoves the back of his head as hard as she can onto my boob. He managed a good latch and ate a nice meal while the lactation lady was here, and I was feeling like a hooter-certified mom until it was time for him to eat again. Then it was no go on the latch, and Zach had to quell two crying babies.

Now Sam sleeps serenely on Zach's chest. A nurse walks in, sees the diaper commercial visual, and announces, "What a good dad." Bitch said nada about me being a good mom, even though

I'm the one who recently excreted the kid out of my body and am now busting a tit trying to, oh, I don't know, sustain his life with nourishment from my very being.

What does a girl have to do around here to feel a little love?

Later

Sam is in his bucket again, and Zach is squeezed in next to me on the hospital bed. I warned him to stay away from the crinkly blue pad underneath me, which may or may not be catching God knows what liquids that are dribbling from my body. I still look about five months pregnant.

"How about this one?" Zach has his laptop out and flips through pictures of me and Sam taken right after I gave birth. We're prepping the obligatory Facebook birth announcement, and I'd like a picture that doesn't say, "I just shat on a table, and all I got was this slime-covered baby."

I veto several shots before Zach suggests, "This one is nice."

"I have a gimpy eye and twelve chins," I note.

"But Sam looks cute."

"This is not about Sam, Zach. Sam is going to look cute no matter what because he is a baby. And even if he doesn't look cute, people will 'like' the picture anyway while reassuring themselves that their babies were way cuter. It doesn't matter. What does matter is that dozens of ex-classmates and three or more ex-boyfriends will be seeing this, and I don't want to look like a hideous, gelatinous troll."

We finally settle on a decent shot (merely two chins, maybe two and a half) where one can only slightly detect that my hair is crusted onto my forehead.

"What should we write?" Zach poises his fingers above the keyboard.

"How about, 'At one forty-three A.M. we welcomed Samuel Schwartz-Jensen into the world—'"

"Wait," Zach interrupts. "Are we sure about the name? This is forever, you know."

"Yes, but technically it's not forever. He can change it when he's older. But why would he want to? It's a good name. Solid. Normal. Now if you had let me go with Starbuck . . ."

"That's a girl's name," argues Zach.

"The original Starbuck was a guy," I offer. Zach and I have had this argument before about naming our son after a character from *Battlestar Galactica,* but we could never agree on any of the names; the characters' real names were boring, and their Viper pilot call names (Starbuck being one of them) would have tempted ridicule for the rest of our kid's life. Zach and I chose Sam, after the S of his father, who was Stewart. I like to pretend Sam still has its roots in geekery: Samwise Gamgee from *The Hobbit,* Sam Winchester from the television show *Supernatural,* and Sam, a Cylon from *Battlestar Galactica.* Luckily we didn't have the baby during our *Harry Potter* binge-watching era, or the baby may have been named Severus.

"Type in Sam. We settled on that a month ago," I command.

"You're right. I know. We're sure there aren't any horrible nicknames someone can make up with Sam, right?" Zach was traumatized as a sixth grader when his bus dubbed him "Zach the Sack," and it stuck well into high school.

"Assholes can sniff out a mean nickname no matter what your

real name is. That's what they do best. I don't think any testicular words rhyme with Sam, though."

"What about poo words? Or fart words?"

"You tell me. You're the expert on those subjects."

"Looked like you were the expert there in the middle of that one push." Zach chuckles.

"Oh my God. I'm never pooing again."

"Don't worry. I'm sure I would shit everywhere if I was the one giving birth."

"If you were the one giving birth, they would've had to knock you out the second your contractions began, the way you whine."

"What? I whine in a very manly manner."

"Uh-huh. Let's post this picture before it's time for Sam's bar mitzvah. 'Sam no-middle-name Schwartz-Jensen.'" My mom didn't give me a middle name, and her mom didn't give her a middle name, so we're continuing the tradition. "But I don't know," I waffle, "I always wanted a middle name. What if Sam feels neglected because he doesn't have one?"

"We could barely agree on a first name. Let's just stick with this for now. Like you said, he can always change it. *We* can always change it," Zach decides.

"Fine. Samuel Schwartz-Jensen, six pounds, seven ounces, twenty-one inches. You have to include the stats. People eat that shit up," I encourage him.

"Anything else? How long you were in labor? How many centimeters you were dilated? How many pints you pood?"

"Don't be a butthole."

"I don't know what you people share with your FaceFriends."

Zach, while working with computers for a living, wants to keep his digital presence to a minimum, therefore he abstains from Facebook. Plus, he essentially hates everyone from his childhood.

"FaceFriends?" I chide.

"You whippersnappers and your newfangled technologies."

"Can you imagine what the technology will be like when Sam is our age? People will be living on the moon and ordering food from their walls."

"And then the lion in Sam's playroom will eat us," Zach muses, referencing a favorite Ray Bradbury story.

"We can only dream," I concur. "Post it."

2 Days Old

"One hundred fifteen likes. Wow, that's pretty impressive. Even that girl who was a skinhead in high school liked that I had a baby." I'm not ashamed to say I'm obsessively checking my Facebook page for little red alert bubbles every five minutes. Maybe three. Time moves at a different pace in a hospital. Or perhaps I'm just glazed from watching thirteen straight hours of *Call of the Wildman,* a reality show about a man sorely lacking in teeth but not in the chutzpah department. He helps people catch wild animals that wreak havoc in their homes and businesses with his bare hands. I never watched the show before, but it's benignly entertaining, and the Turtleman, as they call him, is surprisingly clever.

"Why are you friends with an ex-skinhead when you were not actually friends with her in the first place? I would never want those fuckwads from my high school looking at my business." Zach cuddles Sam in his arms. "You're never going to show anyone your business, are you, Sammy? No, you're not," he babbles to Sam.

"I like it. It's like we were all reborn as adults or something. I mean, the ones who survived. Did you know there have already been seven deaths from my high school class? I barely knew any of them."

"And now you'll never have the opportunity to look at pictures of their kids or what meals they eat."

"Speaking of meals, I wonder if Doo is eating." Doogan was once a plump cat whom the vet was always trying to put on a diet, but is now a slim senior who we have to make sure eats.

"Your mom checked on him yesterday and said he ate about half his food. Better than none." Doogan's aging is something I hate to think about. Sometimes in the middle of the night I imagine his death and can't stop myself from crying. If I ever become an actress, this is the mental trick I'll use to help me cry on cue. Not that I want to be an actress. You never hear about middle school English teachers breaking into Hollywood at thirty-six anyway.

"I hope he likes Sam. I'll feel really guilty if he doesn't. We've had seventeen years alone together."

"What am I, chopped liver?" Zach asks.

"What are you, a seventy-five-year-old man named Manny? And no, you are not chopped liver, but Doogan was like my first baby, and now he's my old baby and I'm bringing in a new baby and I don't want it to upset him. Remember that woman I used to work with who had that crazy cat with thumbs who somehow figured out how to open their deep freezer and ate all of their ice cream bars?"

"No, but continue," Zach laughs.

"Well, they had to get rid of the cat after they brought the baby home because he kept trying to jump in her bassinet and lick her head."

"Maybe he thought she was an ice cream bar. Besides, we don't even have a bassinet," Zach points out.

"True. But Doogan is half Siamese. What if he's like those cats in *Lady and the Tramp*? 'We are Siamese, if you please.' What if I have to choose between Sam and Doogan?" I panic.

"Obviously you'd choose Sam."

"Why obviously? I only just met Sam. I've known Doogan seventeen years, and—"

"Doogan is a cat, Annie. I love him, too, but Sam is our *baby*, remember?" I well up, and Zach tries to backpedal. "I'm sure it will all be fine. Doogan is an awesome, mellow cat. I'm sure Sam will be an awesome, mellow baby."

"You're sure?" I sniffle.

"Positive." Zach kisses me on the top of my head.

"He better be," I warn. Is it my imagination, or did a maniacal laugh just sound from the bundle in Zach's arms?

Later

My mom stopped by the hospital to meet her first grandchild. Sometimes I feel like my mom is secretly filming a sitcom of her life when she says things like "I'm not going to cry . . . I'm not going to cry . . . I'm going to cry!" Zach documents the moment on camera, and I envision us airing the footage at Sam's bar mitzvah. If either of us makes it that long. I'm still having heaps of trouble getting him to nurse. The stress has forced me to indulge in the splendor of the hospital's food offerings. It's like ordering room service, if budget motel chains offered room service menus with not a single choice of an entrée you actually wanted to eat. I sent Zach down to the cafeteria twice to pick up pudding parfaits. In general, I tend to avoid formless desserts, but pudding in a cup, layered with Nilla wafers and spray-can whipped cream feels like an absolute delicacy. Plus, I've got to bulk up if I'm ever going to get this breastfeeding thing right. That's my new perspective on breastfeeding: I'm going to treat it like a sport. I've got to train. I've got to practice. I've got to fuel up. And someday I'll be one of those women with a six-year-old boy hanging off her boob on the cover of a magazine whom people both respect and think is endlessly creepy.

Now if I can only take a dump. Going to the bathroom is just about the most terrifying thing on earth. I know I should poo, but there are stitches down there that could erupt, creating an ass chasm the likes of which the world has never known. My only friend is this strange little squeeze bottle whose specified purpose is to be aimed at my butt while I'm using the toilet. Is that why this bottle was invented? Was there someone at a hospital-supply design company whose designated job was to create an ass-spraying squeeze bottle? If so, bravo to them, because he did a bang-up job. I don't know why I assume it was a man. Men should do something right by women in the land of maternity, and by gods if this squeeze bottle wasn't it. I wonder if it has a name. The ass-juicer? Butt-squelcher? Hole-sprayer?

Zach has just heard me laughing out loud at myself in the bathroom and assumes I am crying.

"Still no poo, honey?" he calls from his chair.

That just may be the sexiest thing that someone's said to me this week.

To: Annie

From: Fern

Annie!

OMG! You had the baby! He is so cute. You look awesome. Beyonce's got nothing on you. Or Princess Kate. Who just had a baby? I can never keep track. Nor do I care. My four are keeping me busy with various ailments. It seems like Dov is always barfing, Hannah is always pooping, and Jacob has it coming out both ends. Oh the joys of kids! You'll see what I mean.

We'll be back in town in a couple months. I wish we could be there now, but I'm stuck out here in sunny California where everyone thinks 50 degrees is going to give them frostbite. Pussies! I miss Chicago. And you!

Let me know what you need. Send me an Amazon wishlist or Toys R Us or whatever, and I'll send you some stuff.

Enjoy Baby Sam (not short for Samhain, right?)

Hugs!

Fern

Fern is my best friend from high school who, even though she married a wealthy screenwriter in L.A. and has four small kids, still likes to talk about Satan like we did in high school (just a short-lived phase, between our Wiccan period and the house-on-the-corner-psychic era). I adore her and wish she lived nearby. I don't really have any close friends with kids since Zach and I moved to the suburbs a few years ago after he declared he needed more space and was tired of "smelling our neighbors."

My mom lives closest to us, at fifteen minutes away, but pretty much everyone else, including my sister, Nora, and her husband, Eddie, lives in the city. How does one go about making mom friends in the sprawling suburbs? Will I be forced to join a playgroup? Does that involve potlucks? I hate potlucks. So many casseroles with their quivering cream of mushroom soup. Just another way I'll be ostracized from the parenting community. Because most parents actually know what to do with their kids.

3 Days Old

. . . .

They claim we are ready to take the baby home. I have managed to get Sam to latch with a spectacular contraption called a nipple shield. While it's not very shieldlike in appearance (it is a clear silicone cover that fits over my nipple and areola), I suppose it is shielding me from the debilitating pain of the suck. Why did they make these things clear? Couldn't they be jazzier, with wacky patterns or sports teams or band names? Or maybe that would defeat the purpose of trying to get the baby to latch on to my actual boob once he figures out how to latch well with the shield. If it was patterned, then I'd have to start decorating my nips just to keep things consistent. As it is, I already feel like a hooker from the future with these things perched on my tits.

Have I mentioned that my boobs are like boulders right now? Gigantic and rock hard. I look like I might float away at any minute, but their density makes me think I'd sink like a stone if dropped into an ocean. I've been told that cold cabbage in my bra might help, so I'm sending Zach to the grocery store for a head as soon as we get home. And then demanding that he make me some coleslaw.

All of this teat trouble makes me question if my goal of nursing for Sam's first year is complete madness. Isn't all of this complete madness, though? I am still baffled that a human being came out of me, a "human being" who can't do a single thing on his own. Scratch that—he seems to be highly capable of both filling his diaper and crying so people in neighboring counties can hear his nuanced shriek. Does it fill their bellies with panic, too? Do other moms feel this way, or am I completely evil?

I look at Sam, and, yes, I am in awe that he is a real, live baby. *My* real baby. But he is also a complete stranger to me. I knew him better when he lived inside my body, waking me up at night with his hiccups and kicking me as I drove my car listening to speed metal. I was certain I was going to spawn an adorable little headbanger. I looked supercute in my maternity clothes, and everyone gushed at me when they asked what I was having and I answered, with a loving pat to my belly, "A boy." We had a good thing going.

Now they're trying to kick me out of the hospital, as though I'm actually ready to raise a person from start to (my) finish! People do this all the time, yet I never thought about how terrifyingly fucked up it is that before I came here I just had myself to think about and less than three days later I am completely responsible for a human life. How the fuck do people do this? I don't know how to comfort or feed or cuddle him as well as I did when he lived inside of me, perfectly contained and cozy, drinking his own pee. We are strangers, and yet I am wholly responsible for his well-being. Everything I do from now on will be fodder for his therapy as an adult.

Aside from the midwife checking the state of my union (all good, she claims), no one has given me a second glance since Sam was born. Even though I am still wearing my adorable maternity clothes. So this is what it means to be a mom.

Later

Sam is sitting in his car seat. Correction: Sam, the tiny human-like form, is slumped in his car seat.

"Is he supposed to look like that?" Zach asks.

We stand over the car seat, which is sitting on the floor of our hospital room, and assess the situation. I spent weeks researching safety ratings, weight, and color patterns of every car-seat brand known to womankind, and none of it will matter when Sam stops breathing the second the car starts moving because his head is too flopped forward.

"I think we did it wrong. Oh well. I guess we can't take him home." As much as I want to escape from the land of gigantic ice-water refills and too many vitals checks, once we leave this joint we're on our own. Who will help us every time we need to get Sam into his car seat?

For the first time since we checked in, there is no one in our hospital room but the three of us. Why hasn't anyone stopped by to send us off? To check his car seat placement? To offer us permanent residency and a wet nurse?

"I'm going to call someone," I say.

"Isn't that for emergencies?" Zach asks as I approach the all-in-one nurse/remote/bed-adjusting protrusion that dangles violently from the bed.

"The red button is emergency. This orange one is for other things, like picking up room service trays or calling someone to look at what I did in the toilet. They love to look at what I did in the toilet."

I press the button, and a voice answers, "Nurses' station."

"Hi. We're ready to leave, and I was wondering if someone can help us check the baby's car seat."

"Just a minute," the nurse answers.

Fifteen minutes later, a nurse shows up and looks down at Sam, who we hope is merely dozing.

"Looks fine," she assesses.

"But his head . . . ," I point out.

"We did a car seat test on him, and his breathing was normal."

I forgot about the car seat test. They took Sam and the car seat away for an hour, presumably to go on a joyride with a baby in the backseat. He came back unscathed, so maybe that means he will make it home unscathed, too.

"Ready?" Zach asks.

"No," I answer.

But he picks up Sam's car seat, and we're off to the never-ending tunnels of the hospital parking garage. It seems like months since we've been in our car, and I'm surprised that it hasn't sprouted ivy when we manage to find it.

"How the hell did Prince William make this look so easy?" Zach struggles with locking the car seat into the preinstalled base, and I snicker at his royal reference.

"I read that he practiced. At least we don't have that kind of pressure. It's hard enough bringing a new baby home without twelve billion people monitoring it all," I say from my spot in the passenger seat.

"There," Zach declares. "It's in."

"You sure you heard a click?" I check.

"Yes, I'm sure," he confirms. To double-check, he wiggles the car seat.

"Careful! You'll snap his neck!" I warn.

"Jesus, Annie, don't say things like that."

"I'm sorry. It's scary, you know?"

"Yeah," Zach agrees as he slides into the driver's seat. We look at each other anxiously. "Maybe you should sit next to him, just in case," he suggests.

"I was thinking the same thing."

I spend the next half hour with my finger perched inside of the massive pacifier cloaking Sam's face. Every time I feel the tug of his hearty suck, I'm comforted.

First Night Home

Everyone manages to arrive home alive, and while I wriggle out of the car Zach removes the car seat.

"Don't bring him in yet!" I order. "Let me say hi to Doogan first. I read that's how you're supposed to introduce younger siblings. First show the older ones how important they are without the new baby in your arms."

"Not a sibling, but do what you gotta do," Zach encourages me.

I open the door from the garage to the house, the door where Doogan always sits and waits when he hears the grinding of the garage door. There he is, my soft little pal, mewing loyally and tripping me with his back-and-forth leg nuzzles. I scoop him up for a kiss and snuggle. Purrs radiate from his entire body. "I missed you, Doo. Such a good boy." We head butt each other a few times, a gesture I never understood but still partake in. Zach interrupts our moment with a jarring whack as the car seat slams into the door. He plunks the seat onto the floor.

"This thing's heavier than it looks!" he declares, oblivious to the romantic interlude he disturbed. "Hey, Doo," Zach says, and scratches Doogan behind the ears. "We've got someone for you to meet." On cue, Sam begins crying, that grinding, newborn cry that verifies we are indeed ancestors of wild animals. "You want to meet Doogan, little buddy?" Zach asks Sam, and I feel Doogan's reflexive jerk in my arms. I really hope he doesn't scratch me as he flees for his life.

Zach gingerly unhooks the seat belt and takes another two minutes to weave the belt over Sam's arms so as not to dislocate anything. By the time Zach picks him up, Doogan has most certainly lodged himself firmly in the inaccessible corner of the crawl space.

"You can meet Doogan later," Zach assures Sam. "Let me show you around." Zach cradles Sam and familiarizes him with different areas of the family room. "This is where you'll play with LEGOs someday, and here is the TV, where I'll show you all thirty-two seasons of *Doctor Who*."

The niceties last about ninety seconds until we figure out that we need to change Sam's diaper. And feed him. And put him in his bed. We manage to do all three of these things, admittedly at our own pace, and are feeling almost smug as we eat our frozen pizza dinner at six P.M.

"We got this." Zach pats us on the back, and we celebrate our victory with a glass of wine and an episode of *Outlander* that we missed while in the hospital.

Then Sam wakes up. Screaming. We check his diaper. A little pee, so we change him in case he's uncomfortable. I try to feed him, but he wants nothing to do with the nipple shield and only toys with my actual nipple. Zach bounces Sam for a solid half hour until, finally, he is lulled back to sleep, then delicately places Sam in his co-sleeper, and all is quiet again. For about an hour. After that, it's a twelve-hour blur of pee, poo, boobs, shields, tears, and what feel like the least restful spurts of sleep I've had since I tried to stay up all night to finish an essay on barnacles for a mandatory biology class I took in college. I got a C on that paper.

My mind is so shot right now that if I tried writing that paper today, it would read:

Barnacles. That's a funny word. Barnacles. Barnacles. Barnacles. Barnacles. Barnacles. Barnacles. Barnacles. Barnacles. Barnacles. Barnacles. Barnacles. Barnacles. Barnacles. Barnacles. Barnacles. Barnacles. Barnacles. Barnacles. Barnacles. Now it doesn't even sound like a real word.

At one point Sam slept for two hours at one chunk, but I was so afraid that he wasn't breathing I ended up putting my face up to his in order to check for signs of life, and I woke him up.

How do people with babies manage to keep them alive when I can't even make it to the toilet before I start to pee? I almost made it. Does that count?

4 Days Old

I slept for a solid three hours, and that has magically refreshed me enough to go online.

"Are you frakkin' kidding me?" I yell at my computer while Sam flails on my boob.

"He's not latching?" Zach asks, concerned, although I think he's more worried about my mental health at this point than Sam's culinary needs.

"He's fine. He adores his plastic nipple hut. Kelly Shulman still hasn't liked that picture of Sam I posted yesterday on Facebook. The one with his little don't-scratch-your-face mitts on his hands. That picture is fucking adorable."

"Might want to tone down the language around the baby, don't you think?"

"He doesn't know what I'm talking about. And he can learn from this. People are assholes, Sammy. You like all their stupid, pretentious black-and-white pictures of their kids, and what do you get from them? Jack shit."

"Do you want me to hold Sam?" Zach asks nervously.

"He's eating. He's fine."

"And you?"

"I am neither eating nor fine."

"Why don't you just de-friend her?"

"It's *un*friend. And if I did that, I wouldn't know if she were not liking my stuff, then, would I?"

"Don't go joining the debate team anytime soon."

"Watch it, or I'll de-friend you."

"Backing away slowly."

Later

"I talked to my mom. She says she can't wait to meet the baby, so they booked a trip out here next month."

"Next month? Your mom is so weird."

"She wanted to give us some space. Plus she admitted to not really liking newborn babies. I think I traumatized her."

"Would've been nice to know that before having our own baby," I mumble.

"They sent a present," he offers.

"If it's not a new set of working boobs, then I don't care," I gripe.

I'm griping now?

5 Days Old

· ·

I think I've been awake for sixty-six hours. I've lost track of all time and reality. How do people do this? Zach somehow manages to fall back asleep every time Sam wakes up, but after changing him, dressing him, nursing him, and washing the nipple shield, I am more wide awake than that time I drank two five-hour energy drinks in order to finish grading a stack of essays I shirked to watch all of *Orphan Black* over a three-day weekend.

Must try to sleep.

Must fall asleep.

I'm imagining my yoga teacher's voice in my head.

Eyes heavy.

Shoulders relaxed.

Breathe.

Breathe.

Breathe.

Shit.

Baby's up again.

Restart the clock.

Sam's First Doctor's Appointment

Why do they expect us to bring a brand-new baby to a doctor's office? For starters, I look like absolute shit. Second, we just left the hospital. Is this some sort of test so they can see what a bang-up job I'm doing or take the baby away if I'm not? And what about all of these disgusting kids hacking their death boogers all over the waiting room? How is that good for a newborn?

Zach and I (to be clear: Most of the time when I refer to "Zach and I," I technically mean "I," with an afterthought nod of approval from Zach) interviewed pediatricians the last few months before Sam was born. I wanted to find someone highly intelligent, pro-vaccine, but understanding of my irrational fears. And funny. And it had to be a woman because I'm completely sexist. We chose Dr. Zale, a short and sharp Jewish pediatrician with a wonderfully calm demeanor and a few years of crazy parents under her belt.

Zach and I enter Dr. Zale's waiting room, Sam resting in his car seat. My paranoid new-mom vision zeroes in instantly on two children: one coughing directly into the air (get off your fucking phone, mom, and teach your kid some healthy hygiene habits pronto!) and another moaning into mom's shoulder as he's curled up on a chair. I consider draping a plastic sheet over Sam's car seat but reconsider when I realize it probably would not be the safest thing to do. Plus, I left my plastic sheet at home. Zach is about to set Sam's carrier down a mere two seats away from Curlboy, so I violently snap at him with my fingers and make a scrunched-up expression that says, "Do exactly as you're told, and you'll get ice cream afterward." Then I use my best head-jerking skills to redirect him to a chair equidistant from the two sickies. No one else better come into the waiting room while we're here, or I'll have to recalculate our seating.

Coughie and Curlboy are called in first, and I breathe a little easier (albeit not very deeply, so as to avoid inhaling nascent germs). Ten minutes later, a nurse pokes her head out of the door leading to the exam rooms and calls out, "Sam." A ping of recognition hits me that Sam is, in fact, a real person with a name attached. We bring him into room four, and the nurse instructs us to undress him down to his diaper. I try to work quickly, sensing her impatience, but I'm still new to the litany of teensy snaps. Eventually, he of the shriveled, black belly-button monstrosity is undressed and ready to be weighed. I rest Sam into a bucketlike scale, resulting in a wail of mythical magnitude. "Six pounds ten ounces," the nurse reads.

"That's more than he weighed when he was born," I note to Zach. "That means when he's sucking on my boobs, something's coming out."

Dr. Zale examines Sam soon after, but I can't hear much of what she tells us. Aside from the sheer volume of Sam's screaming, I'm still dumbfounded that my body is actually working correctly, that milk is coming out of me and nourishing this baby enough to make him gain weight. Maybe I am capable of providing for a human. At least three ounces' worth, anyway.

To: Louise
From: Annie

Lou, I'm sorry I haven't returned any of your calls. You told me I would be a zombie shell of my old self once the baby was born, and you were right. I seriously think bits of my skin are peeling off. I look that bad. Just behead me now. I'm soooooooo tired. I actually had to delete some of the o's in sooooo because I fell asleep while holding down the key. And then Sam woke me up. Why is he always doing that? Help! I know you can't. I know you're home with Jupiter and baby #2 is going to fly out of you any second, so I have no right to bitch because you will have <u>two</u> people to prevent you from sleeping. I wish I had listened to you when you told me how hard this is.

I'm guessing the answer is no (you get an *I'm about to have a baby* pass), but do you want to come to Sam's bris on Tuesday?

It's BYOP. That was supposed to stand for Bring Your Own Penis, but I realized that makes no sense. Will I ever make sense again?

XOOOOOOOOOOOOOOOOOOOOOOOOOOOOOOO OOOOOOOO

Annie

Louise and I have worked together at Parker Middle School for ten years. So far she is one of the only people who admitted things aren't going to be all baby powder and handmade blankeys. I hope that was just her patented sarcasm talking.

6 Days Old

My mom came over today to help plan the bris. Everyone has their theories and opinions on circumcision, as is evident by the hilarious comments on Facebook. One guy from my high school referred to it as "the worst day of my life," while another shrugged it off as "a snip and a nosh." I'm choosing to do it because it's a

Jewish custom, and supposedly mohels do the cut better than most hospital staff (according to the cautionary tales of my colleagues, and I do love a good cautionary tale about penises). Plus, my aunt Edie already ordered the lox platter. Zach, while not a Jew, is on board the circumcision train because he doesn't want any locker room trouble for Sam later in his life. To which I ask: Are guys really looking at one another's penises so closely that they can detect whether someone is circumcised or not? Why aren't they hiding in the showers or trying to discreetly put on their underwear while awkwardly shielding themselves with their towels like girls do?

The bris is supposed to take place on the eighth day of life, because thousands of years ago someone figured out it is the day the baby will feel the least amount of pain, or something like that, proving once again that people of yore did a much better job of understanding their kids than I am managing today.

Did I mention my nipples are dying?

Zach's moms sent a rather bizarre baby basket today, although I'd expect nothing less. After his mom, Dawn, and dad, Stewart, divorced when Zach was sixteen, his mom went back to school to get her master's in creative writing. While there, she met a women's studies professor, Mimi, with whom she fell madly in love. They've been together, professoring it up in Seattle, ever since. At our wedding, Zach's dad and two moms walked him down the aisle. Zach's dad remarried almost instantly after the divorce to a woman I never got to know very well. Sadly, his dad died five years ago of lung cancer, and his stepmom seemed to think we were going to argue over who got his money. All Zach wanted was his dad's collection of Johnny Cash memorabilia, and he had to fight her on that, even though she always seemed annoyed that his dad spent their money on the collection. The Cash (Johnny, not money) eventually became Zach's, and we now keep our communication with the stepmom to a holiday-card minimum.

Dawn and Mimi are a fun couple to visit, although extremely tidy to the point where staying with them becomes more chore filled than our nonvacationing lives. I've never wiped a bathroom counter after using the sink, but leaving extra water droplets on the tile is a no-no. If only they could see the horror show that is our toothpaste-globbed, watermark-tainted bathroom sink these days. I guess I won't worry about it until their visit next month. In the meantime, we can enjoy their gift basket of feminist baby-raising literature, oatmeal-colored, organic, dye-free onesies, and mother's milk tea that tastes a little like tree bark pancakes. How did anyone discover this stuff ups breastmilk production if they had to taste it first?

Later

Having my mom here was the most magical six hours of my new life. She held Sam, and I showered without fear of him waking up or Zach coming into the bathroom with a question (although showering with my healing ass was still horrifying). Not that Zach's doing a bad job. He hasn't complained about changing a single diaper, even that time he threw up in his mouth a touch, but he is under the impression that I know more about parenting a newborn than he does. Just because I grew this little pumpkin doesn't mean I know how to water and feed it and trim its vines or whatever, and by vines I mean his fingernails. Sam's pediatrician joked that some ignorant parents think biting their kids' nails off is a good idea. I pretended I wasn't one of those parents. Is this natural to other women? Is there something inherently wrong with my physiology?

> To: Annie
> From: Annika
>> Hey Annie—
>> Thanks for the invite to the bris! Is it OK if I bring my new boyfriend, Anders? Do we need to bring anything? Pigs in a blanket? Cocktail Wienies? Band-Aids?
>> Hugs!
>> Annika

Annika is a close friend from college. At least, we were close when we were in college. We lived together a couple of years, took random classes like ceramics and Finnish together, dated several of the same hipsters, and formed a band called the Pee Sharps. Annika was the lead singer, and I played lead guitar. I was never very accomplished, but the chords I did know I played very well. Repeatedly.

Toward the end of school, Annika decided she had no interest in completing her degree, and she moved to Sweden with a guy from our Finnish class. After that ended, she moved to Barcelona to be with a guy she met in Finland. Rinse and repeat. Between college and our current age of thirty-six, I think Annika has lived in seventeen different countries with an equal number of guys. Maybe more. Somehow she landed nearby in Chicago about a year ago, working as a party planner for a nonprofit company, although I've only seen her a couple of times. Working and being pregnant made visiting her in the city complicated. Not that she came out to visit me in the suburbs. We don't quite have the same interests or schedule anymore; I'm more of a "go out to lunch" person, while Annika's social life doesn't start until I go to bed (a reasonable nine thirty on a school night). And she's not quite in tune with the nuances of adult behavior, which explains why she'd want to bring a new boyfriend to a bris. At least she'll get to meet Sam.

7 Days Old

We are running out of options for takeout. Even Doogan seems miffed by the stack of plastic containers (I promise to wash and recycle them when I'm not so tired, Doo). I am very grateful that Zach doesn't mind going out and picking up (in no particular order): Indian, Chinese, Thai, and Mexican. If we ate "official" fast food, I would ask him to pick up a Whopper right now. But we don't eat fast food or even meat, really. Why is that again? Something about chemicals and not wanting to hurt animals, and damn, Zach better get back with that double chocolate fudge sippable sundae from Steak 'n Shake ASAP.

FACEBOOK STATUS

Was anyone else as disgusted by their baby's charbroiled belly button shrapnel as I am?

33

Ten Minutes Later

Did I say I was grateful that Zach doesn't mind picking up food? I meant jealous. Sear-his-brain-out-with-my-angry-eyes jealous that he gets to leave the house and I have to stay here with the Screamer. LalalalalalaIcanthearyou!

Another person just changed her Facebook profile picture to an ultrasound. Why do people do that? a) It is not a picture of you; and b) Let's face it, ultrasound pictures are at most abstract and at the least semidisgusting. I don't want to see inside of your body. If it's a reaching attempt at getting six thousand likes at the fact that you are pregnant, why not post a clever status update. Mine was, "Looks like I won't be climbing Mt. Kilimanjaro this summer because instead I'll be HAVING A BABY!"

Man, that was fucking stupid.

I just posted another obligatory picture of Sam. Six comments already, three of which claim he looks "just like Zach." Why do people think I want to read that? What mom is like, *I just housed this human for ten months and then wrenchingly squeezed him out of my lady hole, which made me so hormonal that I sweat through three t-shirts and pairs of underwear every night, but I'm so glad my baby looks like my husband and not me.* Throw me a bone, Facebook! Who are you, Jenny Krakovitz, anyway except some girl I went to high school with? I don't think we said two words to each other as teens, and now we're "friendly" enough that you can throw insults at me like "He looks just like Zach" on my Facebook page! Fuck you, too! Weren't you a cheerleader? Didn't I *hate* you in high school? Well, I hate you now!

I think he looks like an old man with a receding hairline, Cheerleader.

Take that, Jenny Krakovitz.

Zach is finally back with my grilled cheese and shake from Steak 'n Shake, and I am praying that no one saw that Facebook comment before I deleted it.

Middle of the Night

I have misplaced my nipple shield. I shake Zach awake. "Zach, I can't find my shield!"

"Your what?" he answers groggily. He is not allowed to be groggy.

"My nipple shield. It popped off after I fed Sam, and now I can't find it."

"We'll look for it in the morning."

"No, we will not! I have to wash it off, and I need it for his next feeding, which you will also be allowed to sleep through. Help me find it. I always help you find your contact when you drop it. Think of this as a giant contact lens for my boob."

Zach fishes under the bed for a flashlight. He always pulls out a flashlight when looking for items, one of his most redeeming qualities.

After a good ten-minute search, a glint of light reflects off the shield, which has somehow affixed itself to the side of my dresser.

"Kind of like a wacky wall walker," Zach notes.

"More like a tacky titty tumbler," I laugh, but Zach has miraculously fallen back asleep in the amount of time it took me to concoct that joke. I wash off the shield in the bathroom sink and try with no success to fall back asleep before I have to put it to use again.

8 Days Old—Bris Day

What kind of asshole makes people host a penis trimming at their home eight days after giving birth? This means I have to put on a bra! Thank God my mom came over and helped Zach straighten up. I still can't walk completely normally. The midwife told me my "bottom" might be stiff for a few weeks. I thought that sounded ridiculous. Who calls a butt a "bottom"? But it's not my butt, and it's not my vag, but somewhere in between. "Bottom" seems to cover it nicely. What I want to know is, how did Princess Kate walk so normally in front of billions of people when they showed her leaving the hospital after giving birth? Is there anything that woman does not do perfectly? I'd like to think she had serious "bottom" pain but was ordered by the queen to grin and bear it and walk normally or have her title revoked. This may be my son's bris, but I'm going to be shuffling through it like a ninety-three-year-old man.

I hope I manage to not puke all over the mohel's beard.

Post-Bris

It wasn't so bad. Sam barely seemed bothered by the cut. The mohel was very calm, and he gave Sam a little towel soaked in wine to suck on. One of my mom's mah-jongg friends (of which there are about seventeen hundred) hovered near me during the ceremony, trying to convince me to leave, that moms aren't obligated to stay and watch. By the time she concluded her overprotective nudging, the mohel was finished and wrapping a sleeping Sam in a blanket. "You missed it! I made you miss it!" she shouted wildly. She seemed far more bunged up than I was. It's not like I wanted to watch. I was mostly thinking, a) *Are my boobs leaking?* and b) *I wonder if my mom remembered to buy egg bagels.* The answers: No and Yes, so I'd say bris success!

After everyone has left and Sam is sleeping like a drunk (I'd be a bad mom if I spiked his blankey every night from now on, right?), Zach rubs my back.

"How are you feeling?" he asks.

"Tired. Relieved it's over. How about you? Any transference of penis pain?"

"I'm trying not to think about it." He adjusts his manhood all the same. "You did great today."

"Thanks? I didn't really do much except eat a lot and try not to cry."

"You were very composed. Very mature when you gave that speech thanking everyone for coming."

"I guess this officially makes us grown-ups." I sigh, resigned to the idea.

"I guess so. We can still go to comic book conventions, right?"

"I hope so. We can dress Sam up in all sorts of humiliating costumes before he's old enough to tell us not to."

"I knew there was a reason we had a baby." Zach squeezes me.

"Not too hard in the boob area. I wouldn't want to get any milk in your eyes." He eases off. "I noticed Annika didn't show. Not that I expected her to. Who brings a new boyfriend to someone's bris?"

"It would be better than when she brought that one guy to my grandpa's funeral," Zach reminds me.

"Oh yeah. That white guy with the dreads. Isn't he an accountant now?"

Zach fishes around in his pocket. "I got you something."

"I really hope that's not Sam's foreskin," I joke.

"Annie," Zach reprimands my grossness. "Here. It's a push present. I read about it online."

"You read about it online, huh?" I smirk at the thought of Zach reading relationship articles on his computer while pretending to watch *Breaking Bad*.

He hands me a tiny cardboard box with a hand-stamped logo on it. I open it, and inside is a silver "S" framed with a gold heart. "It's for 'Sam.' I thought it kind of looked like the Superman symbol, except with a heart."

"It's beautiful. Thank you." I open the clasp and slip it around my neck. Zach kisses me on the lips, and for a moment I pretend we're a perfect little family.

Dear Aunt Edie,

Thank you very much for the savings bond and the lox platter for Sam's bris. His penis seems to be healing very nicely.

Next time I see you, can you remind me where you bought that tuna salad? It was delicious. Capers—brilliant!

    Love,

    Annie

To: Annie

From: Louise

    OH MY GOD I MISSED THE BRIS! I am such an asshole! I am so sorry! Can you do it again, so I can see it? Just kidding. I wrote it on the calendar, but for *next* Tuesday. Will you forgive me? Attribute it to baby brain. Four days and counting, and they slice this be-yotch out of me. Can't wait! (to be un-pregnant. I can wait for just about everything else. Except for the smell!!! New baby smell!!! You better at least be enjoying that.) Hopefully we can talk on the phone when I'm in the hospital. It's the only time I'll be away from Jupiter. She never lets me near my phone—either I'm on it, and she talks the entire time no matter how many conversations we've had about Mommy being important, too, or she's on it playing games. (Don't look at me like that. I see your smug superiority through my computer screen. Just you wait until you have a four-year-old!) Speaking of, I have to go, the battery's about to die on my phone.

    Wish me luck with my c-section!

    C-ya later!

    Lou

10 Days Old

. . . .

Doogan the cat seems rather annoyed with Sam, and I can't say I blame him. Every time Doogan and I try to get snuggly together on the bed, Sam bellows from his little co-sleeper and I have to move. Pretty soon Doogan will be so perturbed that he'll stop snuggling with me altogether. How tragic. Seventeen years of snuggling instantly replaced by this pooping, screaming, squiggly creature. It reminds me of a song I listened to in junior high by Faith No More called "Zombie Eaters." It's sung from a baby's perspective to his mother, and Mike Patton, the lead singer, teases the mom with lines like "Hey, look at me, lady, I'm just a little baby. You're lucky to have me. I'm cute and sweet as candy." I thought it was hilarious when I was a teen. Now I'm ready to cry at the relatable lines "But I really do nothing, Except kickin' and fussin'." Is this my penance for listening to music like that? I imagine Doogan's half of this conversation, "Bloody hell," because in my mind, Doogan has a British accent. "What is that scrawny thing? No fur, can't even crawl to his food bowl, and he makes more noise than the neighbor's schnauzer. I've got it in my right mind to climb into his bed and rest my giant, furry butt on his blotchy face. *Lady and the Tramp* was quite accurate, you know."

Someone suggested I introduce the baby's scent to Doogan to get him used to it, so I tucked Sam's hospital hat into Doogan's bed. The cat hasn't gone near his bed since. Ironically, Doogan can't seem to get enough of Sam's bedroom rug, though. I've already tripped over him twice on my way to the changing table. So I put the hat into Sam's baby book instead. It does have that delicious new-baby smell. I think I must inhale Sam's head at least sixty times per day. Why does it smell so good? Is it an evolutionary tactic so that a mom, no matter how harried and confused and depressed she is, finds some inkling of comfort from snorting her baby's skull?

Is it possible to form an addiction? Do they have support groups for baby head huffing? Is this the main reason Michelle Duggar wants to keep having babies? Because she has an addiction to the scent, and at some point it goes away and she can't possibly live without it, so she submits to having sex with Jim Bob for the twelve millionth time just so that she will be able to sniff in that sweet baby goodness?

I think I just answered one of the most vital questions of our time.

FACEBOOK STATUS

I'm worried that I might erode a spot on Sam's skull from sniffing his head so frequently.

11 Days Old

The doorbell rings while I'm putting Sam down for a nap. When I eventually open the front door, I find several garbage bags filled with gifts from my colleagues at Parker Middle School. I can't believe how much they bought for him—clothes, bottles, toys.

There are hundreds of dollars in gift cards (enough for a plane ticket out of here—not that the thought crosses my mind). Strangest of all is a handmade blanket from the superscary math teacher with whom I try to avoid all interaction, particularly when he's fired up about the union at our faculty meetings. A note with the blanket reads, "Congratulations on the sweet, new addition to your family. Enjoy the time you have at home. They grow up fast." Did he knit the blanket?

I'm giddy with the generosity of my coworkers until I remember I have to write them all thank-you notes. I figure I have until the end of my maternity leave. Five months should be enough time, right?

> *Dear Parker friends,*
>
> *Thank you so much for all of the amazing gifts for my baby Sam. It's nice to see that all of the money I've contributed at faculty baby showers actually pays for some nice things. Keep up the good work, social committee!*
>
> *See you in a few months,*
> *Annie*

12 Days Old

"We need to finish the thank-you notes," I tell Zach over a tuna sandwich.

"Have we started them?" he asks.

"*I* have. You get to at least write thank-you notes to your people."

"My people? I thought we don't differentiate between my people and your people since we got married."

"That's money. We don't differentiate between my money and your money. *People* is a different story. Your people are the ones who sent Sam a BB gun so he can jump on hunting practice at the ripe old age of two weeks."

"Yeah, my uncle Roger really missed the mark on that one."

"How do they not know you were a vegetarian for fifteen years?"

"They know, they just don't care."

"And what is that thing your aunt Jessa made?" I crumple up a sandwich wrapper and throw it in the trash, already overflowing with carry-out wrappers. "Can you take this out, please?"

"It's a head cozy. Like a tea cozy for your head." Zach stands up and ties the garbage bag into a knot.

"Isn't that called a hat?" I ask.

"Not in my family."

I jot down a list of people Zach needs to thank. The list is short, only five thank-you notes long. "You're lucky your family is so small. I not only have my mom's side and my dad's side, but my mom's mah-jongg friends use up an entire box of thank-you notes. Not to mention her knitting group, beading beauties, and Canasties."

"Canasties?"

"The friends she plays canasta with. I always wonder, if a group of people go in together on a gift, can I write them the exact same thank-you note? Or are they going to think that's tacky and lazy?"

"No one's sitting around, comparing your thank-you notes, Annie. I don't even think anyone expects thank-you notes after a baby's born. I mean, you're all crazy and forgetful with your baby brain, right? It's an accepted excuse."

"No way. My mom told me that the other night at mah-jongg several people asked if we received their gifts. They weren't sure since they hadn't gotten a thank-you note yet. We're talking a week after the baby was born."

"Your people are weird."

"See. I have my people, and you have yours."

"I'll get on those notes as soon as I take out the garbage," Zach promises.

Mom's Friend Thank-You Note Template
Dear [Insert mah-jongg, canasta, knitter, beader friend's name here],

    Thank you so much for the _____. Sam loves it and [circle one]

    Wears it

    Plays with it

    Sucks on it

    Reads it

whenever I put it near him. It was so thoughtful of you. My mom is lucky to have a friend like you.

    Sincerely,

    Annie, Zach, and Sam

Half Hour Later

Zach has been outside with the garbage for a year. What the fuck? If he really doesn't want to write thank-you notes, then he doesn't have to. In the meantime, I've changed a poopy diaper, watched Sam pee in his own face (and laughed just a bit), changed Sam's clothes, changed my clothes due to residual pee trickle, unsuccessfully fed Sam, cried, successfully fed Sam, burped Sam, wiped two tons of spit-up off the carpet, changed Sam again because I hate the sour smell of spit-up, and put him back down to sleep.

Finally, Zach saunters in.

"Where the hell were you?" I blast him.

"Whoa!" He holds his hands up in surrender. "I was just talking to Gary next door. He was mowing the lawn."

"How nice for you. If you didn't want to write thank-you notes, you should have just told me."

"Thank-you notes? I was talking to our neighbor." Zach points toward the door, confused.

"And I was up to my eyeballs in bodily fluids."

"Um, gross?"

"Just write the frakkin' thank-you notes!" I scream.

"Okay. Okay. If it's that big a deal to you, I'll do it. Do we have any cards?"

"Ugh!" I scream.

"Whatever. I'll write them on toilet paper. Sheesh." Zach slinks away.

I poise myself at the kitchen table with a stack of thank-you notes and a pen.

And then I fall asleep and wake up an hour later to the baby screaming over the monitor and the word *dear* printed backward on my forehead.

> Dear *[six different knitting friends—do not forget to duplicate]*,
>
> Thank you very much for the Chicago Bears, Cubs, White Sox, Bulls, and Blackhawks mobile. We thought perhaps you would have made us a beautiful blanket with your combined powers of knitting, but a mobile about sports is very nice.
>
> Yours truly, Annie, Zach, and Sam

13 Days Old

My brain goes to crazy places in the middle of the night.

> Why does Chicago radio play so much Billy Joel?
> Why does it feel like I'm on vacation every time I visit a new Walgreens?
> Would Sam be better off with a saner mother?

To quell the voices, I've started turning on QVC while I'm nursing (and in between, and while I catch a few winks and continue to dream about television shopping). I realize in this day and age there is an infinite number of choices for TV in the middle of the night, but there's something so warm and calming about QVC. Everyone is so damn nice. They want to better my life. Take, for instance, the name of the program I'm watching: *Everyday Solutions*. Every item in this show can help make my life easier. I have already purchased a set of encryption rubber stampers to wipe out the threat of identity theft, serrated knives, and a new set of pots. But buying things isn't my favorite part. I am particularly enamored with the testimonial line. People call in to say how much they covet the products, and they're so complimentary and kind, and the hosts are so encouraging and enthusiastic. If everyone were as loving to each other as they are on QVC, there would be no war.

Ooh! An olive tree!

Daytime

Mom came over today to drop off some more gifts from her friends. I've heard her kvetching about forking over money for all of the obligatory baby and wedding shower gifts, not to mention the bar and bas mitzvahs, and finally I am the one to reap the rewards. If only those rewards didn't come guilt infused with promises of thank-you notes.

My mom and her friends are single-handedly allowing the United States Postal Service to remain open on Saturdays. That reminds me: I need to buy stamps. Now there is a great idea for a new baby gift.

14 Days Old

. . . .

My friend Louise just had her baby. She went through a shitload of fertility testing, had two miscarriages, and suffered through an entire pregnancy's worth of shots for her four-year-old daughter, Jupiter. I felt horribly guilty that it took me and Zach only three months of trying to get pregnant with Sam. So many people I know have gone through fertility issues. My older sister, Nora, has been trying for three years to get pregnant. She's had two miscarriages so far, plus one pregnancy that looked successful but ended at eighteen weeks owing to complications from chromosomal abnormalities. She still hasn't completely recovered from that one. I was terrified to tell her about my pregnancy with Sam. Zach and I found out I was pregnant right before Rosh Hashanah, the Jewish New Year, and we were overjoyed until we realized we'd have to break the news to Nora and her husband, Eddie. Would she hate me? Scream in my face? Grit her teeth, then curse me out to our mom every chance she got?

Zach and I planned to make the announcement to our families at Rosh Hashanah dinner. It was Mom's night to host; she has three sisters who rotate hosting gigs for every holiday: Rosh Hashanah, Thanksgiving, Hanukkah, and Passover. Zach's moms flew in that year for Rosh Hashanah, a rarity since we usually fly out to Seattle for Christmas. But Dawn and Mimi were readying to take a monthlong cruise along the Amazon, and they wanted to try the new-to-them experience of Jewish New Year. It felt like the perfect time to share the big baby news, but I didn't want to surprise Nora with anything in front of a group of people. I called her that morning.

"Nora, I have to tell you something, but I don't want you to be upset."

"Then chances are I will be," she guessed.

"Don't say that! I already feel bad as it is."

"As long as you feel bad, then that should make up for how bad I'm about to feel."

"Nora! You are not making what I'm about to say any easier."

"No, *you* are not making it any easier. You could have just started with, 'I have something to tell you.' You're the one who added the caveat. Now everyone feels like shit, and you haven't even said what you were going to say that supposedly was going to make me feel all bad."

"Never mind," I told her. My nerve had been lost in all of the back-and-forth.

"No, Annie, you can tell me. I promise I won't feel bad."

"You promise?" I double-checked.

"Unless you killed my cat. Or Mom. Did you kill Mom?"

"Yes. I killed Mom. And Dad, too."

"Good for you. I mean, not about Mom, but Dad was a solid choice." Nora still hasn't gotten over Dad leaving Mom for his dental hygienist when we were in high school. "See! We've moved on to patricide. What you have to tell me surely can't be as bad as that."

"What if it is?" I stalled.

"Jesus Christ, Annie, just tell me you're pregnant and get it over with!" Nora demanded.

"What? How did you know?" I was both mortified and relieved that she figured it out.

"What else would you be babbling about for twenty minutes? You never do anything wrong, so I figured this is the one thing you thought would upset me. Plus, Mom already told me."

"She knows? How?"

"You went shopping together last week, and she caught you flipping through a maternity rack on the way to the bathroom."

"Damn her."

"Almost motivation to kill her, huh?"

"Ha ha. So are you mad?"

"How can I be mad? You wanted to be pregnant, and you're pregnant. Now, if you were all, 'Shit! I'm pregnant, and I don't know what to do with this horrid thing growing inside me,' then I'd probably be mad. But I'm happy one of us can be having a baby. Then when I get my baby business figured out, we'll have some cousins."

"Phew," I sighed.

"I'm really happy for you, Annie. Just . . ." She paused. "Don't go around telling everyone just yet. Not until you're really in the clear. I know how awful it feels to tell people you're pregnant and then to have to tell them you're not pregnant anymore, without actually having a baby."

"Okay. I won't. But I'm going to tell Mom, seeing as she already knows."

"She started knitting you a blanket," Nora divulged.

"You're kidding. I thought she was all Jewish superstitious, don't buy anything for the baby until the doctor slaps it on its ass."

"It'll take her longer than nine months to knit it. And doctors don't really slap babies on the ass. At least I read that they don't in one of my baby books."

I swallowed at the thought of Nora and her stack of baby books, worn from rereading over a period of years. "You're going to call me soon with the same news, Nora. I know it. It's going to happen. Kissing cousins and everything."

"Can they just be hugging cousins?"

"For sure." I laughed. "I wish I could hug you right now," I said.

"You can hug me tonight at Rosh Hashanah dinner. Are you bringing your famous yum-yum cake?"

"I made two of them, so there will be leftovers."

"That's my sis."

Nora and I hung up, and a wave of relief washed over me. Zach and I agreed to tell our families once we made it to twelve weeks and the midwife gave us the all-clear. I did confirm with my mom that I was pregnant, and she subtly spent the rest of the night pushing extra turkey on me. "Protein is good for you." She smiled, winking.

I had hoped Nora would soon be able to make a similar announcement, but as yet she and Eddie are still trying. If ever I pray for anything, it will be that Nora gets her chance to be a mom, too.

Afternoon

I speak with Louise for a few minutes in between the doctors prodding her postpartum belly at the hospital. Sam rests on my lap.

"I'm totally flashing back to the big squeeze two weeks ago," I tell her.

"The big squeeze?"

"That's what I call the pushing out of the baby."

"Oh. I guess you could call mine the big pluck." Louise refers to her C-section.

"Like a fine violin," I assure her. "How's it going?"

"Okay, I guess. I'm a little out of it. She's cute, I think. She looks like every other baby, really. For all I know, they gave me the wrong one."

I laugh. "Does everyone keep telling you you did a good job? Every doctor that visited me in the hospital said something like 'I heard you did great.' Was that just for me? Like, I was so awesome at screaming and swearing and punching my husband's arms that word was traveling around the birthing floor? I didn't get it."

"They were full of shit. They said that to me, too, and all I did was lay on a bed while they pulled a baby out of my anesthetized stomach."

"Bastards."

"How's it going with Sam?" Louise asks.

"Okay, I think. I wish someone would come by and tell me I'm doing great at *this*, though. I feel pretty clueless. My boobs are the Antichrist. Antichrists, I guess."

"Yeah, my nips are already cracked and bloody, and I just started."

"Maybe we can compare nips when we see each other."

"Sure. Or I could send you a picture over the phone?"

"Only if I can send you a picture of my stitched-up perineum."

We laugh and commiserate over postbirth grossities until Louise has to go for a vitals check.

"Say hi to baby Gertie for me. Tell her her future husband, Sam, is a big crybaby."

"I'm sure she'll whip him into shape when they're officially engaged."

We hang up, and I pet Sam's head. "Happy two-week birthday, Sam," I say. "I will eat a large piece of cake in your honor." I yell downstairs, "Zach! Can you run to the grocery store to get me a piece of cake?"

What the hell am I going to do when Zach goes back to work next week?

15 Days Old

If there actually is a book of my life, as the Jews believe, then God must have stamped a big ol' FAIL on today's entry.

Sam will not eat right. I have scabs on my boobs, and even the nipple shield is not doing its proper shielding duty because it fucking hurts every time he feeds. I can't stop crying. I'm terrified of my baby's mouth, and it seems like any time I hold him, all he wants to do is attack me. Is this a sign of things to come? Is Sam going to grow up to be a horrible man who attacks women and thrives on their pain? Or worse: a cannibal? Sick little shit. I know I'm not supposed to say that or feel this way. I'm supposed to adore all of his sweet baby quirks and praise him when he does something right. I shouldn't hate him for doing something wrong, even though it's causing me debilitating pain. I should love him because he is my baby, and that's what moms do: They love their babies unconditionally.

But it is so fucking hard when it feels like he hates me.

Later

Latch. Pop off. Latch. Pop off. Latch. Pop off. Every. Single. Time. It hurts like someone is tearing off my nipple with flypaper.

I call my mom to complain, and she tells me, "I've got a case of formula ready for you right here whenever you ask for it."

"You bought a case of formula, Ma?" I'm livid. "I told you I want to breastfeed!"

"It's for emergencies. They had it at Costco. If you don't want it, I'll give it to Marcy's daughter. She's due next week."

"Don't you dare force that on her. Who is Marcy again?"

"I play canasta with her every third Wednesday."

"And you have to get her daughter a present?" I marvel.

"Of course. Marcy bought you that set of sports team teething rings. She said you didn't send a thank-you note yet."

"By all means, give her daughter the formula, then. Goodbye, Mom." I hang up.

Odd Success of the Day:

Sam's belly button scab fell off. And I almost threw up. Am I supposed to save this nasty-ass thing? Don't some people eat them? Or is that the placenta? I think this is technically part of the placenta. I wonder if Zach would notice if I sprinkled it over his pasta tonight.

No, I did not do it.

16 Days Old

My friend Devin, the school librarian from work, called to check in today. Two weeks into my maternity leave, and I'm jealous of people at work. This does not bode well for the five months I have to be home. At least I get to spend more time with Doogan. When he's not running away from the shrieking parasite attached to my boob.

Devin, always the librarian, found a lactation specialist for me only twenty minutes from my house. Her name is Joanne, and she has a storefront lactation shop in a strip mall. I call her, and before I've even paid her she talks to me for a half hour about all of the things I'm doing and what I can do to help my pain. She says I can bring Sam in, and she can help me learn how to make him latch more comfortably. I'm strapping him into the car seat the second he wakes from his nap.

17 Days Old

Joanne worked wonders on Sam's latching technique, but she told me my breasts had "trauma" that would take a while to heal. Little turd has caused me trauma! And now that I'm getting him to latch, I can't get him to unlatch. He is seriously stuck to my boob right now, asleep. Joanne suggested sticking my finger in his mouth to break the seal, but I'm afraid of cutting him with my nail. I'm *afraid* of cutting this delicate flower when he is causing *me* trauma.

See, I'm not entirely evil.

18 Days Old

This morning I opened the door and a box awaited me along with the newspaper. The return address was from a funky-looking kids' store in Chicago, and inside was a onesie that read, "I love boobies," and a frightening-looking clown stuffed animal. A note with the gifts read, "I never know what to get people with babies. The shirt thing made me laugh, and the clown scared the shit out of me, so I thought, why not? Bummed I missed the bris! Love, Annika."

I'm pleasantly surprised she bothered to send me a gift at all. She must have a new, straitlaced boyfriend who gave her the idea.

Doogan wandered off with the clown toy after he spent a half hour stuffing himself into the shipping box. Which makes one wonder if Annika mistakenly purchased a catnip-filled toy for the baby instead of an actual baby toy. Win-win if Doogan hides the thing.

FACEBOOK STATUS

Between the onion in the garbage from last night's dinner, my hormonal sweating through four t-shirts in bed, and Sam's head smelling like Zach's armpit, I'd like to suggest that no one come over today.

19 Days Old

Two days and counting before Zach goes back to work as an IT specialist at a local bank. "What are you so worried about?" My mom holds Sam as I drag a pen along the seams of an envelope. Two half-finished thank-you notes jeer at me. "I raised you kids without your dad around, and you turned out decent."

"I'm not worried about Sam being decent. He barely has a sporting chance, what with being your grandson." I smirk. "I'm worried about generally sucking as a mom," I explain.

"Let me let you in on a little secret: All moms suck much of the time. The beauty about being a stay-at-home mom is that there is no one to watch you fail. It's not like Sam is going to tell anyone. You'll be back at work before he learns to talk."

"Mom, you're wigging me out a little. And yet, you are very wise. You sure you don't want to move in for a few months?"

"Oh, you'd love that. We couldn't spend two days in Lake Geneva without the battle of the air conditioner. No, I'll just be around for support when you need me. At least until I go to San Francisco next month."

"I can't believe you're still going. You have a grandchild now!" I'm worried more about me not having her to help than my mom not seeing Sam, but it sounds better when the baby is the one being the baby.

"He won't remember. And you'll make it without me. What if I were dead? You'd have to do it without me anyway. In fact, pretend I'm dead. It'll be easier."

"Ma! Why do you always have to go to the dark side?" I ask.

"It's part of my charm, I guess."

Doogan looks at me, and I swear I detect a shrug. "She's your mother," he says.

I have managed to take care of Doogan for seventeen years. I'll take that as a good sign. Then Doogan bites me, and I shove him off the couch.

I'm screwed.

20 Days Old

Zach goes back to work tomorrow. I am terrified, scared shitless, and entrenched with fear. I have to be alone with this baby all day, every day, and I don't know if I can do it.

"You're going to be fine. You've been doing it already for three weeks," Zach tries to comfort me as we watch *Supernatural* on the couch. Sam sleeps peacefully on Zach's chest. I give him the stink-eye, just in case he can sense I'm not happy with him.

"I haven't been doing it for three weeks by myself. At first I was in the hospital, and you've been here the whole time, playing a supporting role, as has my mom in her morbid kind of way. Plus—*fine*? I don't want to be fine. I want to be the best, most kick-ass mother on the planet. And beyond. I want to nurse him lovingly whilst I bake cakes and keep the house so clean you can hear little chimes of sparkle ringing from the countertops. I want Sam to learn sign language and ten other languages and to fit all the right shapes into that ball with the shapes cut out that five different people bought for him. Fine wasn't good enough for me before I had this baby, so it certainly should not be good enough when we're talking about the health and happiness of our first-born son!" This would be the start of many a sleep-deprived diatribe on the subject of mama failure. But Zach will soon be lucky enough to get away from it all for ten hours a day, five days a week. Son of a bitch.

Middle of the Night

Full-on panic that Zach goes back to work tomorrow. Thank God for QVC. I don't know what I'd do without the hypnotic beauty of twenty-four hours of gemstones.

21 Days Old

· ·

FIRST DAY WITHOUT ZACH GOALS:

- Feed, clothe, change, etc., Sam.
- Cut fingernails.
- Paint toenails.
- Bake chocolate-chip cookies.
- Take nap.
- Master Moby Wrap.

Zach is gone, and so far so good. Nothing out of the ordinary, and I did manage to write three more thank-you notes. Perhaps I will send them before Sam's first birthday.

I spent much of the day practicing intricate wrappings of the Moby Wrap so I can wear Sam around when I go places. Working with at least twenty feet of fabric to somehow transform it into a safe nest in which Sam will lie seems semi-impossible, but I've made it my quest for the day. Or maybe the week. Why rush these things.

FIRST DAY WITHOUT ZACH ACCOMPLISHMENTS:

- Blah blah blah Sam.
- Managed to knot my Moby Wrap and watched it fall on the floor.

- Fell asleep while on toilet (nap?).
- Ate half a roll of refrigerated cookie dough (baked in my stomach?).

When Zach arrives home, the house is the same mess it was before he left. My face is still the same mess it was before he left. Zach looks like he just returned from a three-week trip to a spa. I pray for a gigantic, dribbly poo to slither into Sam's diaper so I can hand it off to Zach, but for once Sam's baby buns have clammed up. Not that Zach would care. "I missed you so much!" he proclaims to Sam as he swings him around the room.

I should take my act on the road. How much does an Invisible Woman make?

22 Days Old

I am still addicted to my squeeze bottle. I don't know if I'll ever be able to poo without it.

My Moby Wrap skills are improving. I even imagined Ellen was cheering me on from the TV as I pranced around in it. (Sans Sam. I'm not *that* good yet.)

THE SEXIEST THING THAT HAPPENED TO ME THIS WEEK:

Zach came home from work tonight while I was nursing Sam. His latch and my trauma are greatly improved, but he's very touchy about things. If I make the tiniest move, Sam unlatches, starts crying, then I start crying, and this goes on for a good fifteen minutes. It becomes a serious problem when I have to go to the bathroom. Really badly. As I've had to for more than an hour.

"How was your day?" I mouth to Zach as he gingerly closes the garage door.

"Good. Yours?"

"I have to poo," I mouth.

Zach looks confused.

"I have to poo," I repeat.

"You want some food?" Zach attempts.

"Oh, for fuck's sake," I blurt out. "I don't have time for these Who's on First shenanigans. I have to take a shit, and I don't want Sam to stop eating. Help me."

"What do you want me to do? Bring you a chamber pot?" Zach laughs.

"I'll give you a chamber pot on your head," I growl.

"We don't even own a chamber pot," Zach argues.

"Then I'll use a Crock-Pot. Just help me! Come here."

Zach walks over to our big red chair where I like to sit while I nurse. "Help me up while I keep him latched." Zach supports my arms as I use the remnants of my stomach muscles to get out of the chair. I attempt to glide over to the bathroom, and I manage to keep Sam happily eating. Once I'm in the bathroom, I realize Zach is in for a treat.

"You have to pull my pants down," I tell him.

"That's what she said," Zach jokes.

"Yuck it up, Chuckles. This may be the last instance you hear those words uttered in your life," I warn.

Luckily I'm still wearing maternity yoga pants, so it's not too difficult to pull them down. The next part of the process, however, proves to be a tad more complicated.

"You have to squirt me while I poo." I'm on the toilet seat now, and I urgently need to go.

"Squirt you?" Zach asks incredulously.

"With my trusty squeeze bottle. It's the only way pooing doesn't hurt."

"Unh," is all Zach can muster.

"There are stitches down there, and water makes the poo come out easier! Now be a man, and squirt my butt!"

Zach grabs the half-full squirt bottle off the sink and flails his arms around, looking for a place to squeeze it.

"Empty it first, and fill it with warm water. It has to be warm!" I'm trying my damnedest to hold it in, but it's already been too long. "Faster! I'm ready to go!"

"The water won't heat up!" Zach shouts as he repeatedly splashes his fingers under the faucet to check the temperature.

"Hurry!" I shriek. Sam doesn't seem to notice any of the commotion. I imagine he's probably reveling in my discomfort, as he is wont to do.

"It's warm! It's warm!" Zach declares, and fills the bottle to the rim. When it's full, he turns around and yells, "How do I aim it?"

"I'll stand up a little, and you squirt at my ass while I poo. But don't look!"

"How am I supposed to aim it and not look?"

"I'm feeding a human being and taking a shit. Learn to multitask!"

The instant the water starts spraying, I clear out my system in a matter of seconds.

"Done," I announce.

"All that for a three-second shit?"

I sit back down on the seat, relieved.

"Now who's going to wipe?" I ask.

23 Days Old

. . . .

My students just about broke me today. My mom, visiting, found a box on my porch with a note attached. (Does no one ring the doorbell? I would love to speak to an actual human being besides my mother.)

> *Didn't want to wake the baby. Your advisory made this for you with Abby in art class, and I had to drop it off. We miss you! Love to Sam!*
> *—Devin*

Wrapped up was a decoupaged box covered in pictures of my advisees. Inside were letters, written in the formal style I taught them, wishing me happiness and telling me how much they missed me. I handed Sam off to my mom so that I could read sentiments from children who actually care about me and communicate with me. It was positively abstract to imagine Sam would one day be able to do both.

24 Days Old

. . . .

I had an appointment with Joanne today. I may visit her every time Sam needs to eat. Perhaps move into the parking lot outside of her office in an RV. My nipples are looking like booby battle-fields, and Joanne suggested I put olive oil on the scabs to help them heal. I hope next it's something like frosting. I'd smell better. And Zach could lick it off. Just kidding! The next time I let Zach near my nipples, Sam will be studying law in college. Or farm studies. I don't care what he majors in as long as he's keeping his distance from my nipples.

The truly exciting news is that I'm done with the nipple shields. Sam figured out how to latch directly on to the real deals. Perhaps I'll turn the shields into a masterpiece of abstract art and sell it on Etsy. Or better yet, I can put them in Sam's baby book.

A LETTER TO MY DEAR CHILD

Dear Son,

Here are the nipple shields that I had to wear because you inflicted excruciating pain onto your mother. I WILL NEVER FORGET.

To transition from shield to nip proper, Joanne gave me some cooling pads to place over my nipples. They are essentially Dr. Scholl's gel pads, but for nips! They stick pretty well, even without a bra on to hold them in place. When I get home, I spend a good five minutes strutting around in front of a mirror pretending I'm in some warped postpartum burlesque show. I file the moment away as one good reason to be home alone during maternity leave.

To: Fern
From: Annie
Dear Fern,

I'm typing this quickly, as Sam stirs in his crib. I know he is going to want to attack my boobs soon enough. Sometimes it hurts so badly I think I'm going to pass out. I wish it would get a million times better, and he would turn into more of a baby than a lump. I never thought I'd say this, but I think Angelina Jolie was right. She said something lumpy about her baby once, and she caught a lot of shit for it. Glad nobody's interviewing me. Especially because I can't get rid of this zit on my chest, and I desperately need my hair colored. So many grays! Jolie did *not* have to deal with these things, even if she did have a lump of a baby. Remember that glamorous breastfeeding magazine cover? Fuck.

"Lumpy" calls—
Annie

25 Days Old

Friday. Five days of being home alone with Sam, and I'm count-ing the seconds to when Zach gets home from work. Today was very similar to yesterday, as it was to the day before.

1. Wake up (officially, without the goal of trying to fall back asleep, although the desire is still there).
2. Nurse Sam.
3. Put Sam in bouncy seat while I make breakfast.
4. Two minutes later, take Sam out of bouncy seat and hold him as I eat breakfast to prevent him from busting a lung with his screams. While bouncing him.
5. Put Sam down for a nap.
6. Shower with baby monitor on.
7. Let water run until it gets cold or until Sam scares the shit out of me over the monitor.
8. Get dressed in yoga pants.
9. Put Sam on mat.
10. Read aloud from latest Tori Spelling bio.
11. Sing along to Ella Jenkins CD.
12. Nurse.
13. Put Sam down for a nap.
14. Repeat numbers 8–12.
15. Try to take my own nap.
16. Worry that I won't be able to fall asleep.

17. Fall asleep exactly three minutes before Sam wakes up.
18. Repeat numbers 8–12.
19. Take Sam for a walk. Run into "The Walking Man," a neighborhood guy often seen striding by in gym-teacher shorts and tall socks. Friendly hellos exchanged.
20. Look at the clock 16,000 times until Zach walks through the door.

Except that before #20 can come to fruition, my cell phone rings. It's Zach.

Zach: Hey, honey, how's it going?
Me: Oh, the usual.
Zach: You wouldn't mind if I went out with some people after work, would you? Like I used to sometimes on Fridays?
Me: [cold, mind-melting silence]
Zach: Hello?

What am I supposed to say? Is it selfish of me to want him to come home after I've been trapped with this kid for ten hours a day? Am I a horrible person for hating every ounce of his being for having the audacity to ask me this oblivious question? Is it wrong that I think he should automatically know that he needs to come home and that every lonely minute of my day leads up to the very moment that he does? Am I allowed to tell him any of this?

Me: I'd really rather you come home. It's been a pretty long
    week for me.
Zach: [silence. Is it angry silence? Pensive? Did he even
    hear when I said?] Yeah, okay. I'll see you in a little
    while.

We hang up, and I feel guilty. But why? Why is it perfectly
normal in his head that now that we have a kid, he can still do
exactly the same things he did before we had one? We are not
the same people. Our lives are not ours anymore, and I'll be
damned if I give him a pass to freedom—which he already has all
day long—while I'm tethered to this baby for better or for worse.
That was part of our marriage vows, right? So why do I have to
feel like shit? I bet *he* doesn't feel like shit. He's probably driving
home, cursing me out, making some ridiculously antiquated ball-
and-chain reference to his work friends, who then get to make
fun of me for being overbearing and demanding and a hard-ass
and a killjoy.

Wow. I was so mad I didn't realize how far from our house
I walked. Now I really have to pee. My enlarged bladder and
weak Kegel muscles curse you, Zach!

26 Days Old

· ·

Ah, the weekend, where I get to kick back, relax, and sip margaritas by the pool. Except that instead of margaritas I'm drinking prune juice because I'm constipated. And instead of the pool I'm on my bed watching cooking shows and changing my mind about what takeout I want for lunch based on which show is on. Right now it's Mexican for *Mexico: One Plate at a Time*.

Zach is an annoyingly good dad when he's here. Whenever he's around he doesn't seem to mind holding Sam or singing to Sam or changing his diapers. What an asshole. Doesn't he know the better a parent he is, the shittier I feel about my inadequacies? While Zach was at work all week, I tried so hard to be the sweet homemaker mom I'm supposed to be during my maternity leave. I rocked Sam and sang him songs when I could think of one to sing. I tried "Sweet Child o' Mine" by Guns N' Roses, but I was not willing to compromise on my Axl Rose impression, and the loud and screechy parts made Sam loud and screechy. The other ones I came up with seemed so maudlin. "Rock-a-Bye Baby" is bizarre. Why is this cradle in a tree in the first place? Is the baby okay after he falls out of the tree? Then I tried singing "Hush, Little Baby," but I had no idea what the lyrics were so it went something like this:

Hush, little baby, don't say a word
Mama's gonna buy you a mockingbird

If that mockingbird don't sing,
Papa's gonna buy you a diamond ring
If that diamond ring don't shine
Mama's gonna buy you some turpentine
If that turpentine smells bad
Papa's gonna buy you a cow named Brad
If that cow named Brad goes "Moo"
Mama's gonna buy you a stinky shoe
If that stinky shoe's too gross
Papa's gonna buy you a piece of toast
If that piece of toast gets burnt
Mama's gonna buy you some butter that's churned
If that butter that's churned goes sour
Papa's gonna buy you a massaging shower
If that massaging shower's too hard
Mama's gonna buy you a block of lard
If that block of lard's too fat
Papa's gonna buy you a climbing cat
If that climbing cat falls down
You'll still be the sweetest little baby in town.

Sam still didn't fall asleep after that magnum opus, so then I whipped out the saddest song of all time: "Puff, the Magic Dragon." I remember watching the cartoon as a kid and bawling my eyes out at the end. As an adult, I was no different the second I hit the line "A dragon lives forever, but not so little boys." Jesus Christ. Does Jackie Paper die? Or did they mean he just doesn't live forever as a little boy because he grows up into a neglectful dickhead who forgets his awesome dragon friend? Poor Puff, sadly slipping into his cave.

And I'm crying again.

FACEBOOK STATUS

I have a hickey on my areola. Which is a lot less cool than a hickey on my neck because a) a baby gave it to me; b) this hurts like a mother sucker; and c) wait, were hickeys ever cool?

27 Days Old

I hate the middle of the night. Hate hate hate it. I am considering moving to the Arctic for part of the year just so it can be daylight all of the time. Sam is up every two to three hours, and it feels like there is no closure to each day, just an endless cycle of stops and starts and so much waiting. Each time I feed him, I lie awake waiting for the next time. I am so fucking tired. When I ask for advice, be it on the phone or Facebook or the grocery store, people love to offer this nugget:

"Just have Zach feed him."

How? Do you want me to spend what little time I have in between feedings pumping milk from my body? That would defeat the purpose. And people (most prominently my mother) are still pushing the formula angle. I don't want to be all preachy and angry because that's not my style (to people's faces, anyway), but I don't want to give Sam formula. My body was made to nourish him, and damn if I'll let some company pump him full of chemicals to make my life easier. Having a baby shouldn't be easy. Or should it because it's supposed to be natural? But breastfeeding is hella hard and painful, and it feels like the only thing I'm doing right by this baby since his birth. Shit, I have to do something right. I really want to be good at breastfeeding. Like, the same way I wanted to get a perfect score on my SATs. So I will fight through the pain, the sleeplessness, the ravaged nipples. Somebody out there better give me a good grade soon, or I may have to take my mom up on the Costco supply of formula.

28 Days Old

Tonight we had eggs for dinner, which admittedly made me really gassy. Then Sam had a horrible night of writhing and screaming from what appeared to be gas. (Although, frankly, who can tell with babies? Maybe he was wrestling with a demon inside of him who enjoys mauling my breasts and keeping me from getting more than an hour of sleep at a time.) Zach described one particularly bad episode as looking like Sam was giving birth. Served him right. Zach wouldn't subscribe to my demon-possession theory, but it couldn't hurt to call an exorcist. Are they listed in the phone book?

29 Days Old

. . . .

I am not doing so well. Whenever Sam wakes up from a nap, I feel a wave of anxiety well up in my stomach. I don't want to take him out of his crib. I don't want to hear his crying or feel the way he immediately wants to attack my boobs the second I pick him up. I don't want to change his diaper and snap up his baby-sized snaps not made for grown-up-sized fingers. And I most definitely do not want to see that hopeful look in his eyes when he stares at my face, his mama's face, and I don't have the slightest desire to smile at him.

This is not how being a mom should feel.

My mom came over between knitting and canasta so I could cry in the shower for an hour.

Night

Zach noticed I was not myself and suggested we see a movie. We pick a Melissa McCarthy comedy because if anyone is going to make me forget who I am for a bit, it's Melissa. Not that I could possibly forget, seeing as I am wearing Sam in his wrap on my chest.

When we go up to buy the tickets, the kid at the counter actually tells us that no children under six are allowed into R movies.

"He's not even a month old. He won't even be awake," I argue.

"That's our policy."

"Your policy is to allow six-year-olds into R-rated movies but not babies who can't even see past my tits?" I berate the youth behind the register.

"Um, thank you." Zach ushers me away from the whipper-snapper and bypasses the human ticket-buying experience by purchasing our tickets from one of the automatic machines. The ticket-ripping boy isn't as much of a stickler for the "policies" of the theater, and we make it past him without a kerfuffle.

One box of Dots and sixteen thousand fat pretzel bites with fake cheese later, I am feeling pretty good. Until Sam wakes up and starts crying during the last half hour of the movie. I spend the final scenes bouncing him in the aisle near the door. My thighs are going to be speed-skater thick by the time Sam starts walking.

31 Days Old

I am horrid. Someone should come to my house and arrest me and take this baby away to a more suitably loving home environment, because this most definitely is not one. I can't do this. I don't want to do this. I don't know how to do this.

Sam woke up this morning screaming as usual, and after a night of being woken up five times, so many starts and stops and fails of nursing, two diapers filled with shit, and three outfit changes, I am done. I am over this. I want to leave. To run away. To join the circus. To move to Australia. To change my identity and become a different person who isn't the awful, ugly, depressed mother I am.

I screamed at Sam. I screamed at him and about him and on the way to his room and as I threw his diaper on the floor instead of in the diaper pail. I told him he was the worst baby ever. I told him to shut up. I told him he disappointed me, and I wished I didn't have to be home with him. Even Doogan ran away from me.

Sam is now back in his crib, screaming and crying probably, but I wouldn't know because I am in the basement with the monitor off, blasting Slayer on the stereo and vacuuming spots I just vacuumed sixteen times.

I am a horrible person. I don't deserve to have a child.

Later

The consensus is that I might not be that bad.

From my mom: "I'm sure I said things to you that weren't very nice, and you turned out fine. Good enough, at least."

From Fern: "Wait until you have another one. Then you can let them say all of the terrible things you wanted to say to each other, kick back with a shot of tequila, and laugh."

From Louise: "My four-year-old is a giant turdcake. I can't get her to leave the house without having to tell her thirty times to go pee, sixty times to wipe, a hundred and fifty times to flush, six thousand times to pull up her pants, and five million times to wash her hands. Don't even get me started on how many times I have to ask her to put on her shoes. I'm talking instructions for individual feet. Get all your name-calling out while you can. Sam doesn't know the difference. No one's sitting in therapy bitching about how their mom yelled at them when they were one month old.

"Give yourself a break."

33 Days Old

. . . .

Today my mom is taking me shopping for new clothes. I haven't wanted to leave the house in anything other than yoga pants, since my stomach is deflated enough not to wear maternity clothes, but my prepregnancy clothes don't fit me yet. We head to the mall.

"Why are we shopping at a store called Forever 21? I hate to break it to you, dear, but you are no twenty-one-year-old chicken," my mom informs me.

"Do you mean I'm no spring chicken, or are you calling me a chicken for some other reason?"

"You know what I mean." She flaps her hand dismissively.

"Their clothes are cute and cheap. I don't know how long I'll be this size, so I don't want to spend a lot of money."

"I'm paying today," my mom demands.

"You don't have to, Ma," I protest.

"I want to. Let me do these nice things for you before I become an invalid and you have to spend all of your money on a nursing home for me. Or you could always add a wing to the house."

"Ma! You are not going to become an invalid. At least not anytime soon."

"And don't waste your money on a fancy coffin for me. In fact, just cremate me. It'll be cheaper."

"Mom! Macabre much? I'm not going to cremate you. Isn't that against Jewish law?"

"I think God would understand me not wanting to be a burden on you."

"Oy. Let's just shop, shall we?"

"Fine. But if you do cremate me, at least find a pretty little vase with a secure lid. I don't want to be in one of those tacky tins they put pets in after they die. Sweet Nebbie gone, and they return her to me in a coffee tin covered in whimsical paw prints. . . ."

"Got it, Ma, no dead dog coffee tins."

I successfully manage to tuck Sam into my Moby Wrap, and I find myself feeling rather smug as I spot other moms pushing their babies around in strollers. They're probably thinking, *Look at that woman, how bonded she must be with her little one. How sweet.* Or maybe they see through the charade to read the exhausted, blotchy expression on my face, the result of crying half the night as my husband lay snoring next to me.

"That's a nice one." My mom pulls top after top off the racks, and I try not to veto every single one. It's baffling how my mom manages to sniff out the matronly items available at Forever 21. "Ready to try on?" she asks.

"How am I going to try on clothes? I'm wearing the baby."

"Take him off. I'll hold him. You want Grandma to hold you, don't you, Sammy?" Mom coos at the baby.

"If I take this thing off, I'll never get it back on. Plus, he'll probably start crying, and then I'll have to rush and stress out. It's better we just buy them, and I can return the ones I don't like."

As we're paying, Sam starts fussing. "He's hungry." I deflate. "He's always hungry."

"I made you that lovely nursing cover. Why don't you use it? We can find a quiet spot."

"I'm not ready for public nursing, Ma. I can barely do it when I'm sitting in a soft chair with ten pillows behind me, a nursing pillow under him, and my bra on the floor. Let's just get him home."

"But we've only been here a half hour," Mom protests.

"Unless you want him to suck on your boobs, we're going home."

"In my day, they didn't even encourage us to breastfeed. I couldn't figure it out. My doctor was all, 'Meh, that's why they make formula.' And you turned out fine." She likes to say this.

We walk toward the car, trying to carry on a conversation with Sam screaming in my face. "Ma, are we really going to have this argument again? I want to breastfeed him. Period."

"I just wish you weren't so hard on yourself."

I'm starting to get that a lot.

FACEBOOK STATUS

Note to self: Probably best not to purchase ten size small t-shirts four weeks after giving birth without trying them on first.

34 Days Old

Zach wants to go out to breakfast today, a Sunday, which I am vehemently against. Breakfast restaurants are always annoyingly packed on Sunday mornings, and I flash back to the ridiculous hour-and-a-half wait times Zach and I were willing to endure during our hipster tenure in Chicago before we moved to the suburbs. Today we compromise and leave the house at six forty-five A.M., prechurch crowd, since I was already up anyway. Zach wasn't quite as game to miss out on his beauty sleep, but I reminded him that beauty sleep died the day his sperm invaded my egg.

With the amount of shit we bring into the restaurant, you'd think we're moving into one of their extra-large booths for the next three months.

Sam stays in his car seat carrier, and I almost manage to devour my entire Belgian waffle before his face turns from peachy sweet to roaring red.

"What's wrong? What happened?" Zach is still not completely awake, even though he is on his third cup of bottomless coffee.

"He's hungry," I say, sounding a lot like Eeyore. "As always."

"Do you want to try feeding him?" Zach has watched me struggle for nearly five weeks and knows not to say anything that might imply inadequacy in the slightest. But he also really wants to finish his omelet.

"I could. I guess." I'm waffling more than, well, my waffle, because the thought of other people witnessing my complete failure at momness is debilitating. But one of the many reasons I chose to breastfeed was to make Sam more portable and spontaneous. I have to try it sometime, and the restaurant isn't crowded enough for all eyes to be on me. Hell, at this time in the morning the only eyes on me are from senior citizens who woke up earlier than we did. "Can you hand me the nursing cover?" I ask as I gingerly unlatch Sam's seat belt. Zach digs through the diaper bag and pulls something out.

"This?"

"That's a blanket."

He dives in again and holds up another item. "This?"

"That's another blanket."

Three blankets later: "How many blankets do we need in here?" he laments. Zach manages to find the nursing cover my mom made for me out of old Strawberry Shortcake sheets from my childhood bedroom. Attached is an adjustable strap I throw around my neck to hold the cover on, and she even thought to fill the lip of the cover with a bendable wire to give it a tentlike stiffness.

I hold Sam with one arm and throw the nursing cover over my head. I slide myself back into the booth, Sam rooting around my fully dressed chest, the smell of my milk driving him mad. His behavior is so primal and animalistic, I'm a tad creeped out by him. His neediness only adds to the pressure of feeding in public. I flick at the hook on my nursing bra until I feel it release, and I whip the nursing cover over Sam's head so he is now hidden from others' views. I, however, can see him as I look down into the bowed opening. My mom really did a great job. I fumble underneath and pull down the bra cup so my breast is available, then I grit my teeth and hold my breath while I hold Sam to latch.

And he does.

I wait for him to pull off or cry, but he's just sucking away like this is what he is meant to do. After a minute like this, I relax and even manage a few bites of my waffle. When it comes time to switch breasts, Sam cries only the tiniest bit while I flip him around and unhook the other side of my bra. Then he latches again, and we finish our meals at the same time.

An older woman hobbles by with a walker, looks down at me, and says, "You're doing a good job." She smiles and trundles on.

Is she some sort of angel who's been watching me the last month and knows my thoughts on self-loathing? Or is she just a nice woman who says kind things to people? Or is she a crazy lady who thinks I'm smuggling saltine crackers and rolls underneath my cover, and she's commending me on my thieving skills?

Whatever it is, it makes me feel damn good. Better than I have in a long time. As we leave the restaurant, Sam back in his car seat and me blissed out by the elderly compliment, Zach points out, "You're looking a little lumpy. I think you forgot to hook your bra things back on."

"Shut up," I say. "Don't ruin it."

To: Annie
From: Annika

Hey Baby Mama! How's your little guy? How are you? I have to come visit sometime. Or you could always bring him into the city for lunch.

So Kesha is coming in concert, and I know you love her. Why don't we go? Maybe it will inspire us to get the Pee Sharps back together. ☺ You can wear Sam on your back and the guitar on the front!

XXXOOO Annika

35 Days Old

. . . .

Hmmm. I do love Kesha. I think she reminds me of my college self, which would then make a lot of sense for me to see her with Annika. But this show is in Milwaukee, about an hour from my house, and I'll need to bottle some breastmilk for Sam and pump somehow at the show if I don't want to explode or get a breast infection. We'd probably be the oldest hags at the show, but it could work. I'll ask Zach how he feels about having to put Sam down for bed without me.

This is too weird, right? I'm a mom. Moms don't go to Kesha concerts. Moms drop their kids off at Kesha concerts.

My mom reminds me how just last month she went to a Neil Diamond concert, and her hands were raw from clapping so much.

Fuck it. I'll go.

To: Annika
From: Annie
     I'm in for Kesha. Brunch and Pee Sharps reunion will have to wait.

36 Days Old

Zach thinks it's hilarious that I want to see Kesha in the first place, because, as he puts it, "You could be her mom," which is so not true. I mean, I guess I technically could, since I got my period when I was eleven, but whatever. The concert is in five weeks, and hopefully I'll be walking 100 percent normally by then. I have my six-week appointment next week, and that's when I get the go-ahead for all kinds of things: lifting, running, sex. Oy. I can't even think about anyone going in or out of my vagina right now. I'm still completely addicted to my squeeze bottle. I hope my midwife encourages me to keep using it. Forever.

I'm also going to ask her when my massive quantity of hair will start falling out. I know some people love that their hair gets extra thick and lustrous during pregnancy, but I already have a shit ton of hair and having more just makes me look like the Cowardly Lion after he had his Emerald City make-over.

I definitely need to ask about all of this black shit in my belly button. It's like a caked-on layer of crud that I can't pick out, not that I would try. Sticking my finger in my belly button makes me want to heave. But I don't want it to look like I have filthy hygiene habits. Does everyone have crudded-up belly buttons after giving birth? Why don't any of my pregnancy books talk about this? Or the fact that I have so many new veins on my leg that

Google Earth might mistake them as a route to the local 7-Eleven. And is this stripe down my stomach going to go away? It magically appeared during the pregnancy, so can't it just magically disappear now that the pregnancy's over?

One last thing: the bright, shiny, Rudolph-intensity pimple that blossomed a week after the birth smack-dab in the middle of my chest. How long is this douchebag going to hang around?

I better write all of this down and bring it to the appointment with me. Wouldn't want to forget anything important.

37 Days Old

Devin emailed me from work and asked if I wanted to bring Sam to an English Department meeting. At first I was totally game. Why not? I've seen other people do it, and I've taken part in the mass adoration of new staff babies. But the more I think about it, the more I recognize the potential for a clusterfuck. I'd have to see my sub. Everyone would witness my still jiggly belly. Sam would most certainly cry and need to nurse, and then there is the possibility of one of my students or—gasp!—colleagues seeing my breasts. And what if it's a bad latch day? Or Sam poos all over himself? Or all over me? What if he catches some nasty middle school disease? What if he gets lice, and there are itty-bitty bugs crawling around his downy hair?

I better turn down the offer. It sure would have been nice to get out of the house, though.

· · ·

THE SEXIEST THING THAT HAPPENED TO ME THIS WEEK:

I found a new tributary of veins on my leg the shape of Billy Dee Williams (head only).

38 Days Old

Damn. Sam's smile is really cute. He smiles whenever Doogan walks by and brushes his tail over his face. And he smiles at my mom. Way more than at me, of course. He does kind of look like Zach. But I'm not going to tell anyone I think that quite yet.

FACEBOOK STATUS

I love when I fill out a health form for Sam and it asks for his marital status.

39 Days Old

Devin skipped out of work for lunch today because they were setting up for the retirement party in the library.

"I told them I'm allergic to deviled eggs, and the smell was giving me a headache." She offered to pick me and Sam up and take us out to lunch, but with the car seat and all of Sam's crap, I thought it would be easier to meet her.

The way things went, she would have been better off with the deviled eggs. Sam, when not screaming so loudly that I couldn't hear a single word uttered by Devin, was rolling around in my arms so aggressively while I was trying to feed him that I needed twelve more hands just to hold my nursing cover in place lest I flash the entirety of Panera.

I wanted to hear Devin's gossipy goodness from work, since everyone tells the librarian everything (they are the keepers of information, after all), but Sam was not going to let that happen. After a hurried and hellish half hour, I admitted defeat and we parted ways. I suppose I'm going to become her new fodder for a juicy tale: *Annie is a terrible mom.* It will pass around the faculty until even the annoying part-time teacher's assistant looks down on me. I'll have to find a new line of work, dye my hair, change my name . . .

Maybe the circus is hiring.

40 Days Old

Zach's moms are coming to visit in a week. I'm going to pretend I forgot and see if he remembers any of the things we need to do to get the house ready. Sometimes I wonder if that's why he married me: so I could remind him of things he needs to do. Did he ever wish his family Happy Birthday before we met?

41 Days Old

Sam had another crappy night last night, which means I had a crappy night. For a while there we had three-hour/three-hour/three-hour stretches of sleep, so I was averaging about six hours of total sleep, divided up into two-hour chunks (taking into account the length of time it took to feed Sam and then get myself to fall back asleep). Last night I woke after three hours, but Sam slept until four. So I lay awake, waiting. Then, after I put him down, he woke up after one hour. So I fed him and put him down again. Then he woke up an hour later. So I fed him and put him down again. Was I supposed to feed him every time? Was I supposed to let him cry? Who holds the correct answers to all of my fucking questions?

I am painfully tired. Doogan looks so cuddly curled up on Sam's floor that I may have once fallen asleep there next to him. At least I didn't have to walk as far the next time Sam woke.

42 Days Old

Who needs therapy when you've got QVC? I might start buying one of everything just so someone can say nice things to me on the testimonial line.

Today a woman purchased a pair of white, bedazzled capri jeggings, and when she called in to tell the host that she made the purchase, the host actually exclaimed, "I'm so excited for you!" I want someone to be so excited for me and my ludicrous-looking pants. When I told my mom what I bought, she one-upped me and told me she already has three pairs. Is QVC hereditary?

43 Days Old

Sam is six weeks old today. Things I know about Sam so far:

1. He likes to eat from my boobs.
2. He doesn't like to go to sleep.
3. He doesn't like to stay asleep.
4. He thinks Daddy is funny.
5. He likes when Grandma holds him.
6. He giggles when he touches Doogan's fur.
7. He hates me.

44 Days Old

My favorite part of my six-week midwife appointment: I only weigh twelve pounds more than I did before I got pregnant.

My least favorite parts:

When the midwife went near my vagina.
When the midwife said I could start exercising again.
When the midwife said I could start having sex again.

Why did she have to go near my vagina? Hasn't it done its time as whipping girl for this baby? It did not want to open its doors for anyone, particularly one wearing latex gloves and shining an unflattering light in its face. I get the icky shivers every time I remember the speculum greeting.

So now I'm allowed to exercise. I don't get how celebrities start exercising earlier than normal humans. My midwife explicitly told me that I could not do anything strenuous before six weeks because my body needed time to heal. She made this gross analogy of a towel getting stuck in a washing machine and if I tried to pull it out, my insides would never rebound. Or maybe it was that my insides would get messed up like the towel? It sounded grotesque either way, and it was a great excuse not to exercise. Do celebs have different doctors whom they pay off to allow them to exercise earlier than real people? I don't envy them and their obscenely unrealistic need for perfection. Part of me really wants to hop back on the treadmill because I never hated exercise, but the other part of me much prefers refreshing my Facebook page sixteen thousand times and watching *Say Yes to the Dress* from the vantage point of my couch. I'm trying to remind myself how much I loved running and how good it made me feel. Even better than . . . So I'm allowed to have sex now. Do I have to let Zach know?

. . .

Side note: Of course I forgot my list of questions and couldn't remember a single one.

Later

Awaiting me on the porch when I arrived home from my six-week appointment were four enormous boxes, like the type you pack your clothes in when you're moving. Inside: Fern sent me eighteen boxes of diapers of various sizes, because eighteen represents good luck to Jewish people. Attached was this note:

"May your poos always be lucky poos."

Dear Fern,

Thank you for the eighteen boxes of diapers. Instead of putting them on Sam's tush, I was thinking we could use them as extra insulation in our attic. It does get pretty cold around here in the winter.

Love,

Annie

FACEBOOK STATUS

There sure are a lot of people running this morning on Facebook. Am I the only one sitting on the couch eating cereal? I mixed two kinds, if that helps.

46 Days Old

· ·

Did everyone I go to high school with suddenly become marathon runners? How did this happen? Some of them are even doing Ironman races! Are they trying to make all of us who haven't exercised in months feel like shit? Are they trying to motivate us? I have mixed feelings about the motivation. For some reason, looking at really fit women makes me feel like I'll never look good enough. But looking at really fit men, like, say, Channing Tatum, makes me work harder. Is it the muscles that motivate me or the distraction? Whatever it is, it is time. Today I get back on the treadmill. Now where did I put that Blu-ray of *Magic Mike*?

Later

I swear my uterus started falling out when I tried to run. Everything down below felt draggy and heavy and wide open. My uterus, my lady lips, my . . . well, let's just say I took an involuntary bathroom break less than a minute after trying to squeeze my Kegels as tightly as I could while simultaneously plodding along pathetically.

Next time I'll start with a nice, slow trot. Or perhaps a canter. I don't know which is which. I've never ridden a horse. The way they look at me with those sad eyes, like, "Bitch, have you seen how skinny my legs are, and you want to sit on my back?"

I wonder if horses ever pee themselves when they run. This one girl on Facebook posted about her Ironman race and how she had to pee on herself while riding her bike. If I didn't have a baby, would I try an Ironman? Doubtful, but what about a marathon? Half marathon? Who am I kidding? If Sam weren't here right now, I'd be spending eight hours playing *The Sims* on my computer and planning our next summer vacation overseas. We always said we'd go to Australia, but fuck if I'm ever going to be able to sit on a twenty-hour flight with a child. We're stuck taking road trips to the world's largest chicken for the next eighteen years.

Peeing myself during an Ironman looks more appealing by the second.

47 Days Old

The in-laws arrive tomorrow. I don't have the time or energy to do any real cleaning, so I took out a tub of Clorox wipes and cleaned every surface imaginable with them. The house smells like a school bathroom, and there are remnants of lint clumps everywhere. But at least it looks semipresentable in that college-student-cleaning-up-for-their-parents'-visit-so-they-don't-worry-them-and-visit-more-often kind of way.

And, yes, I did strap Clorox wipes onto my slippers with rubber bands and skate over the kitchen floor. Duh.

Middle of the Night
Why the frak will this kid not sleep more than two hours without having me feed him? Not even QVC can make this better.

How many fucking minutes can they talk about self-tanning tow-elettes?

I hope they work. I ordered three boxes.

48 Days Old

· ·

The in-laws have arrived. Thankfully, they offered to stay in a hotel. Dawn, Zach's mom, claimed it was to give our family space, since our nights are so tough. I'm guessing it has more to do with the gross-out factor of our house. I don't think Mimi could handle the random patches of spit-up that we never bothered to clean off the carpet. (I figure we'll get to them all at once when Sam's done with his spit-up phase. Or we'll get new carpet.)

It's hilarious watching the battle of the grandmas. There is a constant neediness emanating from their Chico's jackets. I can tell Zach's mom is trying to be diplomatic, but I also see a fire in her eyes when Mimi wants a turn that burns, "It's my grandbaby by *blood*." Slightly scary. I can't wait until we have dinner with my mom tonight. Three grandmas in one place. I hope Sam still has all of his limbs when it's over.

Dinner

Sam slept through most of the parental dinner at Indian Palace, until I had to nurse him. I'm getting better at feeding him in public, although it didn't help when Mimi felt the need to act as my guard dog and barked, "That's what breasts are made for!" at anyone who dared glance my way. Since I was wearing my nursing cover and most of my torso was concealed by the table, I think it mainly made Mimi look like a raving lunatic instead of a protective mother-in-law.

The conversation between bites of palak paneer and aloo gobi went something like this:

My mom: So I'm Grandma [finger quotes]. What would you like to be called? [Ballsy move on my mom's part to stake her claim on the classic Grandma, but she always thought Bubbe made her sound too old. Plus, her mom was Grandma, so she wanted to continue the tradition.]

> Dawn (Zach's mom): I always thought I'd be called Mimi because that's what Zachy called his grandma.
>
> Mimi: But my name's Mimi.
>
> Dawn: But the baby doesn't know that.
>
> Mimi: The baby doesn't know anything yet, and even if he doesn't know it now, he will know it someday. I thought he could call me Mimi.
>
> Dawn: I understand that Mimi is your name, but it's not your grandma name. My mom was a Mimi, and it is important to me that my grandbaby know his family connection."
>
> Mimi: Are you saying I have no family connection?
>
> Dawn: You know I'm not saying that, nor have I ever said that. You know what I mean. It was my mother, for God's sake.
>
> [Huffy silence.]

Mimi: Your point is valid. I propose a compromise.

Dawn: I'm listening.

Mimi: How about you're Mimi, and I'm Mimi Two?

Dawn: Like we're both called Mimi? That will confuse the poor boy.

Mimi: No. Like Mimi Part Two. The number. The sequel. Kids love sequels.

Dawn: I suppose that could work.

Thus, Zach's mom became Mimi, and Mimi became Mimi 2, the Sequel. And my mom retained her reigning title of Grandma.

49 Days Old

Zach's moms are insisting Zach and I go out for a dinner date. I argue that I have to nurse Sam, but Dawn says we could leave right after I nurse him and get back in time for his next feeding.

"He might be fussy. Dinnertime is his fussy time of day. Well, one of them," I warn them.

"We can handle it," Mimi 2 says as she strokes Doogan on her lap. She has taken to holding Doogan when her turn with Sam is up. I watch Doo try to struggle out of her arms, but Mimi 2 refuses to relinquish her grip. I telepathically send him a message that I'll give him an apple, his favorite fruit, later.

"Sam will be fine. We'll only be gone for an hour." Zach tries to convince me that all will be okay, but I don't know how he can just leave our baby in the hands of people we see only once or twice a year. I can barely get myself to leave Sam alone with Zach, even on those days when I feel like I could leave Sam screaming alone in his crib while I escape through an underground tunnel I'm kicking myself for not having installed. If something goes wrong with Sam when I'm with him, at least I can blame myself. If he's with other people and something goes wrong, what happens then? Would I leave Zach if he accidentally dropped Sam down a flight of stairs? Sue Dawn for letting Sam roll off the changing table? Attack Mimi 2 for feeding Sam organic whole-grain gingersnaps before he's ready for solids?

"I don't think we should go," I say, running through all of the incidents of negative possibility in my head.

"We're going. I already have my shoes on." Zach points to his feet.

"Oh, well, if you already have your shoes on," I say sarcastically.

After taking my sweet time nursing Sam, changing his diaper, and tucking him into a new outfit, I reluctantly put on my own shoes.

"Our cell phone numbers are listed next to the phone," I tell the Mimis.

"Thank you, dear. We also have them programmed into our cell phones," Dawn reminds me. "Because you're not leaving him with a babysitter in 1985."

Zach finally manages to usher me out the door and into the car. Five minutes after we leave the house, I shout, "Wait! We have the car seat base in our car. What if there is an emergency and they need to drive somewhere with Sam? Turn around."

Zach opens his mouth to attempt a calming sentiment but

quickly realizes that this is an argument he does not want to have with me. When we pull into the garage, I unlatch my seat belt and bolt inside, informing Zach, "I'm just going to check in."

My sneak attack proves fruitless, as the Mimis and Sam appear to be in exactly the same position they were in before we left the first time.

"Back so soon?" Mimi 2 asks.

"We took the car seat with us, but brought it home just in case you need it. Not that you will. Just if there's an emergency. Please don't drive anywhere with Sam," I mumble, backing my way into the garage.

On the road again, I remind Zach, "We have approximately 1.2 hours door-to-door."

"I don't understand why we didn't leave them a bottle of breastmilk. We have a bunch stored in the freezer."

"That is only for absolute emergencies, like Kesha concerts and murder mysteries. I'm not wasting it so you and I can go out to dinner. That's liquid gold we're talking about."

"Right. So where are we going?"

"I'm dying for some meat. How about you?"

Zach and I are not technically vegetarians, although we both were when we first met. When I got pregnant with Sam, my cravings steered toward the fleshy variety. Zach had been holding back his own meat cravings for a while, so together we began sporadic indulgences in chicken or turkey. Once Zach ordered a steak, but it was too officially dead animal–like, and he stuck with poultry from then on. For me, if the meat seems at all meaty, I'm out. But there is a barbecue place that serves the most incredible, falling-apart chicken sandwiches that has been clouding my hungry brain. And that is why Zach and I have our first official postbaby dinner date at a place called Porky's Meat Hut.

50 Days Old

Middle-of-the-night feeding. I ordered a floor steam cleaner from QVC because it kills 99.9 percent of germs and doesn't use harsh chemicals. I hate to think of Doogan licking poison from his paws. Maybe someday I'll feel the same way about Sam, too.

51 Days Old

It is becoming a common occurrence for me to sit on the shitter while breastfeeding Sam. Every time I nurse him on the right boob, I have the urge to take a poo. According to my boob guru, Joanne, something about the hormonal rush can trigger nausea in some women. She told me a story of a woman who threw up every time she breastfed. And yet she kept doing it. Are we mad?

52 Days Old

I took a trip to Target today, wore Sam in his wrap, and all went well until he started screaming during checkout like I was ripping out individual toenails from his plump little feet (my favorite part of his body, if someone made me select one at gunpoint). I already had most of my items on the conveyor belt, and the cashier in red and khaki was beeping away and placing the items into my reusable Target bags (you get five cents back every time you use one!). I panicked and began rapidly unspooling the Moby Wrap, whipping the yards and yards of fabric hither and yon until it landed in a floppy purple puddle around my feet. Sam's screaming made me feel harried to the extreme, so instinctually I did the one thing I knew would make him shut up: I lifted my shirt, dropped my bra, and shoved his head at my boob. Instantly he was calm, eating happily as I reached for a box of tissues I was about to purchase. Cradling Sam in my left arm, I ripped the cardboard cover off the tissues and began wiping down the sweat oozing from my forehead and upper lip. I crumpled the used tissue blob and tossed it into one of my red bags. When it was time to pay, I fumbled one-handedly through my purse and eventually managed to extract my credit card from my wallet. The woman behind me in line, a close stander (which meant she was getting an eyeful of boob), commented, "Nice multitasking."

"Thanks," I told her. "You should have seen me in the bathroom this morning."

"What do you mean?" she asked.

Really, lady?

53 Days Old

I awoke this morning with the most disturbing firmness in my right breast. It was too large and developed to scare me into breast cancer territory, but the size wasn't the disturbing part. It was square. I had a square protrusion on part of my breast, and it hurt. Inside and out. I called Joanne, who answered right away (seriously, is this lady the angel of boobs?). She said it sounded like a plugged duct and gave me orders to ice it before I feed Sam, massage it gently while he's eating or if I pump to release the milk, and take ibuprofen to bring down the swelling. She said if it seemed to be taking too long, I could even hold a vibrator up to my breast to help loosen it! I don't know where she gets all of this information, but it's brilliant. When the plug clears, I plan on baking her a bunch of cookies. Or buying some. Maybe a cookie bouquet? What would my boobs be without her?

Later

The square is still there. It's royally grossing me out. I have the inclination to get a piece of tracing paper and do a rubbing of it just to prove the squareness of the situation to Zach, who sounded skeptical over the phone. He also said someone brought Lou Malnati's pizza and cheesecakes to the bank for lunch. I told him he better bring me a cornucopia of theater-sized candy boxes on his way home from work for all the shit I have to go through while he indulges in endless lunch delights and pain-free boobs. I thought about asking how he'd like it if he had to put ice on his testicles every couple of hours but thought better of it if I wanted that candy.

THE CANDY COUNTDOWN:

It's 5:30 already. He better be gift wrapping that candy!

5:33. Where is he? Is he monogramming each individual piece of candy?

5:36. I need something sweet. I've already finished off the only sugary cereal we have, which is Alpha-Bits and barely counts.

5:41. I think we may have some Hershey's Chocolate Syrup. Maybe I can squeeze that onto a saltine.

5:43. Zach arrives home, and I practically knock him to the floor for my Charleston Chews. "Nice to see you, too, honey." I snarl at him as I tear at the chew like a werewolf coveting his freshly killed prey.

54 Days Old

Plug seems to be clearing. Now what to do about the indigestion I've given myself after scarfing Sour Patch Kids, Junior Mints, and Raisinets (fruit!) for breakfast.

55 Days Old

My mom carries in lunch from our favorite local Italian restaurant.

"Your hair looks nice," I note of the newly darkened color and covered roots.

"Thank you. Yours could use a touch-up," she remarks.

"I know. My grays are glowing like a shiny beacon of oldness. But I don't have time. And it's not like it matters. Who sees me except you and Sam?" I stuff in a mouthful of salad.

"Your husband, for one. Don't you want to look nice for him?"

"I have no obligation to look good for him right now. I just birthed him a baby."

"Well, for you, then. Maybe it'll put you in a better mood. You're always so surly."

"Three hours of sleep a night will do that to a person." I glare at my mom. "You know, making me feel like shit about the way I look isn't going to improve my mood."

"Forget I said anything." My mom chews her food superiorly.

I stand up and fish through our kitchen junk drawer. "What are you doing?" Mom asks. I ignore her until I find what I was looking for: a brown Sharpie. I whip it out and march into the bathroom. I remove the cap and spend the next ten minutes seeking out the two inches of gray invading my otherwise chocolaty-brown hair. Each metallic strand is quickly coated in the stench of permanent marker. When a suitable number of grays are marked out, I exit the bathroom and present my newly colored hair to my mom. "Voilà. Is that better?" I ask her.

Mom, the keeper of the perfect beat, holds her tongue for a classy three seconds, then offers, "You can get cancer doing that, you know."

I was this close to drawing a permanent marker mustache on her face.

56 Days Old

I tried running again this morning. Things went well for maybe a minute, but then it felt like the bottom was about to drop again. What a bizarre sensation. I envision my vaginal area looking something like a Hellmouth from *Buffy the Vampire Slayer*, and if I shake it up too much, everything—demons, vampires, fallopian tubes—is going to start flying out into the new dimension I opened. Not to mention the extra sixty pounds of boob I feel like I'm toting around. I don't know if I could run even if I managed to stop up my giant nether-chasm.

Best walk instead. Wouldn't want to sweat too much and agitate the marker on my scalp.

57 Days Old

My mom dropped off a box of Pixies from Fannie May on her way to knitting. "Don't go rubbing these all over your head now. They *are* brown." I might have thrown them at her if I didn't intend to eat the entire box in the coming hour.

58 Days Old

Zach and I are watching a behind-the-scenes flashback show about *Fast Times at Ridgemont High*. I just put Sam to bed, which means absolutely nothing in my cyclical sleep-wake-sleep-wake lifestyle, but it's the time of day when Zach and I get into bed and watch TV as though I'm about to sleep like the sandman intended. I'm enjoying a detailed dissection of Damone and his piano scarf when out of nowhere Zach asks, "Do you want to have sex?" The marker makeover must really be working.

"What?" I'm barely hiding the look of disgust on my face. "What do you mean?"

"You know. Knocking boots. Do the nasty. Sex?" Zach clarifies. I'm not a fan of when Zach uses gross slang for sex. Maybe he thinks it's funny, but all I can think of is the guy I lost my virginity to my senior year of high school offering me the "hot beef injection" à la *The Breakfast Club*.

"I just had a baby," I remind him.

"Two months ago," he stresses.

"I don't know if this area"—I gesture in a circular motion to my crotch—"is quite ready."

"Didn't your midwife give you the okay after six weeks?" He waggles his eyebrows.

"Put your eyebrows in check. We may technically have the all-clear, but Betty Sue has the final say. It still feels . . . different down there." Not to mention my giant dark areolae, the line down my middle, the filthy belly button, and the hideous mass of a pimple that my chest birthed just as I did to Sam.

"Different can be good," Zach notes.

"What are you talking about, Zach?"

"I don't know. Watching this show about teenagers having sex is making me want to. I can't help that I have a beautiful wife who inspires lurid thoughts."

Points for the compliment and use of the word *lurid*. Still, "I'm just not ready, Zach," I say in a gentler tone. "Can we cuddle? Later on you can masturbate into the toilet like Judge Reinhold does as he fantasizes about Phoebe Cates taking off her bikini top."

"I'll keep that in mind," he retorts.

Thankfully, the cuddling was enough for tonight, and Zach fell asleep within two minutes of cuddle time. But how long can I keep him at bay?

To: Annie

From: Louise

This new baby is such an asshole. She doesn't want to eat from me, wakes up a million times a night, and she farts all the time. ALL THE TIME. Her doctor says I should try changing my diet because maybe she's having a reaction to something in my milk, but fuck that! I already had gestational diabetes for this turducken when she was inside me, pricked myself 75 times a day, and couldn't eat a single thing I wanted. A pregnant woman who can't stuff her face is not a pregnant woman!!! Fuck. I'm going to go eat the leftover from Terry's birthday cake. There's about half left. That should be enough. Burn this email after you read it.

xo Louise

60 Days Old

My sister, Nora, came over to snuggle Sam today. She seemed perfectly content, giggling and cooing. Sam was eating that shit up (probably thinking, *You're much nicer than my mom, who can't think of a single thing to do with me 90 percent of the day. Her breastmilk doesn't even taste that good*), but I'm consumed by guilt. How did it happen that I so easily got pregnant and totally suck at this mother thing, but Nora wants a baby so badly and is a complete natural at it and can't get or stay pregnant without having to go through repeated invasive interventions? Why does life work that way? High school girls, crack addicts, and people who didn't even know they were pregnant and give birth on the toilet get pregnant all the time. Babies are born to people who truly do not want them, yet my amazing, responsible, kind, deserving sister can't seem to have a baby. It kills me.

I walk over to Sam and kiss his forehead, trying to appreciate what I have. I sit down on the couch next to Nora, who has Sam propped up on the coffee table.

"Don't you just love babies?" she asks. She's not the first person to ask me this. It's supposed to be a rhetorical question, because what kind of satanic sociopathic sonofabitch doesn't like babies? However . . .

"You mean as a group?" I ask.

"Yes. They're small and cute and smell so good, and they need so much from us."

"Tell me about it." I shrug. "Not really."

"Not really? Why?" I'm surprised that she's surprised by my answer.

"Because saying 'I love babies' is like saying 'I love cats.'"

"Don't you love cats? Look at little Doogan."

Doogan scrunches up in a ball beside me on the couch. I stroke his side for a moment, until he bites me. "Damn, Doogan! Why ya gotta hate?" I ask. I turn to my sister. "I love Doogan, yes, because I know him. That took a while. I wasn't such a fan when he used to knock everything off my dresser in college. Or when he bites me." I shoot Doo a glare. "That doesn't mean I love all cats. Just like I don't love all babies."

"You love your baby, though, right?" Nora holds up Sam in front of her face and babbles, "Mommy loves you. Yes, she does."

"Yeah, of course," I admit. And I think I do love him. "But I've known Doogan longer."

"So are you saying you love your cat more than your baby?" Nora's still talking in baby-babble voice.

"Not necessarily."

"Give it time, Annie. How could anyone not love this little butterball baby? Nomnomnom . . ." Nora eats Sam's belly.

I lean over and rest my head on Doogan's pillowlike frame. "You bite me, and I throw you off the couch," I warn. "How much time am I supposed to give it?" I ask, muffled by Doogan's fur.

"When he starts talking. Or crawling. Or maybe just smiling more. Hopefully something will just click, and then you'll realize what a lucky person you are."

Dig the guilt dagger a little deeper, why don't you? I should just hand Sam over to Nora right now. She's more deserving of him than I'll ever be.

62 Days Old

TODAY'S ACCOMPLISHMENTS:

- Folded three pairs of underwear.
- Ate a bag of candy corn I found hidden in a cabinet (I was the one who hid them, and they weren't all *that* stale).
- Made Sam laugh when I tripped over his bouncy seat.
- Wrote 1.5 thank-you notes.
- Set another lunch date with Devin for next week.
- Cut six out of ten of my toenails.

63 Days Old

I am reading celebrity magazines voraciously. I have a stack of novels on my bedside that I naively expected to devour during my maternity leave, but I can't get through a single chapter without falling asleep. These magazines are vapid crap, yet I am addicted to digesting them. I wish I could go back in time and write a paper for my women's studies classes on the way these magazines try to make women, and moms in particular, feel like ass. What the fuck is wrong with how celebrities look without makeup? Why do I have to care how fast a celebrity who just gave birth lost her weight? It's fucking disgusting. As if we don't have enough pressure to bolster a human life, we also have to look good while doing it? I wish for once there would be a celebrity, a really famous and talented one, who would always leave the house without makeup and be pregnant with mighty tree stump kankles and then give birth and show off her stretch marks and puckered stomach and veiny legs in a bikini, her gray roots showing because she's too tired to get them colored.

I wish for once there really truly was a celebrity who did not give a fuck. I can't decide which is worse: those who pretend they don't care but obviously do or those who try so hard to be perfect even when they shouldn't be. Like pictures of celebs at the airport. How the hell do they not look wrinkly and covered with Coke that spilled on them during turbulence? Do they change on the plane? And if so, why? Why do they care so much? It sucks that they do, because since they care so much about how they look, then, in turn, all of us normal human beings are supposed to feel like losers who cannot possibly look even 15 percent as good as they do.

I wish I didn't care. I wish I could stop buying these stupid magazines and giving money to the cause. I wish I didn't get jealous that these celebrity moms look so good and, even worse, love their kids instantly, and all seem to be able to breastfeed like champs the second the baby passes from their loins.

They must be full of shit. There is no way they are all breast-feeding and traveling and wearing push-up bras without getting plugged ducts and no sleep. I am declaring that all celebrity moms are part of an evil army, and I am out to destroy their un-realistic representation of what it means to be a real mom. I'll start a blog! Write a book! Post pictures to some website where people write hateful comments from the safety of their anonymous hovels!

But first I have to go to the bathroom. I wish these damn magazines would write longer articles. There's not even enough content to last a basic poo.

64 Days Old

My mom brought lunch today, and we spent much of our time on the couch watching Turner Classic Movies. I managed to do two full loads of laundry, run(ish) on the treadmill, shower, and fin-ish painting all ten of my toenails. In a month, my mom leaves on her yearly vacation to San Francisco. And while she drives me insane a good 97 percent of the time, I am freaking out. How will I survive without her?

66 Days Old

. . . .

MY SLEEP SCHEDULE:

Put Sam to bed at 7:30.

I fall asleep while watching *Louie*.

Sam wakes at 9:45. I feed him.

Both fall back asleep.

Sam wakes at 1:45. I feed him.

Sam wakes at 2:45. I feed him.

Sam wakes at 3:45. I feed him.

Sam wakes at 4:45. I yell, "We're closed for business!" at the baby monitor and shove a pillow over my head.

Zach wakes me at 7:30 when he leaves for work and hands me Sam. "I love you," he says, and kisses me. "I hate you," I grumble, and flip on the TV to QVC.

67 Days Old

Today I took Sam on an outing to Walgreens. I spent over an hour plus $67, even though there wasn't anything I actually needed except a trip out of the house. People fawned and cooed over Sam, and he smiled at them. It was all very lovely. If only they knew what evil lurked inside of his terrible mother's brain. At least I have seven new nail polish colors that I will never find the time to apply.

68 Days Old

I finally did it. Today I timed my breastfeeding and relinquished one bottle of liquid gold so that I could get my hair colored. The permanent marker is long gone, and I don't need the grays on top of my sleep-deprived craggy face to add on the years. I wouldn't want anyone thinking I'm Sam's grandma.

My colorist, Carina, along with several others at the salon, loves to share Mexican home remedies with me. While I was pregnant, they determined the gender of my baby based on the shape of my stomach and face. They also had me tie a strand of my hair around my wedding band and dangled it above my belly, and the direction of the swaying confirmed I was having a boy. Accurate, no? Now they're offering up this nugget: "Rub an egg on him," Carina says, squeezing a bottle of creamy brown into my roots.

"An egg?" I question.

"That's what my mom always told me," she says.

Another colorist chimes in, "It takes away any evil spirits that may be possessing him. It will stop him from crying."

"Evil spirits?" Are they insinuating Sam is possessed? I'd thought it once or twice myself, but nobody else has ever seriously mentioned it.

"You rub an egg over his body while you pray for calm, and all of the bad energy will transfer into the egg."

"What kind of egg?" I ask, wondering if I should take notes.

"A regular egg. Uncooked. And you roll it down his head, onto his arms, all around his body. You have to pray the whole time."

"I'm Jewish. Does that matter?" I want to make sure I do everything by the Mexican book.

"I don't think so." Carina shrugs. "It works. I used to do it with my daughter, and she started sleeping perfectly."

I have my doubts, but I listen intently. The other colorist interjects, "I know a girl who rubbed the egg over her baby, and it fell on the floor and cracked. Inside the yolk was completely scrambled. It took the bad energy and made the egg rotten."

"Did the energy escape when she dropped the egg? Was anyone else in the room possessed?" I ask. The colorists look at me like I'm an idiot.

"No," is all they say.

"Try it tonight," coaxes Carina. "Afterward, crack it into a cup of lukewarm water, and watch the bubbles rise."

"And don't forget to drink a beer every morning at breakfast. It makes your milk fill up. I hate beer, but I had one first thing every day with my son. I wanted to throw up, but I did it."

"Beer and eggs." I nod my head. "Got it."

Looks like I need to go to the grocery store.

My favorite part of having my hair colored, aside from taking five to seven years off my age, is getting my hair washed afterward. This particular salon employs reclining chairs at the sinks, so instead of ganking my head back and killing my neck, I get to splay my entire body out, feet up and relaxed. I have a favorite hair washer, Ava, and I wait in line for her magic hands. She is brilliant. I dream of being a wealthy woman and hiring Ava to wash my hair every morning. I think I'd be a different person if someone massaged and pampered my scalp every day for a half hour.

That's right: *a half hour.*

Ava scrunches and kneads and scratches my hair for a glorious, bubble-filled half hour. I've never had a full-body massage that's felt as good as Ava's hair washes.

As I lie in her chair, I attempt to clear my mind of everything—eggs, sleeping, laundry—and just concentrate on how good her hands feel. I use a method from my Rodney Yee yoga videotapes, where I relax each body part from head to toe. I even hear Rodney's soothing voice in my head telling me what to do, and I am in sheer heaven for all of thirty seconds, just down to my ears, when from inside the purse on my lap, my cell phone buzzes. I try to ignore the jumpy grind, and eventually it subsides (I make a mental note to figure out how to shorten the number of rings before the phone goes to voice mail). I begin again: Relax my forehead, relax my eyes—

The phone buzzes again. This time I wonder if something might be wrong but hope it is just two different people calling me. I don't manage to get through even two body parts when the phone buzzes a third time. I open my eyes and dig through my purse. Ava stops washing and waits patiently, while I excuse my tacky behavior. I hate being one of those women not abiding by the "no cell phone" policy pasted all over the salon walls. A picture of Doogan, the caller ID for our home number, flashes on my screen.

"Hello," I growl into the phone.

"Hi." It's Zach. "I was wondering when you were going to be home. Sam didn't nap long, and now he's fussy. I'm wondering if I should give him another bottle."

You interrupt my hair wash heaven to tell me a) Sam didn't nap well, which means he'll be a butthead later; and b) you want me to spare another bottle of my precious freedom juice? "He'll be fine. I'll be home in fifteen minutes. Just bounce him or something." I hope Zach can hear the venom in my voice, but it's probably hard for him to hear anything with the screaming baby he's holding up to the phone.

"What?" he yells.

Now I have two boys shouting at me during what could very well be the most relaxing moment of the next three months. "Just wait for me!" I scream. Now I'm getting glares from the other patrons, glares I know well from doling them out myself in the past. "I'll be home soon." I speak loudly and clearly.

After I hang up, I apologize to Ava. "I have to go," I pout.

"I'll just finish your rinse," she says, and I forgo the blissful head massage I so desperately crave. I tip her amply, as I always do, and leave the salon after a measly two-minute shampoo.

I'm officially entering this on my list of "You are never going to live this down" items. I just have to figure out whose list to add it to: Sam's or Zach's.

FACEBOOK STATUS

It takes a village . . . to get my hair colored.

Later

In the dead of night, I stumble down the stairs to the kitchen as Sam wails in his crib. The light from the refrigerator blinds me, but I know exactly where to feel for what I seek: the incredible, edible egg, which also apparently doubles as a mini-exorcist. My eyes adjust to the light, and I select the largest egg out of the carton in order to maximize demonic containment.

Back upstairs, Sam's lungs in full swing, I sidle up to his crib, armed with a symbol of life, where this whole mess began in the first place. Perhaps that irony will not be lost, and this egg will be the magical talisman that will finally allow me to sleep.

"Ssshh. Sssshh," I say as I approach him with the egg gripped between my thumb and pointer finger. The egg touches Sam's hair, and he is instantly quiet. He watches me skeptically as I roll the egg from the top of his head, along his sides, and down to his feet. As I do, I pray. "Um . . . Dear God, it's me, Annie. Please stop this baby from crying all night and keeping me awake and just being a miserable human being in general. I know that's bitchy and isn't worthy of a prayer, and I should not interrupt you while you are doing other important and godly things, but please have Sam do something that makes me like him more or please change me into a better mother. And please let my sister, Nora, get pregnant and stay pregnant and have a healthy baby."

Sam's interest in the egg has waned, and he breaks into baby howls again. "See, God? Isn't he loud? Can you maybe turn down his volume, or make me not loathe the sound of his voice so much? I'd really appreciate it. I'll make sure he doesn't use your name in vain. Does that really bother you, though? I've always wondered. Not that you can answer me, because I wouldn't be able to hear you over this baby crying!" I'm shouting now and about ready to smash the egg against the wall when Zach walks in.

"Why are you letting him cry? I thought we were doing that attachment-parenting thing." He yawns.

"Your royal 'we' is a royal pain in my ass," I grumble.

"Is that an egg?" Zach notices it in the glow of the night-light.

"Yes?" I confess.

"Were you going to crack an egg over Sam's head?" Zach asks, alarmed.

"I'm not that crazy. I was rubbing the egg over his body and praying so as to rid him of evil energy so he'd stop crying."

"Oh. Well, as long as you aren't *that* crazy," he quips.

"Go back to bed. I'll get him out." I'm defeated and rest the egg in Sam's crib.

Twenty minutes later, Sam is back in bed and I'm on the brink of falling into a light and unsatisfying slumber when I'm jolted awake by a crunch, followed by the familiar unpleasantness of my son's dissatisfaction with life.

"Shit!" I exclaim. "I left the egg in his crib."

When I return to the scene of the scramble, the egg is dripping from Sam's hair and smeared into his sheets. I'll be discovering bits of shell until he moves into his big-boy bed. I guess I'll never know if I managed to trap the devil inside the egg. I'm guessing not, because neither Sam nor I fall back asleep.

Life would be so much easier if I were the possessed one.

69 Days Old

I haven't watched this much TV since I had free cable in college. I've already re-binge-watched *Battlestar Galactica,* and I'm halfway through re-binge-watching *Buffy*. In between episodes, usually while I'm making food, I watch daytime TV. Zach and I vowed we wouldn't let Sam watch TV until he's two, as research suggests it's not good for developing brains, and he's not technically watching. But in my grand tradition of beating myself up for being a horrible mother, I have to wonder if some of the noise from the TV—future weaponry from *Battlestar* or chilling screams from *Buffy* or canned laughter from sitcoms—is going to cause irreversible damage to Sam's brain. Am I causing ADHD as we speak?

Maybe I should start watching with the closed-captioning on instead.

Later

I now have a wicked headache from playing Bach on the stereo (to regenerate Sam's brain cells) while reading the closed-captioning on the TV. Perhaps I'll invest in some wireless headphones. Or a book.

71 Days Old

I have no idea what I'm supposed to do to entertain a two-month-old. I read him little books and sing him songs. (For the life of me, I still can't come up with any good kid songs, so I've started singing Sam "One" by Metallica. At least it starts off slow, and he doesn't need to know it's about a war veteran who lost all of his limbs and wants someone to relieve his misery by taking him off life support. Doogan always slinks off after the chords change and I start headbanging.) At this point, the one thing Sam truly enjoys, besides sucking the life out of me one boob at a time, is going in the Moby Wrap while I walk around the neighborhood. But how will I binge-watch TV if I have to leave the house?

Later

Compromise: I downloaded a bunch of fan-geek podcasts that I can listen to while I walk. Nerdery be thy savior.

73 Days Old

Zach and I are watching TV during the postbedtime, pre–second bedtime Sam sleep. We're loving *Orange Is the New Black*, but I'm hoping the girl-on-girl action isn't putting any sex ideas into Zach's head. I'm still not at 100 percent, or at least it doesn't feel that way during my attempts at morning treadmill runs. During one scene where Nicky goes down on a new inmate with bulbous breasts, I interrupt with, "I was watching QVC last night, and I'm considering buying a new bed. Or at least a mattress topper."

"From the TV? How do we know it's going to be comfortable?" he asks.

"There were a lot of testimonials."

"We don't know what kind of mad bed users these people are. They probably pay them to call in anyway."

"Don't you dare challenge the validity of the QVC testimonial line! Anyway, we can send it back if we're not one-hundred-percent satisfied."

"How do you send back a bed? We'd have to pack the thing up and bring it to a post office and pay a shitload on shipping. Please don't order it. I let it slide when you bought the olive tree, but we do not need a home shopping bed."

"Okay," I agree as the sex scene stealthily passes us by.

We watch for another few minutes, when Zach sneak attacks me with some neck kisses. "What are you doing?" I ask, trying to wriggle away.

"I'm kissing my wife. Sam's asleep. Now would be a good time for . . ." His eyebrows dance the language of nookie.

"For eyebrow dancing? No thanks. I'm good."

"Don't you want to, Annie?" He gives me the same look he uses to convince me to bake him cookies.

"I don't know. I still don't feel ready," I admit.

"What if we don't do everything? Just a little," he suggests.

I shrug. "I guess. But you can't touch my boobs because they're too sore."

"Okay. Can I look at them, at least?" he asks.

"I suppose. But don't freak out by how big and floppy they've gotten," I warn.

"I've seen them when you're nursing, and they are not big and floppy. Well, maybe a little," Zach zings. I elbow him.

"And you can't go down there, either." I point to my crotch.

"Why?"

"Because I already said I'm not ready! My vagina is scared. Respect the vagina."

"So what are we talking? Backdoor action?"

"Jesus Christ, Zach. You think I'm going to start letting you in there just because I won't let you in anywhere else?"

"Then what?" he asks, more confused than dickish. I feel a tinge of guilt, but I remind myself that I'm the one who carried, birthed, and feeds our baby, and I need to have some say in what happens to my body and when for a change.

"Let's start with kissing. We can work our way up from there."

"Kissing's good. I seem to remember a time when all we did was kiss," Zach reminisces.

"Yeah," I commiserate. "Our first date. Then it was all downhill from there." I smile at the memory.

"And what a fun trip downhill it was." Zach leans in for a make-out session equivalent in chastity to my sophomore year in high school. It was fun and frisky, but I could definitely sense Zach wanted more. When will my vagina stop being such a pussy?

74 Days Old

Mom and Nora visited today, and aside from nursing Sam, I managed to not hold him for a good five hours. I refuse to admit that something felt missing from my body.

"So you're still going away, Ma? Even with this little poochie here?" Nora presents Sam to my mom, and I allow her to give my mom the guilt trip she deserves.

"Sam will still be here, and he's so young he won't know the difference," my mom dismisses.

"But I will," I chime in. "What if I can't handle being alone with him every day of the week? What if I go insane, and by the time you get back I'm sitting in a corner scratching pictures of forest animals into the drywall?"

"What are you going on about?" my mom asks. "You will be fine. Nora will be here."

"No, she won't. She lives in the city and has a job and a husband and can only come out here when she doesn't have anything better to do."

"Hey!" Nora contests. I mouth, "Sorry," and continue my defense. "You're sure you can't stay home just this one year?" I press.

"Honey, my sister and I are getting older. It is important for me to spend this time with her. I have complete faith in you that Sam will be okay—even thrive—without me here. Plus, I'm going to take care of him when you go back to work. This can be like my vacation before I start my new job as Sam's caregiver."

"It's not technically a job if she's not paying you," Nora points out.

"Just wait until you have a child you don't know how to take care of, and Mom abandons you," I tell Nora as I escape to take a shower. "And for your information," I call back, "I had sixteen-foot-high brick walls built around the house while we've been sitting here, so neither of you will even be allowed to leave again. Get comfy."

75 Days Old

. . . .

Even the batteries in the carbon monoxide detector don't want me to get any sleep.

To: Annie
From: Louise

    Holy shit turd and a half. What the fuck was I thinking having another kid? Jupiter is on top of me twenty-four hours a day. She won't let me sleep. She keeps having nightmares and coming into my room. Last night I just put the baby down, which took me a good forty-five minutes, and I close my eyes for one minute before the apparition of Jupiter appears and says, "I had a nightmare about an Old Navy mannequin. I looked at it, and then it moved!" That is some freaky shit right there. And now I have another place I can't take the kids if I need to run errands. Better off anyway. How many of those stupid stuffed animal balls can I buy from the checkout just to keep my kid quiet for three minutes while I bleed money?

Hope you're faring better than me in the sleep department.

Lou

77 Days Old

. . . .

I went walking with Sam today in the Moby Wrap. I listened to a particularly dorky *Harry Potter* podcast, although there's only so much one can say about a book and movie series that I've read sixteen times and watched hundreds more that is even remotely revelatory.

Then I realize that there will come a day when I can read *Harry Potter* aloud to Sam.

A rush of joy burns in my stomach that I haven't felt since his birth. Or before his birth, when I was hopeful and naive. I almost believe he will not be this age forever. At some point he will start to talk and walk and share in countless pop cultural milestones with me.

I have something to look forward to.

Sam and I round the corner, and I'm veritably beaming with my new discovery, when we run into the Walking Man.

"Hello." He nods.

"Hi," I reiterate.

"Hard work there." He addresses the lump in my wrap.

"Hmmm?" I clarify, as I'm not quite sure to what he's alluding.

"Exercising with a baby. Good for you!" he commends me, and heel-toes speedily away.

A future with *Harry Potter* and a compliment? Somebody pinch me.

(But not on my nipples, please. You don't want to know what I'd do to you if you did.)

78 Days Old

When I first became a teacher, I told myself I could buy one fancy thing with my first paycheck. That thing? A boxed set of all of the *Monkees* episodes in existence. *The Monkees* was my favorite television show as a kid, when they celebrated their twentieth anniversary and aired on several channels from local to MTV. My mom took Nora and me to a reunion concert when I was merely seven, and I cried when they sang "Daydream Believer." At the time I thought it was a sad song, since Davy (may he rest in peace) was telling sleepy Jean to cheer up.

I pull out the box set, untouched for several years, and pop in the first disc. Immediately I'm transported back to elementary school, when Nora and I danced around our living room to her cassettes and she made out with classic photos of Mike. (Never mind that the Monkees were well into their forties at the time of their reunion. They will forever be etched into our brains as the romping foursome of the TV show.) Sam seems to enjoy the sound of the show, and he gives an extra oomph to his neck extensions during tummy time.

Could I be doing something right?

79 Days Old

Has anyone seen my ass? I seem to have misplaced it while giving birth. Or maybe it's just reattached itself to my stomach.

> To: Annie
> From: Annika
> Ready for Kesha? I'm painting my nails for the occasion. You should consider some crazy makeup, too. Can't wait!

80 Days Old

Some mornings, I love to see Sam smile at me, and I whisk him out of bed with a snuggle. Other days he's so whiny and grumpy that I'd rather leave him in there and beeline for the Dunkin' Donuts drive-thru for a finsky of Munchkins.

81 Days Old

Last night Sam was up five times. *Five times.* Five times of cry-ing, feeding, and wrestling him down to sleep. When I'm that tired, the middle of the night is so scary. I remember reading Roald Dahl's *The BFG* when I was a kid and he wrote about three o'clock being the Witching Hour. I am not supposed to be awake at three o'clock. Something happens to my mind, and it is not right. I am not right. My thoughts spiral out of control to a dark, terrifying place, a place I would never admit I go to anyone. I think about doing terrible things to myself, or to Sam, hating my-self for feeling that way, hating Sam for the guilt and for coming into this world and making me turn into this monster. Picking him up from his crib and wondering if I can control myself from doing something atrocious. Feeding him without feeling love.

Then morning comes, and I don't feel as bad, and I make it through the day and Sam makes it through the day and Zach gets home from work and things feel like they might be getting better.

And then it's the Witching Hour all over again.

82 Days Old

"There are three bottles, just in case. You might only need two."
Tonight's the Kesha concert, and it will be the longest period of
time I've been away from Sam since his birth. The concert is in
Milwaukee, which is about an hour's drive from our house. Between those two hours of driving plus the two to three hours of
the concert, I'm going to have to pump breastmilk in the car lest
I get another plugged duct. I've never had to use the pump's bat-
tery pack, and I'm nervous that it won't have enough juice to suck
the milk out of me. Not to mention the sheer awkwardness of having my boobs attached to miniaturized farm equipment in a car
parked out in the open. I'm not as anxious about having them ex-
posed near Annika; we had enough changing room shenanigans
in college that it doesn't seem all that strange. Plus, I'll be wearing a cover.

Half the contents of my dresser are now on my bedroom floor as
I try to find something to wear that a) does not scream, "I'm too old
to be here!" and b) fits me. I settle on a distressed, oversized black
t-shirt, worn thin from my college days, and a pair of shorts that
don't squeeze my stomach too much but hang enough that they
don't look like mom shorts. I finish the look with green Converses,
cool and timeless (although I know I'll regret them later when my
old-lady feet and back scream at me for not wearing more support-
ive shoes).

By the time we leave the house, I'm toting my pump bag,

backup batteries, empty bottles, a cooler, my boob cover, and enough makeup to cover a transvestite cabaret. I convinced Annika to drive, since with my months of minimal sleep I don't know if I can be trusted to helm long car rides. And this way I can liberally apply ridiculous makeup along the way.

I look up the concert venue beforehand and see there is an opening act. Based on previous Kesha concert reviews, I estimate we can get there around eight thirty and we won't miss any of her show. I'm too old to be hanging out for an opening band.

Annika and I arrive in Milwaukee around seven thirty and grab a bite to eat before the concert. She regales me with tales of adventure and romance, delicious food, and mass quantities of alcohol. It doesn't seem very different from our lives in college, except now she's not living off her parents' insurance. Since all I have to talk about is boring stories of sleep deprivation and boob pain, I let her do all of the talking. Around eight, we decide to find the venue and a discreet place to park for the breast-pumping preshow event.

We drive through Milwaukee, down alternating bright and busy thoroughfares and dark and desolate industrial streets. I don't want to park on the breast-exposing bustling streets, but I'm afraid to park on the empty ones because there is something sinister about abandoned buildings on unlit roads. I'd hate for the suction cones on my boobs to slow me down in the off chance I'll have to make a quick getaway. We settle on a side street near the venue, kitty-corner from a well-lit McDonald's but directly in front of a darkened assisted-living facility. Annika pumps us up with music from her iPad while I pump the milk out from underneath my boob cover. It's all very surreal and odd and nothing

I'd ever envisioned the two of us doing together in college. I'll pretend the whole thing is subversive and file it away for parallel life performance art potential.

I spy a disheveled man drunkenly wandering across the street, and I pray he doesn't make his way over and knock on our windows. I double-check the door lock just in case. Luck, be a titty tonight! I manage to pump without incident (or so I hope; one never knows what may sneakily make its way onto the internet).

When I'm finished (an ample five ounces!), I store the milk in my cooler, and we stuff everything in the trunk. "I hope no one is watching," I say. "What if they think I'm stowing some kind of refrigerated drugs in your trunk, and they break in and steal my breastmilk?"

"I don't think anyone saw." Annika shrugs it off, as she often does.

"That breast pump cost over two hundred dollars. I wonder what they can get for it on the black market. And think of the boost to their immune systems if they drink my milk!" I'm laughing at my breastmilk humor, but Annika doesn't seem, or even try, to get any of it.

We drive around in circles in an attempt to find street parking. Annika is certain we can score a free spot, but I'm leery of the possibility of getting stuck in Milwaukee if our car gets booted or, worse, towed with my breast pump in the trunk. "Why don't we just pay for parking?" I suggest.

"Why would we do that?" Annika balks. I might have, too, fifteen years ago, but we are adults with jobs and there is a $20 parking lot directly across the street from the venue.

"If you don't want to spend the money, I'll pay for it," I offer.

"It's the principle," she argues.

"The principle is that we are thirty-six years old, and we don't need to be dealing with parking bullshit like seventeen-year-olds visiting the city for the first time. Park in the lot. We're going to miss the show."

Annika concedes, and we give my $20 to a shifty-looking man with a wad of cash. He wraps our bill around the rest and points to a space in a lot that I'm hoping is kosher and not just some dude collecting money and leading suckers into a tow zone.

I'm suitably dolled up in face paint, and Annika looks doubly the part in preposterously uncomfortable-looking footwear. She staggers into the venue, and we scope out the joint.

I remember a time when I'd wait outside for hours before a show to ensure my body was pressed immediately against the stage and every person surrounding me. Tonight, older and germophobic, I don't want to touch any of the people here who seem to have started drinking sometime in the afternoon. Yesterday.

We decide to use the bathroom before the show starts, my practical suggestion, and we find a line in the bar area. A motley crew of "older" women wait in line, all completely trashed. I marvel as a ratty-haired gal digs into her bra and extrapolates a pouch, similar to a Capri Sun, filled with vodka. I know its contents because she proceeds to tell the entire line about her purchase and how the drinks here are too expensive and the concert tickets are so expensive and I'm afraid she's going to drop trou and pee on the floor, we've been waiting so long. Finally it's our turn for the bathroom, a single, as it turns out, and I invite Annika in with me. It seems like the right thing to do in this situation (and by "situation," I mean being surrounded by drunk Milwaukeeans also too old to be attending a Kesha concert and getting shit-faced on boob package liquor).

Annika and I stop by the merch stand, and I take advantage of the babyless shopping experience and purchase a t-shirt emblazoned with a picture of Kesha's cat, a Siamese bearing an uncanny resemblance to Doogan. I tuck it into the back of my shorts, and we make our way inside the hall.

The concert is held at what was probably once a beautiful, ornate dance hall used for swank, polished events, as many concert halls once were. Now, as we stand close to the back so as to remain untouched by the seething mass of sweaty bodies, a girl vomits white goo not ten feet from us and, consequently, passes out. As her friends drag her away, I think three things: a) *This is a far cry from the tux and tails this place once saw;* b) *Why would you get so fucked up after you paid for concert tickets that you end up missing the show;* and c) *Damn, I'm old.*

Kesha comes onstage, approximately the size of a Tic Tac from where we stand, and Annika and I spend the next hour dancing, sweating, and watching people slip on that girl's puke. I'm almost transported back to a time when I felt free to dance and not care how I looked to anyone. Or maybe I cared a lot more how I looked, since I was probably single back then. Either way, I most definitely felt better than I did now: older, bags under my eyes, heavy, milk-loaded boobs inhibiting my dance moves. I wager with myself that I'm the oldest person in the room, until I spy a seventyish-year-old man. He's not dancing so much as swaying, and for all I know he's a child-stalking perv, but for now I give him the benefit of the doubt that he's just an aged Kesha fan who doesn't give a crap what people think of him. I try to follow suit and let the glitter fall where it may.

After the concert is over, we haul ass back to my house so I can feed Sam before my boobs burst.

I change out of my sweaty concert clothes, and Zach grills me about the show. I tell him about pumping in the car, the barfing girl, and Old Man Kesha. He tells me that Sam seemed tired, so he put him down after we left and he's been sleeping ever since.

Five hours.

The second I put on my pajamas, Sam is up screaming. I nurse him and lay him back down to sleep. Two hours later he's up again. And another two hours after that.

I guess this is my punishment for taking five hours for myself.

FACEBOOK STATUS

I pray I do not look as old as James Spader.

84 Days Old

I woke up on the wrong side of the bed today. Does it really count as waking up if I never really fully had a night's sleep? If my life is a series of unfulfilling naps that fail to invigorate me? If I look ten years older than I did a mere three months ago?

Do they have mom and baby couples therapy?

85 Days Old

· ·

Sam is twelve weeks old today. He smiles. He holds his head up to some capacity during tummy time. He laughs when his daddy makes silly faces. He plots maniacally against his mother each day as to how to make her life an aging, depressing, sleepless hell in which she will rot eternally for not knowing how to love this human she brought into the world. And he poops quite a bit, too.

86 Days Old

· ·

In preparation for her trip to San Francisco (eleven days and counting), my mom drops off the Costco case of formula she's been keeping in her trunk the last two months. "Just in case," she notes.

"I'm not going to use it." I grit my teeth. "But thank you anyway. Why are there some missing?"

"My mah-jongg group was over, and we wanted to try it. Zelda was insistent it was going to taste like Ensure."

"You drank baby formula?" I laugh. "How was it?"

"Disgusting. I mixed it with a little vodka, but that didn't seem to help."

"Vodka and baby formula? So that's why you're always bustling off to a mah-jongg game."

"We know how to have a good time. What can I say?" Mom shrugs.

87 Days Old

Because of my, shall we say, lack of pleasantness (and because I look like a bulldog), Zach suggested we sleep-train Sam. He brought home a book called *Healthy Sleep Habits, Happy Child*, with a foreword by noted baby expert Cindy Crawford. I open the book, read two sentences, and throw it across the room. Well, I try to, but I'm so fucking tired that the book arcs downward in a pathetic rainbow.

I have no interest in reading a book about sleep when I am not getting any. I give it to Zach and say, "If you want to help, you read the book. I might be tempted to club someone over the head with it."

89 Days Old

Two days later, Zach approaches me. "I read the sleep book. Some of it. It's a lot. The guy seems very focused on a baby needing sleep, and we're doing him a disservice by going to him during the night. I don't know if I agree with that."

"a) What about *Mom* needing sleep; and b) *we?*" Zach may be a great dad, but he is an even better sleeper. Not to mention his lack of mammories.

"Hey, I read the book," he tries to defend himself.

"Yes, and you also got me pregnant," I note.

"Speaking of which . . . ," Zach starts.

I don't let him finish. "You want to get me pregnant again? Do you hate me that much? I can't even take care of one kid, and now you want me to have two? This soon? My body won't be able to handle it! I'll go into the hospital and have to be on bed rest for months like Tori Spelling!"

"Whoa! Calm down. I was just going to say it was nice making out that one night and see if you wanted to do it again. I'm not asking for another baby. I barely know what to do with this one."

It surprises me to hear Zach sound insecure about parenthood. He always appears, at least through my sleep-blurred eyes, like it all comes naturally to him. "Really? Because you always seem to know what to do, or when to hold him, or when he wants a song or a silly face. He never laughs at me." I pout.

"That's because you're always making faces like that. And as funny as I think you look, the comedy is not quite broad enough for Sam's palate."

"You think I look funny?" I ask.

Zach engulfs me in his wide chest. "I think you look beautiful. A little tired, but even that's beautiful because you're a tired mom. You're not just my tired wife anymore. In fact, I would have to say that being a mom has made you even more beautiful. Thank you for giving me our little son, Sammy." Zach sounds overcome with emotion, as though he might cry. What is it about me that makes all the males in my life such crybabies?

90 Days Old

. . . .

UGLY REPORT:

> Bags under my eyes.
> Black shit in my belly button.
> Zit still on my chest.

And now my hair is falling out in mass quantity. I read that this is all of the hair that did not fall out during my pregnancy. I don't mind losing the hair, but the problem is that in order to not clog the drain, I can't just let the hair fall where it may. So I untwine the nest from my fingers and stick my hair to the wall until my shower is over. After I dry off, I use a toilet paper wad to wipe the hair off the wall and toss it into the garbage. Only, by the time I'm done with my shower and start to dry off, Sam usually wakes up crying. Then I forget about the hair installation, and by the next morning the wet hair that was once stuck to the wall has now dried and fallen all over my shampoo and conditioner bottles. In order to get the hairy mess off my bottles and hands, I end up rinsing it down the drain anyway. Zach has already had to make two runs to Target for extra Drano.

File under: Stuff they don't tell you about in pregnancy books.

91 Days Old

My mom calls to check in during a break at her mah-jongg tournament.

"We got in trouble," she whispers into the phone. "They told us we needed to be quiet while we listened to the rules, but who doesn't know the rules already if they're at a mah-jongg tournament?"

"Quite the rebel, Mom. I'll get you a leather jacket with a mah-jongg tile on it for your birthday."

"Make it three bam. That's my lucky tile."

"I can't believe you're leaving me here all by myself in a week," I bemoan.

"Not this again. Anyway, we can Scope while I'm gone. It'll be just like I'm there."

"It's Skype, and it'll be nothing like you're here. Say goodbye to my sanity. I doubt it will be here when you get back."

"Gotta go—the game's about to start. Love you!" She hangs up.

I can't wait until I'm old enough to abandon my adult children.

93 Days Old

My vagina seems not to hate me quite as much as it used to during my treadmill time. I managed to run an entire five minutes. The worst part of my workout are the Kegels. Someone should make a workout video for Kegel exercises. I'm envisioning constipated, twisted expressions on the instructors' faces while they squeeze their inner lady parts. The hilarity of that makes me pee a little bit.

To: Annie
From: Louise

I am going fucking insane. It is beautiful and sunny and 72 fucking degrees outside, and all I want to do is curl up under my covers and hope it all goes away. Gertie cries all the time. Like I'm feeding her, and she's crying while I'm feeding her. I don't want to take her to the doctor because all they'll do is ask me a bunch of questions and then have zero answers. Plus, they'll be all, "She's getting so big," and I have to pretend I give a shit. And if I have to take Gertie to the doctor that means I have to bring Jupiter, and every time we go to the doctor's office Jupiter feels the need to take a shit. It's like some Pavlovian response to the office. And I have to take her into that bathroom where all of the disgusting sick children go to puke and touch everything. Not to mention I still have to wipe her ass after a poo, so I'll have to stand holding Gertie while I wipe Jupiter's ass, then wash her hands, and somehow wash my hands while attempting not to drop the baby in the toilet.

FUCK.

—Lou

94 Days Old

I made plans to get together with Louise because she seems like she needs to get out even more than I do. We meet up at a park near her home in the city.

"I swear I'm going to pack up and move without telling Terry." Lou's been threatening, to me, at least, to move out of Chicago for years. "Another house on our block foreclosed, and don't tell me that wasn't a crack pipe we passed while coming to this park. Of course we bought the house before the market went to shit, and now it's worth half what we paid for it, even though we put a buttmunch of money into it." She takes a deep breath, lets it out, and slowly smiles at me. "I'm sorry. It's just so nice to get to bitch to an actual person, and not a computer screen."

"I don't mind. It makes me feel better to hear someone who hates their life more than I do," I admit.

"Does it sound like I hate my life?" she asks guiltily. "Because I don't. Not all the time. I just don't feel like I'm doing anything right. It's hard enough with a baby you can't communicate with, but wait until Sam's an actual kid and you really fuck him up. My guilt cup runneth over."

"I can't wait until Sam can talk. Right now he's this roly-poly ball of poo. I don't know what he wants. I don't know what to do with him. He has the attention span of a donut." I pause.

In unison, Lou and I ask, "Do you want to get some donuts?" We giggle.

"Watch me, Mommy!" Jupiter yells from the monkey bars.

"I'm watching, honey! She can't do anything without someone watching," Louise asides to me.

"It's more interesting than watching a baby try to lift his head up. Why is this so hard? Why do people love being moms so much? I'm terrible at it. I hate being terrible at things. Give me the days when I was acing tests and job interviews and traveling the world on ten dollars a day. Now I'm spending hundreds of dollars on crap from QVC just so that I have someone to talk to."

"Watch me, Mommy!"

"Seriously. We're eating lunch, and every bite she takes she's like, Watch me eat this spoonful of cereal. And I'm like, Why? Why the fuck do I need to watch the way you eat every single bite of food? Once is cute, and that is it. I have no patience for this shit." Louise takes a sip of water from a Nalgene. "How exactly do you talk to QVC?"

"I call in. Order over the phone. Once I was even in a queue to give an on-air testimonial, but they ran out of time." I sigh dejectedly.

"You know there's this little thing called the internet. Makes spending shitloads of money really easy."

"It's not about the shopping. It's about the human interaction," I counter.

"Okay, so there's this place called a mall . . . ," Lou starts.

"I know, I know. But I'm not up for *that* much human interaction. QVC is a happy medium. I don't have to get dressed or, even worse, get Sam dressed and pack up all his crap. I don't have to deal with him crying in public or having to breastfeed him in front of people—"

"Watch me, Mommy!"

"I'm watching! For fuck's sake. Shit's exhausting. Speaking of breastfeeding, do you mind if I whip out the old milk jugs? It's time for Gertie to eat."

"I don't mind," I say. "How do you know she's hungry? She's not crying," I observe.

"Yeah, the one thing that keeps her from crying is being outside. She loves the sun. But that means I have to leave the house. Some of us don't have the luxury of loathing our kids in the privacy of our own homes."

"Hey, I'm the one who came to you. Besides, if taking her outside stops her from crying, isn't it worth it?" I ask.

"I'm not going to be coerced into leaving my house by someone who does her shopping over the phone like it's 1925, and you've flipped open your Sears, Roebuck catalog, thank you very much."

"Fine," I yield. "Be miserable inside."

I'm surprised when Louise takes Gertie out of her stroller and proceeds to lift up her shirt and pop out her breast without the use of a cover. She catches me looking at her. "What?" she asks.

"You don't put anything over yourself?" I ask.

"Nah. I did with Jupiter, but now I'm too droopy and tired to give a shit. I'm not half the MILF I used to be."

"That should be the title of your memoir, *The MILF I Used to Be*. We snort.

"You look great, honey! You're a superhero!" Louise calls to Jupiter, and I can see the love for her kids behind all of the grumbling.

Sam wakes in his stroller and commences his bloody murder bellow.

"Damn. He *is* loud," Lou acknowledges.

"Yes. I am so proud." I take Sam out of his stroller and fish around for my nursing cover.

"You don't have to wear that around me, you know," Lou informs me.

"I know. I'm not quite as comfortable with the public breastiness. I'd like to keep the minuscule air of mystery my boobs have left. After giving birth, I feel like my vagina has its own TV channel." I loop the cover over my head and help Sam latch. I wince at the initial tug.

"He's still hurting you?" Lou asks.

"Yeah. Not all of the time, but he latched badly yesterday, so now I have to wait for it to heal again. I will not miss the neverending cycle of boob pain."

"But you're going to stick with it. Fight the good fight?" Louise is definitely more outwardly aggressive about the importance of breastfeeding.

"I'm going to try," I say. A man, probably around sixty, walks past and looks our way.

"Good morning." He nods, and I watch as the recognition

grows on his face that he just saw a woman's breast. He turns his head speedily in the other direction.

"Hope you got a good look, pal! If it offends you so much, go to a different park!" Lou yells after him. The man walks faster.

"Impressive. You just harassed a man for saying good morning."

"Yeah, right. He's heading home to jack off at the memory of the women in the park with babies attached to their boobs."

"Mine are covered," I remind her. "Do you really think guys get off on watching women breastfeed?"

"Oh, sure. There's probably a subgenre of porn dedicated to lactating women. That dude totally subscribes."

"If it's by subscription, then maybe we can make a little extra money," I propose.

"Watch this, Mommy!"

"Jupiter is supercute, by the way. And so smart," I offer my praise to Louise.

"Yeah, the doctor started recommending gifted schools for her yesterday. But I don't have the money for that."

"So you ended up going to the doctor?" I ask.

"Yep. It turned out Gertie wouldn't stop crying because she had an ear infection. She's on antibiotics and is a billion times better already. I'm the worst fucking mother on earth because I didn't take her in sooner."

"Watch this, Mommy!" Jupiter deftly climbs a mini rock wall, turning around to check the status of her mom's attention.

"Obviously, you are an amazing mom. Look how Jupiter's turning out."

"Just wait until she starts stealing my car and using that crack pipe we found on the sidewalk."

"Well, I think you're doing a great job. You have to stop beating yourself up about things." I dole out the advice I've heard a thousand times over.

"I will if you will," she bargains with me.

We nurse our babies in silence and watch Jupiter as she hops from one piece of playground equipment to another. Two moms, doing the best we can. And possibly starring in a porn video coming soon to a computer near you.

95 Days Old

Sam has his first cold. I don't want to trace its origins, so I'll pretend it had nothing to do with our day at the park. I'm awake most of the night trying to keep him upright so he can breathe. Thank goodness I'm not sleeping, or I would have missed this classic QVC sales pitch for a pair of stretch pants:

"This is an antigravitational zone! No more wiggle, no more jiggle!"

I totally bought them.

Not that I've even worn stretch pants in public.

The woman on the phone was really nice.

I bought two pair.

96 Days Old

I return to work in two months. I hate myself for looking forward to it. I miss the regular, quantifiable success of students learning. I miss the intellectual challenges of lesson planning. I miss showering on a daily basis.

I still don't know what I'm supposed to be doing all day with a baby. Sam is awake enough now that I have to find ways to entertain him. But what more can I do with a three-month-old? Am I missing something? We do tummy time, listen to music, I read aloud from a Stephen King novel (he has no idea what I'm saying, right?) to let him hear language, and I hold and feed him. A lot. What else can I do?

Annika texted me the other day and asked me to drive into the city for brunch. I told her I couldn't, not bothering to explain why. She doesn't seem to comprehend that a baby complicates scheduling a tad more than the days of the Pee Sharps. I have to time everything correctly with naps and feedings and diaper changes. I have to make sure I have all of the necessities—toys, diapers, wipes, covers for both my boobs and gross public bathroom changing tables. And even then there is no guarantee that Sam won't cry the second I walk into the hipster brunch joint where people with all the time in the world spend two hours waiting to eat overpriced, underwhelming waffles (which I can get tastier and cheaper at our nearby truck stop), so we won't be able to eat there even after driving a tortuous hour in the car. Did I mention the death-defying drive where I have to keep one hand on the steering wheel and the other arm flanked over the back of the seat like a sideshow contortionist in order to hold the pacifier in Sam's mouth because he spits it out every five seconds even though it seems to soothe him when he bothers to keep it in place?

Text to Annika:
Sorry. Can't today. Maybe another time?

Like when Sam's in college.

97 Days Old

Today my mom makes her annual trip to San Francisco to stay with my aunt Mabel for the summer. I am officially on my own. I acknowledge that I have Zach, and I realize I could try to find a babysitter, but by the time I find someone I trust enough not to drop my child or taint the breastmilk I would have had to spend weeks pumping to have enough for our time away, I'll be back at work anyway.

Before Mom left, we had this little exchange:

"Last chance to change your mind, Ma."

"I'll be back before you know it," she assures me.

"Grandma," I speak in a baby voice, "if you go away, I will forget who you are. Don't leave me with this mean mommy."

"They called my flight, honey. Be good. Love you!"

Click

Shit just got real.

98 Days Old

. . . .

Today Zach and I celebrated our seventh wedding anniversary. He gave me a pair of handmade garnet earrings from Etsy. I gave him a monogrammed back scratcher and a *Battlestar Galactica* t-shirt. As we eat our romantic Burritoville takeout anniversary dinner, Zach broaches the delicate subject of sex again.

"Since tonight is our anniversary, and you are in fighting shape—you're looking lovely, by the way—I was thinking it might be a good time to try, you know, a little celebration lovin'?"

Zach and his weird, creepy sex euphemisms.

"I can't even think about sex until we buy some condoms. There is no way I'm risking getting pregnant again this soon."

"Right. Condoms. I forgot you used to be on the pill." Zach seriously considers this. "Can you come with me?"

"You're a grown, married man with a child who desperately wants to have sex, and you can't go out and buy condoms by yourself?" I chide.

"They don't know I'm a grown, married man."

"Don't flatter yourself, dear. You look all of your thirty-six years. And you're wearing a wedding band."

"I know, but it will look cooler if you and Sam are with me. My trophy wife plus the product of our previous intimate times together."

"I have never been referred to as a trophy wife before. Well played. Fine, we'll go with you. We can let Sam pick the style. I'll take a picture and write about it in his baby book. 'The first time I went shopping for condoms was . . . ,' Right next to a picture of him with the Easter Bunny."

"Are we going to get those pictures? Us raising him Jewish, and all."

"I won't tell the Easter Bunny if you don't."

"I don't think he really knows Jesus anyway."

"How did our dinner conversation go from condoms to Jesus?" I ask, taking a bite of my burrito.

"It's my sneaky non-Jew way. I like to get a sprinkle of Jesus in every other year."

The trip to Walgreens is an anniversary special event. Zach refuses to buy the condoms at our local Walgreens because he doesn't want one of the regular cashiers to recognize us and see our purchase.

"Seriously, Zach, they don't give a shit. And I highly doubt they recognize you."

"You don't know how often I sneak off to Walgreens late at night to buy supersized Snickers."

"Really?" I ask.

"I'll never tell."

We drive fifteen minutes out of the way and land at a new Walgreens three towns over.

"Don't you feel like you're on vacation every time you step into a new Walgreens?" Zach asks as we approach the welcoming sliding doors.

"I feel the same way!" I exclaim. "I guess that's why we're still married."

Zach wears Sam on his chest in a BabyBjörn. While I prefer the Moby Wrap, Zach thinks the Björn is easier to use and the black makes it more manly. He told me this one afternoon while brushing Sam's scant tuft of hair with a Cabbage Patch Kids brush.

In order to not just buy condoms (God forbid), Zach wants to pile our basket full of candy and office supplies. "Why not get one of those tiny shopping carts? Then you can look really old, like those cute little ladies who come to Walgreens for eighteen boxes of Kleenex," I suggest.

"Whatever works," Zach insists.

Twelve theater boxes of candy, two packages of highlighters, and a shitload of packing tape later ("It's buy one, get one/half off," Zach notes), we're at the register. A middle-aged woman with cat's-eye glasses and a name tag reading "Mindi" greets us pleasantly. Since I'm alone with a baby 90 percent of the time, I take this opportunity to chat.

"How are you?" I ask, and she looks genuinely surprised by the question.

"I'm doing great, thanks. I get off in a half hour. How are you?" Mindi echoes.

"Doing well, thank you," I answer as I unload the basket. Zach mills about several feet behind me, pretending to admire the last-minute tchotchkes offered nearby.

"Care to buy any Hershey products?" Mindi swipes her hand, game-show-hostess style, toward a candy bar display. "They're three for two dollars."

"No, thank you. I think we've got our sugar fix covered. Let me check with my husband." A line has formed behind me, so Zach moved himself to a nearby display of flowers that dance whenever you play music. "Zach? Want any more candy?" I yell to him. He shakes his head aggressively, as though I'm blowing his cover. "Nah. We're good," I tell Mindi.

She beeps each item as she takes them out of our basket and drops them into a plastic bag. When she gets to the condoms, I strike up the band. "I used to work at F&M, a sort of discount Walmart place that closed before Walmart even existed," I begin.

"I remember that store," Mindi remarks.

"When I was in high school. A friend of mine, well, a girl who I was good friends with as a kid, but we sort of grew apart as teenagers, she came through my line one day. She was acting all sneaky and embarrassed because she was buying condoms." I'm telling the story not only to Mindi now, but to an athletic-looking guy behind me buying two tiny energy drinks. "I could tell she picked my line because it seemed the least mortifying of the choices. So to clear the air, make her not feel so nervous, I say, 'Would you like a bag, or do you want to wear these out?'"

Mindi snickers, and the jock guffaws. I slide my credit card through the slot. As she hands me the receipt and Zach finally decides to rejoin me, Mindi asks, "I'm guessing you want a bag?" to Zach. He's too flustered to answer.

Back in the car, Zach muses, "I can't believe you just did a stand-up act about buying condoms in Walgreens. Weren't you the least bit embarrassed?"

"I don't know. Maybe I just deal with embarrassment differently than you. It's all good. We've got the condoms now. And candy."

"And tape. Don't forget tape," Zach reminds me.

"My sticky hero."

Three hours later, we put Sam to sleep and slip into bed. I'm wearing a giant Ren and Stimpy t-shirt my sister gave me in high school that happened to make for a perfect maternity nightshirt. I don't need to be wearing maternity-sized clothing anymore, but it's hard to give up the aged softness of Ren and Stimpy.

"That's what you're going to wear?" Zach asks me, sounding boyishly disappointed.

"I'm sorry I'm not in my Frederick's of Hollywood feathered robe. I'm not quite there yet. Besides, it's not like you dressed for the occasion." Zach has on the NPR t-shirt he wore today, along with his ten-year-old plaid boxers and ubiquitous black socks. He refuses to wear socks of any other color, even if he's wearing shorts. Which is never.

"Maybe I'm not ready to wear my feathered Frederick's of Hollywood robe, either," Zach cracks.

I slide into bed next to him, and we sink into a cuddle. "Why don't we watch a little TV first to relax," I suggest. And stall.

Game of Thrones is on, and within seconds there's a graphic sex scene between siblings. Zach kisses my neck. "Dude," I say, "I am not being turned on by the brother and sister doing it."

"Do you want to change the channel?" he asks.

"How about you scratch my back?" I suggest.

I flop over onto my side, not able to lie on my stomach because of my milk-laden breasts. I close my eyes for what feels like a second when I'm awakened by Sam over the baby monitor.

Only when I look at the clock do I see it has been far longer than a second.

"You fell asleep when I started scratching your back," Zach tells me, squeaking popcorn between his teeth and staring at *Wipeout* on the TV.

"Oops. Sorry. I guess I was tired. Try again tomorrow?" I ask, trying to sound cutesy and enthusiastic while really I'm secretly relieved that we didn't have to attempt the Great Sex Experiment tonight.

Zach doesn't seem too bunged up about it and can hardly rip his eyes from the idiocy on the screen to tell me, "I'll put you down for a sex rain check."

"Thank you. Enjoy your big balls." I nod to the screen.

"I always do." He smiles, and we kiss before I get the baby and put him to my breast.

And I'm supposed to let Zach near these things tomorrow? Like they're some kind of special edition Transformers: baby food jugs that transform into sex toys. Now all I have to do is figure out how exactly the transformation works. There's nothing about this in my baby's first year book.

99 Days Old

Tried a new lullaby tonight. Poison's "I Won't Forget You." I always liked that song better than "Every Rose Has Its Thorn." Sam seemed to like it until I sang the guitar solo.

Aw, baby . . .

100 Days Old

Still no sex. Sam has another cold, so Zach and I are taking turns on sneeze alert. The booger sucker is all Zach, though. Doogan seems thoroughly annoyed that he's not allowed to get comfortable, since every time he does one of us has to stand up. I try to apologize, but he gives me one of his patented "Just wait until you find the poo I'm hiding for you" faces.

The Sexiest Thing That Happened to Me This Week:

Sam left a big fat green booger on my boob.

101 Days Old

This cold fucked everything up. I don't think I've slept for more than four hours the last three nights. I look like shit, I stink, and my throat hurts—always a precursor to my own colds.

At least no one's talking about sex these days.

Later

I flip on QVC in the middle of the night. The giant guy, David, is trying to sell me chocolates. A fancy tin at fifty bucks a pop. Could they be that good?

"They're *that* good," he tells me. "And think of the many uses you can find for this magnificent tin!"

David is really moaning now over the flavor of these chocolates. Maybe when it's actually time to have sex, I can take a cue from him in the faking-it department.

The chocolate sounds so delicious, I'm almost tempted to order myself a box. Instead, I raid our pantry and find the closest thing we have: a box of Count Chocula left over from last Halloween. The marshmallows are all stuck together, but if I chew and listen to David's expulsions of ecstasy at the same time, I almost manage to convince myself that I'm eating $50 chocolates. I can't taste much right now anyway.

To: Annie

From: Louise

Jesus fucking Mary and Joseph, Annie.

I went to a barbecue yesterday at the in-laws because they can't possibly go a fucking weekend without forcing people to come over to their compound. Don't they ever want to be alone? They put up this front like they have such a perfect marriage, but if it were so perfect wouldn't they want to spend more than two seconds by themselves? They look so polished and stylish, and I look like the Tasmanian devil after he kicked up a dust tornado. I'll write more later. Jupiter's complaining about a stomachache. Mine's not feeling so great either.

—Lou

102 Days Old

. . . .

Today is one of those days where everyone on Facebook has a better life than I do. I don't even know who half these people are—I mean, beyond us going to high school together and growing up in the same zip code. But there they all are, on summer trips and eating homemade salads they cultivated from their backyard gardens. I want to go on cheesy road trips with Zach like we used to do each summer, to Wall Drug and Roswell, New Mexico, and De Grassi Street in Toronto. I want to fly away to far-off countries and freak out on our first attempt at using public transportation. I want to temporarily learn a new language because it's fun to ask where the bathroom is in a foreign land.

I want this damn baby to stop crying.

I rescue Sam from what apparently is his Crib of Hell. He pooped. I change him, and he cries because my cleaning his butt is a wicked form of torture. Really, they should lock me up for the horrible act I'm committing. Damn, dude, are you ever going to figure out that changing your diaper is something I have to do multiple times a day, and unless you're planning on learning to use a toilet in the next month, you're going to be in this predicament for at least a couple of years? Why not enjoy it? I put up a stupid black-and-white picture of farm animals that should be stimulating your brain this very minute!

I've taken to keeping a set of earplugs in a basket near the changing table. I have horrible visions of Sam discovering them and thinking they are marshmallows (not that he knows what marshmallows are, but no matter; in my vision Sam is born both mobile and snack savvy) and swallowing them, and before I can get them out of his mouth he dies all because I couldn't handle the sound of his cries.

I've tried everything to make this more pleasant. Pictures next to his head. A mobile above him. I give him toys, but he inadvertently throws them into the bowels of his bowel movements. At this point we play a game where we try to outyell each other, him screaming while I shout, "Why are you yelling?" repeatedly until the changing is over and I assess the damage of how much poo has glommed on to my hands.

Delightful child.

Finally, he's changed and dressed, and I take him downstairs, still feeling melancholy wanderlust. I turn on the stereo and pop in a mix CD I made in college. I'm having trouble finding music to fit my mood or, more important, my identity. It feels ridiculous to rap along with N.W.A when I'm a mom and teacher living in the suburbs, although I suppose it was always a little ridiculous. I've never been the slightest bit close to being straight outta Compton.

After a Guided by Voices song ends, "Anchorage" by Michelle Shocked begins. I put this song on the CD because my mom was about to take Nora and me on a trip to Alaska, and a song called "Anchorage" felt appropriate. I fell in love with the song, Michelle's deep voice, and the story of two old friends finding each other again as adults, one in Texas and the other in Alaska. As a college student, I thought the lyrics were sharp and clever.

But now, as Michelle sings about nostalgic times with the friend she used to rock out with, I feel that sad pit in my stomach.

It's the sensation I sought out as a teenager, when all I wanted from music was a relatable song of weepy angst. Only this song isn't tragic or angsty. It's me. The words sting when her friend muses about her new life with kids:

> *I got a brand new eight month old baby girl.*
> *I sound like a housewife.*
> *Hey Shell, I think I'm a housewife.*

And I start to cry. Because the Shell who her friend tells to "keep on rocking, girl. Yeah, keep on rocking," was once me. But I am Shell no longer. I am no longer rocking.

103 Days Old

You know when something happens to you and you don't know if you're turning it into something bigger than it actually is? Like when Fern saw that gastroenterologist, and he told her that her body looked good for having four kids. Then he touched her boob. Was he being inappropriate?

Today, Sam and I are at Michael's. I have it in my head that I'm not only going to write things in Sam's baby book, but I'm going to add flair, like stamps and stickers and lace and decoupage. It will never happen, but now I'm buying $70 worth of crafting supplies to make me feel more inadequate.

Sam is being his usual unpleasant self; "fussy" is the gentle term people like to use about babies. Annoying, I say. Does he have to cry whenever I want to get something done? Can't he find his love for shopping, too? By the time I arrive at the register, I am sporting my grumpy bitch face and rolling my eyes heartily at grumbly Sam. The cashier, instead of showing the slightest bit of empathy, starts a royally creepy conversation—with *Sam*.

"Your mommy is so lucky to have you. You are an angel sent from heaven. You are a sweet boy, a gift for your mommy to cherish."

I ignore her, seeing as she isn't talking to me anyway, and try to move the transaction along with my coupons. The building line behind me is no deterrent for her infatuation with Sam.

"I would have a grandchild his age by now," she begins, and I'm ready to give her a sympathy face for what I assume is going to be a story about either a deceased child or grandchild or possible infertility. But, no, instead she continues, "If I had married."

Say what now? She proceeds to carry our shopping bags around the counter to hand deliver them, as though we're at a fancy department store, and touches Sam's cheek with her cash register hands.

I call Louise the second I leave the store and recount the tale. "That's fucked up, right?" I check. "It's not just me being a paranoid bitch, is it?"

"I would maybe have been okay with the whole thing if she did lose someone, but that woman was nuts. You don't say you would've had a grandchild if you had been married!"

"Thank you!" I interject.

"No one has to be married to have a kid anyway. She was full-on projecting craft crazy on you. You should report her," Louise asserts. "So she can't do something like that again."

"I can't report her. She was like, seventy. And she doesn't have anyone, apparently."

"I'd report her," Lou admits.

"I bet you would." I laugh.

"Babies make everyone crazy," Lou pontificates. "Even people who don't have them."

We hang up, and I look at Sam in the rearview mirror. "I bet you're glad I'm your mom and not that whack job at Michael's, right, Sammy?"

Silence.

Is that a yes or a no?

104 Days Old

Tonight is one of those nights when I go to a very bad place. I turn on QVC to drown out my thoughts. I'm in luck. A full hour of Quacker Factory, a clothing line with enough sparkles to brighten up even the Witching Hour. Bubbly sellers talk to happy buyers on the phone. I nearly buy a set of t-shirts, one in every color offered, a different appliqué of jazziness emanating from the chests: an apple for fall, a pumpkin for Halloween, a Christmas tree, a heart. I'm tempted to call and ask if they'll ever make a Jewish star or menorah for Hanukkah. I imagine the on-air chat.

"Quack quack! Hi, Annie from Chicago. Which shirt did you get?"

"I bought all of them!" I holler.

"Smart girl! I am so excited for you!"

"Thanks! I have a question. Do you think you'll ever make any Hanukkah designs? I would love that."

"What a fabulous idea! We'll talk with our designers the second we get off the air! Thank you for your call!"

I'll go down in history as the inspiration for a Jewish line of Quacker Factory apparel.

It'll be nice to have a legacy.

My brain begins to calm, moving further and further away from the despair of motherhood toward a world filled with Happy Quackers. As I'm about to fall asleep, I hear a caller claim, "When I die, I'm going to be laid out in my Quackers." Now there's a visual for my subconscious.

FACEBOOK STATUS

Over the last few days, Sam has been facing one of the four cardinal directions when I go to get him from his crib. It's hard not to get a creepy, *Paranormal Activity* vibe.

106 Days Old

With only nine weeks left in my maternity leave, I have decided to fully begin panicking about hiring a nanny. Or a sitter. Or day care. I don't know which to choose or how to find the best one. Everyone I talked to explained there was no point in hiring someone months in advance because someone waiting for a nanny position isn't going to sit around for a job that starts five months in the future. Even nine weeks is pushing it, but at least I can start researching, get a feel for who's out there. It'll give me a sense of purpose, other than my day-to-day goal of keeping my sanity afloat.

The first step in my research is asking friends, but what I'm already learning is that nannies are regional. Fern, in L.A., shells out thousands of dollars to an agency that then matches a number of nannies to the family. There are background checks and a multitude of interviews, until the perfect match is made. Or what is supposed to be perfect.

"Adam hired this one woman while I was on bed rest after Dov's birth. He said she reminded him of a quirky old aunt. That was all well and good until she took off work an entire day to watch Michael Jackson's funeral."

"You're kidding," I say. "Why is it so quiet over there, by the way?"

"It's eerie, isn't it? Dov's at summer school, Hannah's napping, and the other two are with our new nanny."

"How many nannies have you had?" I ask.

"Six? Maybe seven? There's always something weird about each of them. The last one had gigantic feet."

"You fired someone because she had gigantic feet?"

"Well, no. I caught her stealing my jewelry. But her feet were seriously freakish. Sometimes after she'd leave, I'd go into my closet and try on all of my shoes just to see if she stretched them out."

After Fern and I hung up, I reasoned that things were probably very different in the Bling Ring world of wealthy L.A. compared with the "my only fancy jewelry is my engagement ring" environment of the Chicago suburbs. Still, I don't love the idea of someone being alone in my house. And there's that added piece of taking care of the human life I sired.

Louise has a different approach. "There's a website we use where you post what you're looking for, and people get back to you. I have to warn you, though, that the more part-time you want, the fewer people you're going to get."

My mom has agreed to watch Sam Monday afternoons, all day Tuesday, Wednesday and Thursday mornings, and Friday afternoons (in order to fit in her plethora of clubbing and gaming needs). The complicated process is compounded by Louise's caveat, "We interviewed a ton of really sucky applicants. One was a guy, which, I must admit, the prospect of a manny had me blinded for a moment there. He totally duped me, too, because he looked all fabulous and coiffed in his profile picture. Then he comes over, and he wouldn't even look at Jupiter. He had on a friggin' Brad Paisley t-shirt and he was either seriously baked or coming off a bender."

"So did you hire him?"

"Almost. But then we found this smart Ukrainian girl who was not wearing a Brad Paisley shirt, so we decided to go with her."

After I hang up with Louise, I'm even more confused. Fern paid tons of money, and her people are crazy. Louise interviewed a buttload of wackos before finding someone who seems okay. But how do you know even if they seem okay that they're not some psycho baby stealer? Or a Brad Paisley fan? What if someone is wearing a paisley shirt, not a *Brad* Paisley shirt? Is that the same thing?

How do people go back to work after they have kids? This already feels like the biggest, most complicated decision I've ever made. And I'm not even close to making it.

107 Days Old

Today I'm practicing filling out nanny information forms from various websites. They sure want to know a lot about us. I feel like I'm filling out college applications.

Family interests or hobbies: comic book conventions, science fiction, murder mysteries.

Number and types of pets: 1 cat, ½ Siamese, all awesome.

Will either parent work from a home office while the nanny is with the child? No. Maybe sometimes. You never know.

Do you require the nanny to have own car? No. I mean, yes to drive herself to work, but no to drive Sam anywhere. Am I allowed to take her keys?

Other requests: Please keep television viewing to a minimum, and absolutely no cell phone use while watching Sam.

With the answers I'm giving, I don't think I'd even get wait-listed at my safety school.

108 Days Old

· ·

Sniffing out more nanny advice on Facebook. Someone suggested using Craigslist. Can that be trusted? Isn't that where people go to find free pillowless couches and public bathroom trysts? Do I really want to find a caregiver for my son at the same place where I once got into an argument with someone after I posted an ad for a free stack of 1990s *Rolling Stone* magazines, and they were gone before I came home from work and had time to remove the post? I set up a videocamera for the next week just in case the complainant decided to retaliate. (They were free, dude!)

Maybe I shouldn't go back to work. Maybe it would just be simpler to stay home and take care of Sam. Clean the house. Do the laundry. Make the dinner. Because, as I have already proven to the world, that is so easily accomplished when I am home with a child. Plus, that would mean *I would have to be home with a child.*

I don't know if I can do that. No, I do know—I can't. I love Sam, mostly, but I am not cut out to be at home with him twenty-four hours a day. I need my students, my colleagues, my classroom, my alone time in the car, my welcome-home time when everyone is so excited to see me that we scream and hug and laugh every day.

That's going to happen, right?

109 Days Old

I sat down and did the math of our lives. Without my teacher's salary, the result would be no vacations, no takeout, no college fund for Sam or—gasp!—QVC money for me. I call my mom in San Francisco. "How did you manage to stay home with me and Nora while Dad worked? And why?"

"That's what we did. Well, some of us. Other moms wanted to prove to the world that they could bring home the bacon *and* fry it up in a pan, if you know what I'm saying."

"I have no idea what you're saying, but continue," I tell her.

"Money went a lot further back then. Houses were so much cheaper. And, if you can believe it, I enjoyed being home with you girls."

"So you're saying I'm a shitty mom?"

"Did I say that? Who said that?"

"No one." I sag. "I'm just using you to berate myself some more."

"You get that from your father," Mom says. "I have to go, honey. We're going for dinner. Kisses to Sammy."

Mom hangs up, and I crumple my budget and toss it into the recycling bin.

We can't afford me not going back to work.

Thank God.

110 Days Old

. . . .

NO NO NO. People magazine posted a series of photos of a toddler Prince George and his nanny, and the nanny was picking him up and KISSING HIM.

Did Kate die a little inside when she saw these?

I have to stop with the nanny business for now and just enjoy my maternity leave. It would help if I weren't so bad at *enjoying my maternity leave.*

111 Days Old

. . . .

I am interrupting my complete and utter nanny panic to start freaking out about sleep training now that Sam is three months old. Maybe we'll get him to sleep through the night, and my love for him can finally blossom. Feeling *hopeful.*

112 Days Old

. . . .

Sleep training can kiss my flat ass. We are starting with a cry-it-out at naptime approach. I don't know who's crying more, though, me or him. I wish someone would sleep-train me.

113 Days Old

. . . .

I'm officially over the cry-it-out approach (who can stand all of this crying?), so I spend the day driving around with Sam in the car. When he's hungry, I pull over and nurse him in the front seat. When he's cranky, I hold a passy in his mouth until he falls asleep. When I'm hungry, I seek out a not-as-fast-food drive-thru for sustenance. In fact, I make a day out of finding the best drive-thrus in a forty-five-minute radius from my house. Here's what I come up with:

- Steak 'n Shake. Shakes, grilled cheese, fries. Watch out for ketchup packet pressure accidents.
- Dunkin' Donuts. Good to know for breakfast-craving runs, although donuts have been known to start my day in a downward food spiral.
- Sonic. Tots. Sonic Blast with Reese's. Grilled or fried chicken (depending on how much I hate myself at that moment).
- Deerfields Bakery. This bakery has a drive-thru window where you can order a smiley-face cookie. If only they also offered the service of Swedish Fish and matzo ball soup, I'd wonder if I'd died and gone to deli heaven.
- Portillo's. Chocolate Cake Shake. It's a fucking shake with pieces of chocolate cake in it. I'll go through the drive-thru on a unicycle if I have to.

I'm never returning home again. If I keep eating all this shit, I won't be able to get out of the car anyway.

114 Days Old

To: Annie

From: Lou

I'm so sorry I haven't written in a while. Remember how I ended my last email with Jupiter and a stomach-ache? Turned out that my in-laws poisoned us (not technically, but I consider whatever they did poison because it was either their fault for serving bad food or they passed on some killer rotavirus), and the entire family got the shits, pukes, and everything in between. I'm talking every person at that damned barbecue, not just my family, which is why I'm finally allowed to blame the in-laws. Terry was almost defending his family, as always. I don't get it. I would totally cop to my family tainting the hell out of my food, yet he feels like it's some kind of betrayal to say two bad words about his kin. Please. Don't tell me he wasn't cursing them while seesawing on the toilet (do not make me explain what seesawing on a toilet is). Have you ever seen a baby projectile vomit? We're talking *Exorcist*-level shit. All over the walls. Everywhere. It's been over a week, and I know there is puke somewhere waiting to be discovered at Jupiter's sixteenth birthday party. Our house reeks. I'm seriously considering hiring someone to clean the place from top to bottom, but two things are stopping me: 1) Bringing someone in to clean would mean hours of me picking crap up off the floor first; and 2) I can't decide if I'm embarrassed at what a hole my house is. Should I be? It's not *Hoarders*-level disgusting, but it's to the point where I don't feel comfortable using the five-second rule if a morsel of food falls on the floor. Anyway, even though Terry won't officially blame his family for our vomitous situation, he turned down an invitation to eat at their house for the first time in forever. I chalk that up as a victory for me. To the victor goes the lack of explosive diarrhea. Isn't that how the saying goes?

Call me if you get a minute. I'll try to pry the phone out of Jupiter's hands. Am I a bad mother because I let her play games on my phone while I read a book?

<3 Lou

116 Days Old

Sam has been incredibly needy lately. More so than usual. He's almost four months old, and I still don't get him. Sometimes he smiles at me, and I'm not in the mood to smile back. Does he understand? Does he feel bad? Does he hold it against me, and that's why he's always crying? The more he cries, the more vacuuming I get done, so there's that. And it seems to stop his crying for a bit, too. Maybe he's already some kind of baby neat freak, and he's developing obsessive-compulsive disorder and I'll never be able to keep the house clean enough for him and therefore he will be miserable the rest of his life and spend all of his days in expensive therapy and counting the hours until he's old enough to go off to college and leave us forever.

Or maybe he just has gas?

117 Days Old

POSTBABY BODY REPORT:

- Stomach is . . . there.
- Boobs are ginormous and droopy, and my nipples look like they got into a barroom brawl.
- I still have that black shit in my belly button. What gives?
- Line of color leading down to my filthy belly button still there.
- Massive pimple still on my chest.
- My hair continues falling out en masse. I'm making a beautiful hair art sculpture on the shower wall. I may start taking pictures and posting them online. A blog about shower wall hair art. Has that been done before?

I can't believe how simultaneously bored/tired/stressed/depressed I am. I go back to work in less than two months. I don't want to admit to anyone that I'm counting the days, but several of my coworkers posted on my Facebook wall after Sam was born and they all wrote variations on the same theme: "Time goes by so quickly, enjoy every minute of it." "They grow up so fast. You never get the time back, so enjoy it while you can." "You'll blink and they'll be in college." "You'll never want to go back to work."

As of now, it all reads like bullshit. These four months have been the longest of my life. I don't want the time I've already had back if that would mean the lack of sleep and self-doubt that's plagued me from the very beginning. It is super fucking hard to give every single ounce of yourself—your time, your health, your body, your previous life—over to a person you just met and who doesn't seem to have any interest in giving any of it back. Am I the most selfish mother who ever lived?

Maybe a relationship with a child is supposed to be like an arranged marriage: We'll probably love each other eventually, but for now we're strangers and have yet to settle into a happy life together. I click on a talk show to gain some perspective. How is it that there are this many people in the world who are *not* the father?

118 Days Old

. . . .

I think I'm ready to have sex tonight. Not really, but I've been watching episodes of *Girls,* and they have so much sex that I'm reminded of that period in my life when I, too, enjoyed it. Maybe all I have to do is jump back on the horse, and it'll be like old times. Or the bicycle. I don't know. I don't particularly want to have sex on a horse or a bicycle, but they're both things you're supposed to get back on. And darned if I'm not going to try.

We manage to get Sam down to sleep after much screaming and soothing and readjusting. "Maybe he's teething?" Zach suggests.

"Maybe he's just an asshole," I say, and then have to spend the next fifteen minutes apologizing to Zach because he will never be on board with saying bad things about Sam. What is it with guys? Do they think they're above petty blame and name-calling? Please. If they had half the brainpower and intuition that women have, not to mention one-quadrillionth the obligation and guilt mechanism, they wouldn't bat an annoyingly long eyelash at a little harmless venting. It's not like I'm calling Sam an asshole to his face (much).

I try to remember what kind of look implies I'm in a sexy mood, but apparently I choose the wrong one because Zach asks, "Are you mad at me?"

I sigh. "No, I'm making my sexy face. I'm leading you into the bedroom seductively. Pretend you can tell."

"Ah, yes, I recall that expression. It's been so long, I'd nearly forgotten," he says, smirking.

We stand next to the bed and kiss. Pecks at first until we find our groove, and the memory foam of love starts bouncing back. We recline onto the bed, and that's when things, shall we say, turn less sexy.

Zach grabs my breast, which in the past would have turned me on in a manly, take-charge kind of way. Tonight? "Ouch. I've just gotten over a plugged duct, and it's still sore," I warn him. He switches breasts, and that one is no better. "No, not that one either. Sam latched badly the other day, and my nipple is tender. Maybe you should just stay away from the breastal area today."

We kiss and roll a bit, removing articles of clothing and giggling with joy and awkwardness. Then Zach slips his hand between my legs. "Whoa there!" I command. "I don't know if I want your hand in that area. What if things feel weird?" I ask.

"Like weird how?" he asks, sounding slightly disturbed. I'm a pro at the turnoff, I'm discovering.

"It's just that there were stitches, and maybe the area is a different shape or size. You probably knew it better than I did. I wouldn't want to gross you out or anything."

"You just did, and it's not because of anything I felt," he points out, then clarifies, "I'm not thinking about any of those things. I just want to make love to my beautiful wife." He lays it on thickly, and I vow to myself to stop sticking my foot in my vagina.

"How about we get to the act? Maybe a quickie for the first go? You know, dive right in?" I suggest.

"If that's what you want, then I am not going to say no." Zach doesn't seem nearly as uptight about this process as I am, and in a second he's on top of me. In another second, he's inside of me, and . . . It's not that bad. It's not that good, either, but I don't tell him. Maybe the ol' vageroo just needs a few test runs to get up to speed.

Zach is thrusting and moaning, and I'm happy he's enjoying himself. I try to remain still, just in case anything down south starts to, I don't know, go south. Several minutes of work on Zach's part, and he stops. "What's wrong?" he asks.

"Nothing," I answer.

"You don't seem to be enjoying yourself," he notices.

"I'm enjoying myself just fine," I say, not at all in a way that would convince someone I was, indeed, enjoying myself. "I'm just a little tense, is all. Keep doing what you're doing," I tell him.

"I don't want to if you're not feeling it," he complains.

"Oh, I'm feeling it. It's just . . . Never mind." I shake the thought away.

"What?" he presses, and I'm worried that he's going to lose his erection and won't complete the task at hand.

"It's just that I keep imagining you picturing a baby's head squeezing out of my vagina," I admit.

Zach rolls off of me. "Annie," he moans, and not in the manner of David and the QVC chocolates.

"I'm sorry. I don't completely feel like myself yet. I don't know if I ever will. My body has turned into a baby factory—making him, housing him, feeding him. My back hurts, and my boobs hurt and my face has aged about sixteen years since Sam came out of me. I'm worried that I won't ever be as attractive as I once was."

"You are. You're even more beautiful because you're a mom."

"You're just saying that because you're supposed to. I feel heavy and squishy and old, and I see Alfred Hitchcock staring back at me every time I look in the mirror. I'm glad you claim to not see it, but in order for me to feel sexy to you I have to feel sexy to me, too. And that's not happening yet."

"I get it," he says disappointingly. "How soon are we talking here?" He rolls onto his side and smiles at me encouragingly.

"It doesn't hurt that you want to have sex with me, so keep trying and hopefully one day soon I'll be like a sixteen-year-old gymnast again."

"You were never like a sixteen-year-old gymnast," Zach informs me. "Which is good because I'm not interested in having sex with a teenager."

"How about a twenty-something yoga enthusiast?"

"I'd be happy with a thirty-something English teacher," Zach says, and he gathers me into a cuddle.

Instantly I'm asleep.

I have a dream wherein I'm having decent sex with several of the characters from *Battlestar Galactica* (not at one time; they morph from one character to another, as people do in dreams). I take it as a good sign. As though somewhere in the future I'll be having decent sex. Now I just have to make it happen with my husband.

119 Days Old

Nora spent the day with me and Sam, and it was a welcome break from the chaotic monotony of my life. Of course, after she left I felt like a traitor to womankind, but that seems to be more common than not since I became a mom and Nora is still trying.

"I've started fertility testing," Nora says as she lies next to a calm and content Sam on the floor. Doogan is tucked against me on the couch. "It's god-awful. Every time I step into the office, I want to throw up. And then the things they do to me make me want to throw up even more. I screamed, 'Fuck!' at the top of my lungs the other day while they were shooting iodine up my cooch.

It took forever. So much blood taking and timing things and keeping track. It's the most unnatural, unsexy, uncomfortable process. It makes me question whether or not I'm supposed to even have a kid."

"Of course you are!" I was overdoing the encouragement, but my guilty, evil soul was eating away at me. Just last night I was saying terrible things under my breath to Sam when he refused to go back to sleep for the third time. "There's no sup- posed to or not supposed to. If you want a child, you will have a child."

"But don't you believe in fate, things happening for a reason, God giving us what we can handle?"

"And God will give you a beautiful baby that you will be able to handle. Maybe three or four at once if you don't stop asking for it. God probably knew I couldn't handle going through what you're going through. That I'm not strong like you are or pa- tient. Maybe he was like, Enough already! Here's a baby. But I'll make him extra whiny just for you."

Nora massages Sam's tummy in an instinctual way that I would never have thought to do. He loves it and basks in her gentle touch. I stroke Doogan just to prove I'm good at some- thing. He bites my hand. "Ow! When do they tell you the results of the tests?" I ask, extracting myself from the couch in order to down a sleeve of Thin Mints I hid from myself during Girl Scout cookies season.

"In two weeks. What if they say I can't have a baby?" She con- tinues rubbing Sam's belly like Buddha for good luck.

"You can. I know you can. You managed to get pregnant.

More than once, even! You just have to make one that's worth keeping. I'm sure those other two—"

"Three," she reminds me.

"Sorry—*three* were going to be serious underachievers anyway. Like, Blue Bird reading group all the way. Plus they were really ugly. Like tiny troll dolls."

Nora snorts out a laugh. "Can you imagine if I gave birth to troll dolls?"

"And everyone would have to pretend that they're cute because God forbid someone says a baby is ugly."

"I'd go to the park with the troll baby in a stroller, and old ladies would crouch over to ogle him and then hobble away screaming." We're both laughing now.

"What do you name a baby that looks like a troll doll?" she asks, sniffing.

"Olga?"

"How about Grunderson?"

"Ooh. That's good. Snorbert?"

We spend the next ten minutes coming up with appropriate troll names for her ugly troll doll babies. We laugh, and Sam laughs along with us. And there is nothing like the sound of a baby's laugh to clear the pain from the air.

I bet even troll doll babies have cute laughs.

120 Days Old

· ·

To: Annie

From: Annika

Hey girl! Where've you been? Gallivanting around the local mall? Eating bon bons on the couch while you watch those god-awful talk shows? Why don't you call me? We should meet for brunch one day. My treat!

Gotta run. Busy busy busy!

XOXO Annika

That is not the first email I've received in this vein from Annika. She seems to think I'm not doing jack shit while I'm on maternity leave, and while it may be true that I've accomplished very little, not a moment goes by where I'm not either doing or attempting to do something but am quickly thwarted.

I write a hasty reply because it doesn't seem worthwhile trying to explain motherhood to her. She has vehemently announced that she has no intention of ever becoming a parent because she thinks kids suck, which she usually tells me in that way of people who always think what they're saying is fact, even if it is very much coming from a place of opinion. Plus, why would I agree with her when I just chose to give birth to a kid? Even if some of the time I do think he sucks. But I'd never let her know that.

To: Annika

From: Annie

Hiya! Busy here, too! Sam's a love who won't let me put him down. Trying to enjoy my maternity leave. It'll be over in less than two months! We'll have to get together before then.

Annie

I refuse to let Annika get to me. Instead, I watch daytime QVC and buy $200 worth of Joan Rivers jewelry that I will probably never wear. But I do it to honor Joan, and that's what's important.

122 Days Old

If I have to read about another celebrity who says how great it is to be a mom, I am going to drown myself in my arsenal of stored breastmilk. Don't tell me, obnoxious, holier-than-thou super-model, that you're such a great mom because you're "multitask-ing" while you breastfeed in a hoity-toity makeup chair while someone else holds a cup with a goddamn straw for you and three other people fix your hair. Multitasking is hanging on to a baby while taking a shit and then realizing there is no toilet paper left on the roll. So, pants down, baby on tit, you rifle under the sink for more, but there is none there either, so with your pants still around your ankles and baby dangling you have to shuffle/hop your way down the basement stairs without falling in order to dig a package of toilet paper out of the closet, puncture it open with a leaking pen, carry the roll back upstairs, and wipe your ass, not to mention flush, pull your pants back up, and attempt to wash your one hand that isn't trying to prevent your baby from falling onto the tiled floor as he rips your nipple off on the way down.

#MULTITASKMYASS

123 Days Old

It's the middle of the night, and I can't sleep. Sam is going on four hours, but I'm so used to waking up that I can't manage to doze off.

There's a woman on QVC selling personal stair machines. It's 2:53 A.M., and there are three hard-bodied women, half-dressed, demonstrating how using the Sky Stepper will magically transform my gelatinous stomach into a rock-hard washboard.

None of the women are even remotely close to dripping with sweat. In fact, they're barely glistening.

"How do you do it?" I ask the TV. "How do you look so toned and glamorous at three in the morning? I can't look like that after a makeover at the MAC counter at Macy's and three pairs of Spanx. You're on live TV, for fuck's sake."

"I haven't had anything to eat but energy drinks for the last twenty-four hours," one woman admits, and I detect a twitch in her eye.

"I run Ironman every year," the second woman tells me. "Walking on a step machine in the middle of the night is like laying on the couch for you."

"Oh. That makes me feel better," I groan. "And what about you?" I ask the third exerciser.

"I don't have much of a choice. My husband lost his job, and I have three kids at home who need braces."

"Man, that sucks. Well, if it's any consolation, you look great for having three kids," I tell her.

"I'd rather look like you and be in bed than be here, wiping sweat off my forehead every time they turn the camera away from me."

"I knew it!" I shout. At that moment, Zach rolls over in his sleep and asks, "Is Sam up? Are you on the phone?"

"Go back to sleep," I tell him, something I never have to say twice.

On the TV, the three women work out as though we hadn't just bonded. In their honor, I sneak down to the kitchen for a stick of string cheese, celebrating the fact that I can.

124 Days Old

To: Annie

From: Louise

Dear Annie,

Right now I am locked in the bathroom with my phone, and my two kids are outside the door screaming their fucking heads off. Literally, if I open the door, which I may never do and you can come over in three weeks to identify my decaying body sitting on the toilet, I expect to see both of my kids with their heads on the floor. Which would totally be an improvement because they won't SHUT UP. I just yelled that as I typed it. My kids are going to need so much fucking therapy. SO AM I (yelled again). The baby is in a bouncy seat, and Jupiter is seriously scratching at the door and rolling on the floor. I don't understand. How hard is it to sit and watch a cartoon while your mom has to take a shit? Sometimes I wish I had more in the bathroom besides nick-proof razors and infant Tylenol.

Help.

Lou

125 Days Old

I can't tell, but I think Doogan isn't eating as well as he used to. Maybe it's been years since he has. When he was a young cat, he was so rotund that we had to put him on diet cat food. Eventually we bought a food machine on a timer that spits out the right amount of food two times a day. The motor inside whirs before the food comes out, and Doogan used to perk up at the sound of it, then zip straight to the bowl for his meals. He hasn't done that in a while. Months? Years? He's been with me so long, it's hard to differentiate. His eating slowed down once before, right around the time Zach and I were married. We were so busy with the wedding preparation, we didn't notice until we went on our honeymoon. Doogan stayed with Fern, at her lavish apartment with more bathrooms than bedrooms at the top of a skyscraper in Chicago, with pristine white carpeting that Doogan promptly puked on the second Zach and I boarded our plane for San Diego (part of our honeymoon was spent at Comic-Con, the rest on a road trip up the California coast). It turned out Doogan had hepatic lipidosis, where his fat started invading his liver or something like that. Whatever it was, Fern had to take him to the vet, and I spent half our honeymoon on the phone with the vet (and several thousand dollars) making sure he was okay. Doo is such a sweet cat, the vet actually went into the clinic on her off-hours just to hang out with him. I guess he was at death's door, and the vet saved him, gave him seven years more and counting. We send her holiday cards every year.

At seventeen, Doogan's been a senior for a while, and his vet said, maybe it was a few years ago, that it's normal for his eating to slow down. But maybe I should take him in. I'll see how he's doing later this week and make an appointment for next week. I'm sure he's fine. Just older. He's purring on my lap right now. I'm sure nothing's wrong. Right, buddy?

126 Days Old

It's time to try again. Sex, that is. I can feel the need emanating from Zach's body every time we watch an episode of *Game of Thrones*. Hell, I can feel it coming from him when we watch *Ghost Adventures*. Or maybe part of that is me? Maybe I'm feeling that need, too? I can't figure out if I'm horny or if I just really have to pee.

Tonight we watch a reality show where a hillbilly husband talks to the camera about how frisky he's feeling. He lights scented candles for his wife, but apparently they're the wrong scent. So he changes it up to candles that smell like food, and she gives it up.

"What kind of candles would you want?" Zach quizzes me. He knows I don't care for candles, and it's obvious he's of the mind that if these yokels are doing it, there is no reason why we shouldn't be, too.

"Barbecue chips and Slim Jims," I jest. "Got any of those candles in your sexy arsenal?"

"Remember when you used to go to those sex toy parties your friends threw? You'd come home with all sorts of smelly stuff."

"Those parties were such a pain in my ass. I always felt obligated to buy crap because my friends forced me to so they could get their pyramid-scheme kickback. How many feather ticklers and warming balms does one woman need?"

"Do we still have any warming balm?" Zach inquires.

"Yeah. I think that stuff expired four years ago. You don't want to mess with rancid warming balm."

"No," Zach concurs.

"And Doogan appropriated the feather ticklers as cat toys."

"So I guess we'll just have to do with what God gave us." Zach nudges me, and I try my hardest to look relaxed. He rubs my arm gently, then moves onto my back. "You get a very short massage tonight. I don't want anyone falling asleep prematurely."

"And——" I start.

"Steer clear of your breasts. Got it." He slides his hands down to the hem of my sleep shirt. "Can I still look at them?" he asks. I nod, although my inclination is to warn him to look away. They aren't the breasts of yesteryear. He slips my shirt over my head and doesn't comment, so he's either pleased with what he sees or smart enough not to say anything if he isn't.

He kisses me, and I try to pretend this is normal and I've done it a million times. Which it is, and I have, before my body became engorged with a human and then expelled it and is hovering somewhere between the two. I am so aware of all the new and subtle nuances: the darker areolae, the line down my belly, the pimple that won't retreat, the not quite as confident pee-holding ability. All of those things add up to a more lived-in version of my body with whom I still haven't quite made friends.

"How about we turn the lights off?" I suggest. As common as this appears to be on television and in movies, Zach and I never partook in the lights-out, good-feelings-by-only-feeling kind of sex.

"Do I look that bad?" he asks, and when I begin to argue the opposite, he says, "I'm just kidding. If that would make you feel more comfortable, I'm all for it. Anything that will result in me getting laid by my wife." He grins.

"You really need to study your seduction techniques. 'Getting laid' when you're pushing forty is not on that list."

I reach over and click off the lamp on my nightstand. Zach does the same with his and scoots across the bed to spoon with me.

"Thirty-six is not pushing forty," he argues as he kisses the tip of my ear, my earlobe, my neck . . .

"Whatever, old man Schwartz-Jensen."

"I love it when you call me by my hyphenated last name." He gently rolls me onto my back and kisses my mouth.

At first, I try to be me in the moment, remembering all of the moments just like this that came before. But my head quickly travels to me and Zach timing our sex to correlate with ovulation, peeing on sticks, trying again, lying with my legs propped up against the wall to give his semen an easier swimming job. Not sexy thoughts. I joggle my head to see if I can jar them loose, and Zach notices.

"Everything okay?" he asks. He has already rolled my undies down and off, and automatically I reciprocated. I can feel how hard he is, and a tiny spark of hope tickles my tummy as I recognize the desire to have him inside me.

"Yep. Do you have the condom?" It has been one hundred years since I've asked anyone that question, and the youthful request is another boon to the occasion. Crinkle crinkle.

"You put it on me," Zach directs, and I do, harking back to many a tryst in my twenties.

Things are going smoothly—not to the point where I think I'll have an orgasm, but certainly better than full-on panic that he is near my vagina (*Don't think about your vagina . . . Don't think about your vagina*)—when Sam erupts in cries over the baby monitor.

"Ignore it!" Zach grunts, and I'm taken aback since I'm always the one who demands we turn off the monitor when I want to pretend for one squink of a second that I'm not at a tiny human's beck and call.

Sam must know we're putting him off, and his screams escalate.

Zach is carrying on with his rhythmic business, and I'm trying dutifully to keep time, but it's not easy with the distraction.

"Why don't we turn the monitor off?" I suggest. Together, Zach still inside of me, we rock our way toward the nightstand. I stretch my arm over to reach the monitor button, and the struggle knots a kink in my neck. *Play through the pain,* I coach myself. *Just get in one good orgasm! You can do it!* I'm quite the cheerleader, but it's no good. The interruption and job injury leave the twenties me at some bar with a tall, dark hipster I just met, and the mid-thirties, postbaby me prays my husband doesn't notice and finishes his business quickly.

He must realize I'm not on my way to happy town because he asks, "Are you gonna—"

"Nah. But you go ahead."

Zach makes no attempt at the obligatory double check and comes almost immediately. The benefit of almost five months (plus pregnancy time) of celibacy.

I don't bother to stick around for postcoital cuddling bliss, seeing as there wasn't really any from my side of the bed anyway. I attend to Sam, buck naked, and the one man in my house who's allowed to touch my boobs does so voraciously.

My body has officially ceased being my own.

127 Days Old

· ·

I'm on the phone with Fern, a rarity and not always an enjoyable experience. I adore her and miss hearing her voice, but between four kids screaming in the background, that horrid high-pitched-child-voice cell phone reverb, and Fern interrupting us every one to three seconds to either a) remind one of her kids that Mommy's on the phone or b) admonish one of her kids for hitting one of the other kids, I get in only ten to twelve words total. Somehow I manage to broach the subject of the complications of postbaby sex. "You must know something about it, since you managed to have four kids."

"Ah, but two of them are twins," she reminds me. "And I am freakishly fertile." Fern doesn't elaborate, but I assume she's perhaps alluding to having sex only the bare minimum per pregnancy, which doesn't bode well for my sex-life improvement.

"Have you tried fantasizing? Role-play? Jacob! Do not touch your sisters right after you touch your penis!" Fern yells directly into the phone, then picks right back up with, "Adam and I used to do that all the time. Costumes and everything. Highly recommended. Put the knife block down, goddammit! I have to go." Click.

I consider Fern's role-playing idea. I did do a little improv in high school, and Zach played *Dungeons & Dragons* all through college. Maybe it could help?

My thoughts of chain mail and sex games quickly shift to Doogan. His automatic food dish dumps out a new load of pebbles, but Doogan is too lethargic to get up and snarf them down. I really should make that vet appointment. Part of me is too scared to find out anything.

128 Days Old

Six weeks until I go back to work. I know I should be heavily researching nannies, but with Doogan acting differently I'm not in the mood. Zach suggests a trip to the county fair. Nothing says summer like gorging on corn on the cob and funnel cakes, then going on a Ferris wheel and realizing my stomach is aging as gracefully as my face. Sam slept peacefully through it all. Is that what it takes to get him to sleep? Is there a county fair supply store nearby where I may purchase a Ferris wheel for our backyard?

Or maybe I could just hire a carny as a babysitter. The toothless woman at the pick-a-duck game seemed particularly enamored with Sam.

Being at the fair did lift my spirits. I always equate it with *Charlotte's Web* and Templeton the rat scavenging the garbage and singing, "A fair is a veritable smorgasbord-orgasbord-orgasbord!" I try not to dwell on the ending, which makes me weep in both the book and movie formats.

We peruse the animal pens, but most of them are being auctioned for slaughter and I find myself down again. So we move on to the award-winning produce, and my mood brightens at the rainbow of ribbons adorning the vegetables and baked goods.

The county fair is a lot like life: up and down, tragedy and joy, winners and losers. Plus a whole lot of cotton candy. Or is that just my life?

FACEBOOK STATUS

Babies never seem driven by coolness.

129 Days Old

Doogan's stomach looks saggier than usual. I'll take him to the vet tomorrow. In other news, I told a girl in a Girl Scout vest who was acting like a little shit outside of the grocery store that she wasn't behaving in a Girl Scout way. I am both old *and* hilarious.

Later

No sleep tonight. A combination of multiple Sam wakings and nerves over Doogan's vet appointment. I watch two hours of Southwest jewelry on QVC. I don't know how the hostess manages to talk about essentially the same thing—a silver piece of jewelry with some variation of turquoise—for two hours straight. I am mesmerized and completely in awe of her skills.

"What's your secret?" I ask the woman on the TV. "How do you stay so happy when all you're doing is taking money from lonely people in the middle of the night?"

"It's all in the way you look at it, sugar," the hostess answers, adopting a southern accent that wasn't there a moment ago.

"I'm not taking people's money. They're getting something out of it, whether it's a nice brooch or necklace that someone may compliment one day in the future, or just a warm feeling from talking to me when they don't have someone else to talk to. Remember 976 numbers? People spent a buttload of money, pardon my French, on phone psychics back in the day. I'm selling happiness, sweetie. Looks to me like you could use some yourself."

"Fine," I concede. "I always wanted a turquoise-encrusted belt buckle. Now's as good a time as any to buy one."

"You deserve it, cookie," the woman sweet-talks me. "Remember: It's all in the way you look at it. And that's advice I'll give you for free. Well, $49.58 plus $6.73 in shipping and handling, honeybunch."

Sold.

130 Days Old

Our vet, Dr. Irving, asked when was the last time I brought Doogan in for blood work. With the pregnancy and all those doctor's appointments and then the baby and all his appointments, we might have forgotten to bring Doo in for a checkup. But he's always been fine.

His stomach is distended now, and he's hobbling. How long has he been like this and I failed to notice? How could I not have? How could I not see my best friend struggling? All because I've only been able to look at this new edition, this baby.

The vet ran some lab tests and will get back to us with results in a day or two.

Sam has been strangely snuggly and calm today. Maybe he knows something is wrong.

131 Days Old

The vet is sending us to a specialist for an ultrasound this afternoon. Zach took off work to go with me. I am petrified about what they're going to find.

I may have yelled at Sam to stop crying in the middle of Target when I got off the phone with the vet. Which made me look like a psychotic hypocrite, since I was bawling myself. We made quite the pair.

Later

Doogan has cancer. He has cancer, and he's had it for months, and I just found out about it now. I could have found out about it a long time ago, but I was too up my own baby-making ass to take care of him. Dr. Irving says even if we knew a long time ago, would we want to subject him to treatment and tests and surgery? He's not a young cat. She gives us options, the first of which is draining his stomach to possibly make him a little more comfortable but would only prolong things a week or two. The cancer is everywhere, and even if it weren't, it would be a lot to subject him to. He won't have the chance to live a comfortable life either way. Dr. Irving says our other option, and the one she thinks is best for Doo, is to put him down. Before he gets so bad that he can't eat at all, and he's in so much pain that he cries and cries, and he can't control any parts of his body. His life is in my hands, and I don't know what to do. Sam is crying, and all I want to do is hold my furry friend, my friend whom I've known longer than my husband. My friend whom I have to put to sleep.

132 Days Old

Zach and I talked and decided against draining Doogan's stomach. Doo doesn't want to eat, but I'm coaxing him to have a few snacks by leaving out some of his favorite treats: tuna, yogurt, apples. I hide behind a chair so as to not disturb him and cheer at the victory of him eating a teaspoon of food.

This is no way for him to live.

I call Dr. Irving's office to schedule Doogan's death. Saying it like that makes me sound horrible, and I feel that way. I'm deciding to end someone's life. The vet says I am doing the humane thing, and they offer a service where Dr. Irving can come to our house for the procedure. I say we will pay for that, as I can't imagine sitting in the waiting room with Doogan, surrounded by other animals just going in for a checkup. Bringing him in, and not bringing him out. I went through that once with a childhood pet cat, as my mom and I carried her into the vet's office on a pillow while she died in the waiting room. I screamed out, "She's dead!" It was tragic and humiliating. I can't have that happen again.

The euthanasia is scheduled for tomorrow afternoon. I will give Doogan as many kisses as I can before then. I want him to know how sorry I am that I didn't take care of him sooner, that I didn't see how sick he was. That I was so consumed with having a baby that I lost sight of my old friend. I hope he understands. I hope he knows how much I love him.

133 Days Old

Doogan, Sam, and I spend the day watching wedding shows on TV. I tell my boys about Zach's and my wedding, about the cake and dancing and the human-sized challah we had for all of our guests. I give Sam advice for choosing a bride and treating women as they deserve to be treated. "Right, Doogan?" I ask. I imagine him answering in his British accent, in pain but able to laugh at the absurdity of giving wedding advice to a baby.

Zach comes home from work early, puts Sam down for a nap, and together we cuddle Doo the best we can without hurting him and wait for the vet's arrival.

Around five thirty, we watch a black car pull into our driveway. The longest day, awaiting this moment, is finally coming to an end. I shudder as I carry Doo down the stairs. Dr. Irving brought a young vet assistant with her and a doctor's bag of death.

Zach and I prepared a blanket on the floor in a sunny spot in our living room we know Doogan likes. I place him there, and even in his weak state he is smart enough to try and get away from what is coming. I pick him up and set him back in his place, then I lay my head on him and he settles. Dr. Irving says the first step is to make him fall asleep, so he won't be awake when he actually dies.

"Our house won't feel like home without you," I whisper to Doogan.

I don't look as Dr. Irving injects him with whatever horrible concoction she brought, and after a minute she whispers, "He's asleep."

I look at Doo, so limp, not in the cozy, curled ball of sleep that I have seen him in for the last seventeen years. He already looks dead, even if he isn't. I let out a guttural cry and move away into Zach's arms. I can't watch the next part.

As I weep and shudder into Zach's shoulder, Doogan is put to final rest. I sob uncontrollably and violently at the loss of my old friend. Dr. Irving takes him away, and we sign a release to have his ashes returned to us. She leaves the house, Doo wrapped in a blanket.

When I finally return to a semblance of normal breathing, Sam's cries crackle over the baby monitor.

"I can't hold him right now. Can you get him?" I whimper to Zach.

He wipes his own eyes and tells me, "Sure."

My cat, Doogan, is gone, and left in his place is this baby I barely know.

In the middle of the night, after three wakings and so much screaming, I am not right in the head. The fourth time Sam wakes up, I run into his room and shout into his crib, "Why are you here? Why are you here, and Doogan, who was my friend for seventeen years, is not! All you've done is scream at me and hurt me and make me feel like complete and total shit! I hate you!"

Zach stands silhouetted in the doorway. "I'll get him. Go back to sleep."

"I can't go back to sleep because I am never fucking asleep!" I can't stop crying or yelling.

"Annie, go downstairs and turn on the TV. You don't need to be up here."

"We killed him, Zach. We killed Doogan, and we can't take it back. He's gone." I fall to my knees on the bedroom floor. Zach comes over and lifts crying Sam out of his crib.

"We made the right choice, Annie. We didn't want him to be in pain." I can barely hear Zach speaking over Sam's cries.

"Give him to me," I mutter.

"Annie . . . ," Zach starts, but I'm demanding.

"Give him to me!"

Zach hands Sam over. His body feels warm and falls into a comfortable position in my arms. I lean him into me, and his crying subsides.

"He needed his mama," Zach says.

I lightly kiss the top of Sam's head, my tears matting his wispy hair. "I'm sorry, Sam. I don't hate you. I don't hate you, baby," I repeat.

I lie down on Sam's rug and tuck him into my body. I kiss his head gently over and over, as I had done to Doo so many times.

"I love you, Sam," I whisper. "I love you." We snuggle each other until we fall asleep. On his floor. The way Doogan once had.

134 Days Old

. . . .

Nora calls to offer her condolences.

"Doogan was a great cat, Annie. I'm so sorry."

"Thank you. Are you going to send me a muffin basket? I always send people muffin baskets when someone dies," I tell her.

"I think that's usually reserved for human deaths," Nora suggests.

"Well, Doogan was almost human. Better than most humans, I'd propose."

"True," Nora concurs. "Can I share some good news?" Nora is a sweetheart for treading lightly on the cat death. She knows all too well how traumatic pet deaths are, as she also lived through the childhood waiting room cat incident.

"Good news is always welcome here." I stroke Sam's catlike hair as he eats from me.

"It's mostly good news. I got all of my fertility test results back, and there's nothing wrong with me."

"That's awesome news!" I enthuse.

"Yeah, except that I don't have any babies, and the buttrod doctor at the fertility clinic is pushing fertility drugs."

"Why would she do that if there's nothing wrong with you?"

"She's in the business of getting people pregnant, so she treats it like a business. She told me, 'You can start taking Clomid and triple your chances of conceiving.' I felt like I was obligated to say yes. I put her off by saying I'd give it a few months and then get back to her, but . . . fuck. Couldn't she let me feel the least bit successful? Like, I'm sure there are women who go in there with all sorts of things wrong and interventions needing to happen if they want to have a baby. But we just spent a month assaulting my baby-making innards, and they are in perfect condition. I think I deserve a gold star on my uterus, not a C minus and a makeup exam."

"You said her job was to get people pregnant, so she's used to people being in a hurry and demanding her magical baby-making drugs. It's all part of the fucked-up pharmaceutical business anyway. She probably has a quota to fill of how many women she gives Clomid to, and when she meets it she wins a trip to Barbados." I chuckle and try to lighten my sister's mood. Like me, she does not like to fail.

"I don't want to take drugs if I don't have to take drugs. I want to make a baby naturally. Like you did."

"Don't bring me into this. It makes me feel all sorts of guilty." I switch Sam from one breast to the other and give him a peck on the forehead. Nora always brings out the guilt kisses in me.

"It would be awesome for us to have kids close in age. Best-friend cousins!"

"It *will* be awesome," I correct Nora. "It will."

"So say we all," Nora quotes *Battlestar Galactica*'s iconic affirmation.

"So say we all," I reiterate, as they do on the television show.

I really hope Nora gets pregnant soon. We need to start raising our dork army.

136 Days Old

"Don't get rid of it. Not yet," I tell Zach. We're staring into Doogan's litter box, one of his belongings still remaining in the house, along with various catnip pillows, scratch pads, and realistic toy mice that he never once played with but I occasionally find and scream about until I realize they're not real.

"Can I at least clean it out?" Zach asks. I dare not tell him I'm thinking of saving the poo, just in case it can be used for cloning.

"It's probably not great to have stale cat pee out in the laundry room," I decide. "Go ahead and clean it."

The phone rings, and I answer it as Zach commences his final scooping of Doo's litter box.

It's the vet's office, and Doo's ashes are ready to be picked up.

"That was fast," Zach notes.

"How do they do it? I keep picturing them putting him on one of those big pizza paddles and sliding him into a brick oven."

Zach laughs. "Something like that, I guess. What a weird job. And speaking of jobs," he segues, "I have to go to work. I can pick up the ashes on my way home, if you want." He brushes my hair with his palm.

"That's okay. It'll give me and Sam something to do today." He continues his petting. "You do realize you just changed the litter with that hand," I tell him.

"It's not like I scooped it with my hand." He pulls his hand off my head anyway.

"If there's something lurking in cat pee dangerous enough that I wasn't allowed to change the litter during my pregnancy, then I'd rather not have your cat pee hand on my head all the same."

"Such high standards you have," he jokes. "I love you." He kisses me good-bye.

"I hope those aren't cat pee lips," I say.

"Now you're just being gross."

"Doogan would have wanted it that way."

Later

After Sam wakes up from his nap, I dress him in a green onesie with a cat in sunglasses on the front reading, "Cool cat." We have a drawer full of cute onesies, but I rarely bother taking him out of his pajamas. I have to admit he looks quite dashing. His legs, so chickenlike when he was first born, have filled out with an array of fat rolls. The hair on top of his head is still almost nonexistent, but his eyelashes and eyebrows, empty at birth, are a light shade of brown. His eyes remain blue, unlike my dark brown ones, but I've read they can still change. Zach has blue eyes, so there is a possibility I could have a little blue-eyed son. In honor of Doogan, I wear my Kesha concert t-shirt with the Doogan look-alike. It breaks my heart a little to look at the shirt's reflection in the mirror. Good thing I steer clear of mirrors for the most part these days.

Sam and I drive up to the beautiful wooded lot of the vet's office. It took Zach and me a long time to find a suitable vet for Doogan when we moved out of the city. We were eventually lucky to find a country vet who made old-fashioned house calls. If only they delivered the ashes, too. I hadn't anticipated how hard it would be to pick up Doogan's ashes. Sam is tossed up on my shoulder, my favorite position in which to carry him, where Doo used to love to ride, too. The waiting room is busy with two giant, fluffy dogs who look more ursine than canine. Cats in small carriers hiss periodically, and the desk staff chitchat happily to each other as if I'm not about to ask them for my dead animal in a box.

When it's my turn in line, I speak quietly so as to not draw attention. "I'm here to pick up my cat's ashes." Right as I say this, one of the bear-dogs barks loudly.

"What?" the desk woman asks.

I repeat, "I am here to pick up my cat's ashes." Again, the bear-dog rudely interrupts with a deep bark.

"What? I can't hear you." The desk woman has a ridiculously inappropriate smile on her face for what I'm asking, but she has no idea what I'm even trying to say because of this huge fur ball who won't give up the floor.

This time, I take no chances. I shout in bullets, "I'M. HERE. TO. PICK. UP. MY. CAT'S. ASHES."

Even the bear-dogs shut up for that.

Desk lady goes to a back room and comes out with a small shopping bag. "I'm sorry for your loss," she offers.

"Thank you," I say.

I'm ready to walk away when she asks, "Who's this?" At first I think she wants to know who was burned up inside of the shopping bag, but I realize she's referring to Sam.

I flip him around so she can see his face. "This is Sam," I introduce her to the baby.

"He's adorable. Hopefully we'll see you two again under happier circumstances."

I nod and try to control the welling tears at the prospect of ever having a pet to replace Doo.

Sam and I leave quickly, and I sob quietly as I strap him into his car seat. I place the bag with Doogan's ashes on the floor next to me.

When we arrive home and Sam is down for a nap, I open the shopping bag with Doogan's ashes inside. Just as my mom predicted, there is a small white tin with black paw prints dotted whimsically about. Who decided this was the standard tin for dead animals? Why didn't I get a choice, like people with coffins?

I'm curious to see what's inside. As a child, Fern had a pet dog die whom they had cremated, and when his ashes came back they included a tuft of his fur. I wish I had saved a tuft of Doogan's fur, the very fur I attempted to use as my focal point during Sam's birth. Maybe there is some inside the tin. I gingerly pop off the lid and envision the scene from *The Big Lebowski* where Walter and the Dude scatter Donny's ashes off a cliff, only to have them fly back into their faces with a gust of wind. No wind here, but I am struck by how bad the ashes smell. The instant I recognize no sign of Doogan's hair, I shove the lid back in place. Maybe I imagined the smell. It's incredible how a sizable cat can be reduced to such a scant, pungent pile of ash.

I place the wacky tin on the mantel between a wedding picture of Zach and me dancing and a piece of Acoma pottery we bought on a long-ago road trip. "You're home again, Doo," I pronounce. I kiss my two fingers and touch them to the tin, then curl up in a ball on the couch and fall asleep.

137 Days Old

∙ ∙

"Are you okay, sweetie?" Mom's huffing over the phone as she tackles a San Francisco hill with Aunt Mabel.

"I'm okay, I guess. I still can't believe he's gone. Every time I open the door, I expect him to trip me."

"What did you decide to do with the remains?"

I'm reminded of a conversation my mom and I had several years ago, where I told her when the time came we wanted to bury Doogan under the apple tree in our backyard to honor his love of apples.

"You don't want to do that," she warned. "Elana, you know her, the one whose husband ran off with his golf instructor—*a man*—she buried her cat in her yard and less than a month later she found a red fox digging it up. Had to shoot at the thing!"

"Elana has a gun?" I asked. It was a scary thought, envisioning one of mom's mah-jongg crew with a gun.

"Well, it was a Nerf gun, but it was very traumatic."

"I'll take that into consideration," I told her. The point became moot when Zach and I had the apple tree removed after years of finding worms in our apples but not wanting to use harmful pesticides. We recognized the environmental irony of taking out a tree, but I'm still not able to eat an apple without chopping it into minuscule bites just to be certain there are no squirmy green freeloaders inside.

My mom sounds relieved when I inform her, "We had him cremated."

"Well, that's good. Did you get him back already? Did they give you one of those tacky tins?"

"Yeah. Paw prints and all." I sigh.

"Well, we can't have that. I'll see if I can find him something classier out here. Maybe in Chinatown. They have a fabulous Chinatown in San Francisco, you know."

"I know, Ma."

Sam's alarm sounds over the baby monitor. "I have to go, Ma. Sam is up."

"How is my Sammy? Give him a kiss from his favorite grandma. I already bought him six t-shirts."

"He'll love them, I'm sure. I'll give him a kiss. We miss you," I tell her.

"I miss you, too, honey. Love to Zach."

We hang up, and I gather Sam from his crib. "Grandma asked me to give you this," I say, planting a squeaky kiss on his cheek. "And here's one from me." I add a second kiss to his other cheek. "Shall we go for a walk?" I ask. "Yes? Okay, then."

Only 180 minutes until Zach gets home. I got this.

How I Spend 180 Minutes on My Maternity Leave
by Annie Schwartz-Jensen

180 minutes left. Change Sam's diaper. Readjust tabs
three times to make sure his penis is tucked correctly.
Change him into onesie and shorts. Spend five min-

utes trying to find matching socks. Settle on one green and one red.

160 minutes left. Put on my shoes, put hair in ponytail. Realize I have to go to the bathroom.

150 minutes left. Fill water bottle for me, gather blankey, diapers, wipes, and toys to put in bag. Diaper bag is too heavy to carry on walks.

130 minutes left. Sam is cranky, so I nurse him. He fills his diaper.

120 minutes left. Poo explosion. Full outfit change. More sock drama.

105 minutes left. I'm hungry. Slice up an apple and eat with peanut butter. Chase with Little Debbie Zebra Cakes.

90 minutes left. Walk around neighborhood. Run into Walking Man. Exchange pleasant greeting.

60 minutes left. Arrive home. Wash hands of outside germs. Wash Sam's hands of outside germs. Nurse Sam. Put him down for nap.

30 minutes left. Take shower. Put roast in oven. Kidding! Put frozen pizza in oven.

Zach walks through the door. "How was your day?" he asks. "Do anything interesting?"

What the hell kind of loaded question is that?

138 Days Old

· ·

Fern called this morning, which is highly unusual. With four kids, emails and texts are more convenient modes of communication, and I don't mind. It can be frustrating having so many interruptions, of which I'm sure I will be just as guilty as Sam gets older.

"Annie?" I detect a waver in Fern's usually strident way of speaking.

"Fern? What's up?" I ask.

"I'm sorry to bother you. Is now an okay time?"

Fern's formality has me worried. "Is there an intruder in your house? Are you being held hostage? Do you need me to call 911? Code phrase: menstrual cramps!" I blurt.

"No." She chuckles. "It's just . . . I found a text on Adam's phone. I'm not sure if it's anything, but I'm kind of freaked out about it."

"What did it say?"

"It was from a phone number, no name connected to his address book, and all it said was, 'Had such a good time on set with you. Looking forward to dinner.' It could be anything. Anyone. But, ever since we moved to L.A. I hardly see Adam and he's always surrounded by gorgeous women and everyone here thinks infidelity is part of your marriage vows."

"Do you really think he'd cheat on you?" I don't know Adam very well. He's always been incredibly focused on work, but he's struck me as a good match for Fern, someone who works hard and feels an almost 1950s obligation to provide for his family. I'd hate to think he could be so easily swayed by the glare of Hollywood lights.

"I think anyone would cheat if they had the chance," Fern admits. "Don't you?"

"No. Not at all. What's the point of getting married if you assume your husband is going to cheat on you? That sounds miserable. I think you're just saying that to protect yourself. From, hopefully, nothing. Maybe it's a group dinner. Maybe it's from a guy. A really old guy. With bladder issues."

"Maybe. Should I confront him?" Fern wonders.

"I don't know if 'confront' is the right word. Maybe approach him? Have a conversation? You barely see him, right? Tell him you miss him, and you want to know what he's been doing and you want him to want to know what you've been doing. Reconnect. That's probably important to do sometimes when you have four kids."

"I guess so. I don't totally mind that he's gone so much because I like doing things my way, and when he's home it's more about his way. But, fuck, what if he's really cheating on me and then he's never going to come home again and I have to raise four kids by myself?"

"That is not going to happen," I blindly assure her. "You found one not very conclusively sleazy text. Just talk to him, Fern. For the kids. For you. For the old guy with the bladder issues," I jest.

"It would have been funnier if you said shingles," she points out.

"Duly noted."

"Thanks for listening, Annie. Everything okay with you?" Fern asks, but before I can answer she interrupts. "Crap. Dov just peed into the aloe plant again. I have to go."

"Let me know what happens—" I start, but she's already hung up.

When Zach arrives home this evening, instead of an exhausted, annoyed hello, I greet him with a kiss and the aroma of freshly baking cookies.

"Whoa." He steps back. "Did I walk into the wrong house?" He looks around.

"Ha ha. I just wanted to let you know that I love you, and I'm glad you are an IT guy at a bank who loves his wife and son very much."

"That I do," he agrees. "You baked?" He inhales the air.

"Yep. Well, they're the break-apart freezer kind, but I did painstakingly put them on a tray and turn on the oven. There were oven mitts involved."

"You spoil me," he gushes.

"You deserve it," I tell him. And I mean it.

139 Days Old

I signed Sam up for a baby music class. It's supposed to be for six months old and up, but at six months I'll be back at work, so I lied about his age on the park district website. I hope this doesn't start him on a trajectory of fake IDs, early promiscuity, and experimenting with illegal substances.

FACEBOOK STATUS

> Sometimes, like right now, after another night of waking up with Sam six times, I think of him as the spawn of Satan. But since he came out of me, wouldn't that make me Satan?

140 Days Old

I walked extra far this morning with Sam on my chest, so I reward myself by stopping at the local coffee shop, Latte Love. I order an iced coffee and wait for them to call my name. A gaggle of blond children, all under the age of five, use me as a pole from which to play hide-and-seek.

"Hey!" I reprimand them in my most authoritarian, annoyed-sounding grown-up voice. It's the same one my middle schoolers ignore, too.

"Sorry . . ." The equally blond mom saunters over and offers a chill apology. "How old?" she asks, alluding to the package on my chest.

"Four and a half months," I answer.

"You guys come here a lot? We could meet up. My kids love babies."

She's awfully quick on the social draw, and frankly, I'm not enamored with the idea of her many unruly children "loving" my baby.

"We don't have a whole lot of time. I go back to work in a little while." I offer what I think is a viable excuse.

"What? No. Don't go back to work." The woman throws her arms back and seems genuinely put out. I'm so confused by her aggravated reaction that I say nothing as she argues, "You'll regret it. This is why we're put on this earth. Our kids need us. You can't go back to work and leave this sweet little guy"—she makes a move toward Sam, but I back away protectively—"with a complete stranger. It's so much more important for us to raise our families than work. In fact, it is the most important thing we can do as mothers."

How dare this woman with two hundred ass-can kids tell me what I should be doing with my life? She doesn't know me. For all she does know, my husband could be dead and I have no other family and if I don't go back to work, both Sammy and I will starve. I have it in my right mind to—

"Annie!" the barista announces, and instead of calling her out on her high-horse bullshit, I grab my drink and hightail it out of Latte Love without saying a word.

I'm so fired up, I walk home in record time.

As I unwrap Sam, I tell him, "I am going back to work for you, Sammy. For us. You'll see what a good job I do, and we'll both be happy and so glad to see each other at the end of the day. This is what's best for us." I think I've managed to convince him. Now how to convince myself.

141 Days Old

· ·

How the hell is it that I go back to work in only four and a half weeks? I call Louise, panicked.

"What the fuck? Only four weeks left, and I have accomplished absolutely nothing!" I lament.

"There is that little human sucking at your teat. That's not nothing," she drowsily points out.

"You sound tired. Are you tired?" I ask.

"Will there ever be a moment again in my life when I'm not tired? This time I'm dizzy, too. Maybe I need to up my iron intake. I think I have a raw steak around here somewhere."

"I haven't even looked for a nanny," I admit.

"You better get on that shit, or you'll be left with the dregs of sitter society."

"God, don't make me freak out even more. I'm already terrified of leaving Sam with a stranger. Some bitch at Latte Love yesterday told me not to go back to work. That staying home with our kids is the most important thing we can do as mothers."

"What a cunt. She probably has a rich husband and hangs out at Latte Love with her stay-at-home-mom agenda because it's the only way she can feel a sense of power in her pathetic suburban-wife existence."

"Hey, watch it. I live a pathetic suburban-wife existence."

"Yeah, but you can make fun of it, so you're cool."

"Do you ever feel just a little bad about leaving your kids home? Like, after you had Jupiter and went back to work?"

"Of course. I'm not a total monster. But then my students come in, and I'm busy and I'm successful at my job. And I come home, and my kid sees that I have a life and I'm fulfilled, so I become a role model for her. You'll see. It won't be so bad. Most of the time."

"What about the times when I feel guilty and horrid and just want to hold Sam for ten straight hours?" I ask.

"Have you *ever* felt like that?"

"No, but maybe if I'm away from him I will."

"That's what sick days are for. Use them wisely. Going back will be a tiny transition bump, and then it will just feel like—life. Because it is. It's the life you choose and the life you're building for your family."

"Um, hello? Did I call the wrong number? You don't sound anything like my cynical booby buddy Louise."

"Booby buddy?" She laughs.

"I just made that up."

"Clever mama. I gotta go. PB and J time."

"Hope you get some sleep," I say.

"Same to you."

I feel a lot better about yesterday's Latte Love encounter after talking to Louise. I still spend an exorbitant amount of time fantasizing that I ordered an extra-hot drink and threw it in that woman's face, shouting, "Mother this!" My zinger may need some work, but I do feel a little better.

142 Days Old

. . . .

It is time to bite the nanny bullet. As much as I would like, I don't think Sam is quite self-sufficient enough to take care of himself. Plus, I really don't want to go to jail. Who would take care of Sam if I do? This is confusing.

I've been researching questions to ask potential nannies for when the interview time comes. Here are the few I've narrowed down:

- How long have you been watching children?
- Any other newborns?
- Did you like them?
- What is your favorite age to care for and why?
- What special training do you have? CPR, ESP, Heimlich, tourniquets, kung fu?
- What is your highest level of education? Why did you stop there?
- Do you currently have a job? Why are you leaving? Are they making you leave? If we do the same, will you leave us?
- Are you going to leave us if you find a better position?
- Are there any activities or responsibilities you won't do? That you want to do but we won't let you?
- Do you exercise regularly? Kids require a lot of energy. Please outline your exercise regime and your diet.

- Have you ever been convicted of a crime? What did you do? Is jail anything like *Orange Is the New Black*?
- How do you feel about writing down everything you do with the baby for the entire time you are here? I will provide a handy chart for your convenience.

Deal breakers:

They try on my clothes.

They give Sam fast food.

They let Sam watch violent TV.

They let Sam watch porn.

They make a porn film in our house.

They hurt Sam.

They steal from us.

They steal Zach from me.

Note: Hire an old, toothless nanny.

Zach and I talk, and using a nanny agency is way out of our price range. We decide to go with the website Louise used, where we can post our own listing and the applicants will flock to us. At least I hope they will.

SEEKING PART-TIME NANNY for one adorable, sweet, mostly pleasant five-month-old boy. Must have previous experience with age group. Looking for someone connected to the arts, preferably with a music and/or education background. We keep a child-healthy home, so minimal television watching and only healthy snacks allowed once child is of age. Must be comfortable reheating and feeding mother's pumped breastmilk. Looking for long-term help, with time off for summer vacation. Please send résumé and three letters of recommendation to . . .

What if no one thinks we sound cool? What if no one applies? What if the only applicants we get are unhygienic psychopaths who, after we interview them in our house, become obsessive stalkers who kidnap Sam after we fail to hire them?

How do people do this?!

143 Days Old

A couple of nibbles on our listing. So far, I'm not overly impressed. But who would impress me? I'm of the mind to write up a truly perfect description of a nanny, rip it to shreds, send it into the fireplace, and wait for Mary fucking Poppins to arrive.

I don't want to interview people who only seem okay. I want someone who speaks three languages and is putting herself through medical school to become a neonatal specialist. How do I know if any of these people are going to take care of my kid the way I want him taken care of when I'm not around? Am I going to be one of those people who installs nanny cams strategically placed in dismantled teddy bears throughout our home? I'm sure they have systems that I can access directly from my smartphone.

What if I'm so busy addictively checking my phone for Sam's progress that I get fired from my job?

At least then I wouldn't need to hire a nanny.

144 Days Old

The nanny pool is still very slim. Four applicants.

"These two sound fine," Zach says over dinner, a new Thai restaurant. This one cuts their tofu into cute little cubes.

"Fine? *Fine?*" I scoop out a cashew with my fork and bite into it. "This is good," I note of the food. "But fine? How can you possibly be even remotely comfortable with having a merely fine person taking care of your only heir?"

"I never thought of Sam as an heir before. You are the son, and the heir . . ." Zach recalls a song by The Smiths. "You're right," he says, resigned. "But I don't want you to worry so much. They wouldn't let people answer our ads if they were raging lunatics, would they?"

"It scares me when you are that ignorant, Zach. Seriously. Maybe they faked their résumés. Maybe they've concocted completely false identities and use nannying as a front for their human trafficking business. Or maybe they're going to turn our house into a crack den," I suggest, pointing wisely with a baby corn at the end of my fork. "The question is: How do we know? Will we ever get to a point where we really truly know this person who has our son's life in her hands?"

"Jesus. Maybe *I'll* just quit my job," Zach grumbles.

"Don't think I wouldn't use the nanny cam on you," I threaten.

"I'd count on it."

I pout over my golden cashew nut until Zach says, "Why don't you set up one interview and see how it goes? Maybe you'll be pleasantly surprised."

"In all the years you've known me, how many times have I been pleasantly surprised?"

"We're in trouble, Sammy," Zach asides. When he sees I'm deadly serious, he says, "Annie, this isn't like you. I mean, fretting over every detail until it's perfect is, but I'm kind of surprised you didn't choose a nanny months ago."

"Fuck, Zach. Do you know how big of a douche you just sounded like? Why is this all on me? We'll both be at work! If I didn't do this, where did you think *our* kid would go? And this isn't like me because I'm not just *me* anymore. I'm me plus a mom, and that trumps everything! What makes you immune?"

Zach looks stunned, frozen mid-chew. "I'm sorry?" he tries.

"I know. But don't give me shit about this. It's huge. Bigger than anything. Our kid's life will be in someone else's hands, and I'm not going to fuck it up."

"I know you won't. That's why I rely on you too much in these situations. In pretty much all situations, actually."

"As long as you're aware of your colossal dependence and my obvious superiority."

"I'm well aware because you rarely let me forget."

"Don't overcompensate for your inadequacies by making me feel insecure about my perfectionism! It's not about you, Zach. It's about the baby. Finding the right person for the baby so we don't regret the choice later. Because everything we do from now on until the end of us is about him. And if your only help is going to be criticizing my awesomeness, then I don't want to hear another word."

"Damn," Zach surrenders, "you are a mother."

"And don't you forget it. *I can't,*" I add.

145 Days Old

. . . .

Even though I won last night's argument, Zach made a good point about scheduling a single interview. I set up an interview with one of the four applicants, chosen because she has an undergraduate degree from her native Ukraine. To me, this says intelligence and ambition. She also has held two nanny positions already, so she has experience. Her emails were somewhat brief, if not also stilted, but I chalk that up to the younger generation's penchant for abbreviating everything and for the curse that is autocorrect. She seemed nice enough, and thankfully she is currently between jobs and can come by as early as tomorrow. Our interview is set for nine A.M.

What do I wear? If I dress in my normally schlubby attire, she won't respect me as an employer. Or she'll think I'm cool and laid-back. If I dress like a grown-up, maybe I'll scare her off. Or she'll take me seriously and know I mean business.

I'm so anxious, I go twice through the Dunkin' Donuts/Baskin-Robbins drive-thru: morning for donuts, after lunch for ice cream. Who was the genius who thought of that double necessity? I wish I could hire her to be Sam's nanny.

146 Days Old

. . . .

The interview was a total bust, and frankly it made me feel like a royal asshole. Polina seemed very nice. I answered the door, she presented herself professionally in a tidy dress and sensible flats. She cooed and smiled at Sam, who did not hesitate to smile back. But when it came time to ask my arsenal of Very Important Questions, that's where we ran into trouble. Polina and I had a very large, some might say cavernous, communication gap. That is, neither of us could understand a word of what the other said. It reminded me of my travels to Italy, when I naively believed I could talk to people because I took three years of high school Spanish. Occasionally one word would be understood, and it was like we won a consolation prize on a game show—we were so happy to connect, but then we'd recognize that one word wasn't as exciting as we thought.

The interview was brief, and there were a lot of friendly nods and misfired handshakes.

Was I being too picky? Close-minded? What if she was a great nanny, she just spoke a different language? And her English would surely improve over time. She did arrive in the United States only two months ago. But if we didn't understand her, how would she know what I needed from her? How would I know what she did with Sam all day? What if there was an emergency, and things went from bad to worse in the amount of time it took for the two of us to figure out what the other was saying?

Discouraged, I checked the website. No more nanny applicants as of yet.

I'm fucked.

I wonder how you say that in Ukrainian.

147 Days Old

I go back to work in three weeks. Time has not flown, yet I cannot believe I go back to work so soon. Even without a nanny in place, I still have to get my breastmilk stored up for my imminent departure. I also have to figure out how I am going to fit in pumping between classes at work. I designed a schedule for myself during grading periods so I can pump twice a day, ensuring my milk supply remains up and I don't get too uncomfortable. The only place I can think to do the pumping is the supply closet in my classroom. I know colleagues have pumped in the bathroom, but how does that work? I sit on the toilet and have my naked breasts hanging out in a stall while someone sits on the pot adjacent to me taking a shit? No, thank you. And I know from the Kesha concert that the pump requires gobs of batteries to operate. Instead, I'll drag a student desk into my supply closet, along with my iPad for watching movies to distract me from the awkwardness of being topless so close to hundreds of pubescent boys. I think it will be okay. As long as nobody goes searching for a classroom set of *The Old Man and the Sea* while I'm in midpump.

To: Annie

From: Louise

Subject: HOLYFUCKBASKETJESUSCHRISTOHMYGOD-
WHYWHYWHY

Annie, I am in hell. God and Satan are laughing at me, and I am ready to visit them both and punch them in the balls.

I'm pregnant.

I AM FUCKING PREGNANT.

How the fuck did this happen? Terry wanted to have sex, and I was like, sure, whatever, and with Jupiter and Gertie I didn't start getting my period again until after they turned one, so I didn't even think about using birth control and NOW I'M PREGNANT AGAIN and I am way too old and insane for this. What if this baby is an even bigger asshole than my other two kids? What if I never take a shit by myself again? All I envision are three zombies clawing and groaning outside the bathroom door. I'll tell you one thing I'm never doing again: having sex. Terry can hire a prostitute or we can add some sister wives because this vag is closed for business. Oh, Annie, wake me when this nightmare is over.

HELP!!!!!!!!!!!!!!

To: Louise

From: Annie

Dear Lou,

I cannot believe it. I am in shock. I screamed when I read your email. All I can say is that everyone says the more you have, the easier it gets. Maybe the third will be the sweetest and nicest and most well-behaved. My friend Fern has four, and she told me her third and fourth are the best. Little comfort, I realize. Call me if you want to talk. We can yell over our crying babies.

xo,

Annie

FACEBOOK STATUS

Sam is napping going on two hours, and I am wasting these unheard-of precious minutes by reading a Tumblr page called "Duggars Confessions."

To: Fern

From: Annie

I've been thinking of you and wondering how it's going with Adam. Remember my friend Louise from school? She had a baby right after I did, and she just found out she's pregnant again! I don't know what I'd do if I were pregnant again so soon. I think my vagina started crying at the thought.

Call or write when you can.

xo Annie

148 Days Old

Today is Sam's first music class. I try to dress him in clothes that make him look older. His Harley-Davidson onesie from the in-laws gives him that rough-and-tumble look, but the ridiculous (albeit hilarious) assortment of plaid shorts he owns aren't helping the cause. Maybe I could draw a mustache on him.

Sam and I arrive at the park district building three minutes before class is set to start. I find the classroom number, and a warm woman with a soothing voice welcomes the gaggle of parents and kids waiting outside into a carpeted room, sans all furniture but a table in the corner. There are four other moms, one dad, and one man who must be a grandpa or else a seriously old dad. Of course, I instantly imagine him having sex. Definitely the grandpa.

As I scan the room, I can't help but compare Sam with the other kids. He is certainly in the upper echelon of cuteness, although he may be neck and neck with a boy sporting the most hair I've ever seen for a six-month-old. The teacher, who presents herself as Miss Randi, gathers us into a circle on the floor. We introduce ourselves and our babies, two of which are named Jackson, although one is spelled J-a-x-s-o-n, the mother notes. I silently question the use of both an x and an s. When it's my turn, I tell the group my name and Sam's, and Miss Randi mentions, "He's so tiny."

I quickly concoct a lie to cover my age flub. "He was a

preemie." Damn. Now I'm making up medical history for the boy. All I wanted was for him to get a little music education!

The class is fun and awkward, and there are plentiful instances of humming, rocking, and spinning. I can tell everyone feels like an idiot, but we also don't want the teacher to notice. So we attempt to sing, and I remain composed even when marching in a circle and singing about goober peas. By the end of the class, I've learned two things: Some people have wretched singing voices but don't seem to care; and I have incredibly veiny legs, as witnessed by the world as we sat crisscross-applesauce on the floor. Sam seemed oblivious to it all and mostly just stared at people with a concerned look on his face. I'm glad I have already instilled in him the gift of suspicion.

149 Days Old

I walk through the neighborhood, Sam strapped facing outward on my chest. I'm trying to savor moments like this, ones I imagined I'd have as a mother. Me connected with my kiddo, literally if not always figuratively. The care of Sam when I'm not at work weighs heavier than the growing boy hanging off my body. I tick through the possibilities: Convince my mom that other people's parents watch their grandkids full-time; endure a painful round of potentially fruitless nanny interviews; or spend a chunk of Sam's meager college fund to hire a company, which still won't exempt me from having to conduct interviews. There is always plan X: Quit my job and stay home from work. Maybe Righteous Latte Love Mom was right. Maybe I was meant to do this. But as much as I enjoy walking around the neighborhood with Sam, something about being at home all day every day doesn't feel like the right choice for me. Just because I go to work doesn't mean I'll never get to walk with him; I can do it after work, on the weekends, even before work if I force myself to wake up that early. I'll still nurse him before school, after school, and at bedtime (not to mention a veritable smorgasbord of times during the night). I'll be gone during the day, but he'll still crawl, talk, and walk when I come home, too. Speaking of walking, whom should we encounter once again but the infamous Walking Man. Does he ever stop?

"Hello." He smiles.

"Hello," I greet back.

We both slow down, two lonely daytime souls looking for adult communication. At least that's my take on it.

"Boy, is he getting big."

"You don't have to tell me or my back."

He chuckles. "You go back to school soon?" he asks.

Had I told him I was a teacher? Is the Walking Man omniscient of everyone in the neighborhood? In the world? Is the Walking Man God?

"Less than three weeks," I say, and pout my lips in the way I'm supposed to show I'm sad about it.

"What are you going to do with this guy?" the Walking Man asks, twiddling Sam's toes. I appreciate how he doesn't touch Sam's hands; too often people think they have the right to play with a baby's fingers when I don't know where their hands have been.

"My mom's going to take him part-time, but I'm still searching for someone the rest of the time."

"Have you talked to Maureen?" he asks. He does know everyone, doesn't he?

I shake my head. "Maureen?"

"She lives . . ." He pauses to count. "Seven houses down the block. She runs a day care out of her house. Really nice woman. Retired from teaching five years ago and now has this business."

"Do you happen to know if she's licensed and everything? CPR?" My questions sound preposterous as I ask them, because why would the Walking Man know? But he answers, "Yes, it's a full business. We talked when she set up her corporation. I'm a retired accountant," he asides. Could God really be an ex-accountant? How unassuming. "And yes also to CPR. We took a class together last year through the park district." Naturally.

"Do you know if she has room for another child?" I ask, hope growing inside me.

"I'm sure. She tends to have more kids during the summer while their parents work, and some after-school kids. But why don't we go ask her?"

"Really? Right now?" I'm delighted at the prospect of discovering a hidden day care gem for Sam in my own neighborhood. It all feels too good to be true, which scares the shit out of me. Still, the Walking Man . . .

"Come on," he says, and I follow him up the block to a ranch house with a small porch on which stands a dress-up goose. I tried to convince Zach we needed one on our porch, too, when we first moved to the suburbs, but he was adamantly against it. I decided it was a small war I'd let him win (and a victory I lorded over him for several years after).

The Walking Man rings the doorbell, and after a minute or so a gray-haired but not particularly old woman with a round face and matching round belly answers. She wears an apron over a faded school district T-shirt. "Irving!" she greets the Walking Man with a hug. "You're early for bridge night by about four days." I hear children playing from inside. "Come in. And who's this?"

We step into the foyer, and I realize he doesn't know my name. Or at least I assume he doesn't. "I'm Annie Schwartz-Jensen, and this is my son, Sam. We live a couple blocks away."

"Nice to meet you. I'd shake your hand, but I've got grape jelly all over mine. I was just making lunch."

"Annie was wondering if you have room this fall for part-time day care for Sam," the Walking Man, Irving, tells Maureen.

"I do," she answers cheerfully. "In fact, as of now I only have one baby, about a year, and a two-year-old brother and sister during the day. We would love to add this little guy."

I'm stupefied and unprepared without my list of interview questions, but she doles out plenty of information without me even asking.

"How many naps does he take? I have three cribs set up, each in a separate room. My kids moved away, and I took over their bedrooms. They like to complain about it, but I tell them they'll thank me when they learn what their student loans could have been if I wasn't making the extra money. You'll have to tell me everything: number of naps, when he likes to eat. Are you breast-feeding? Pumping?"

"Yes. Both," I answer, overwhelmed.

"Good for you. I have a nice fridge just for the kids' foods. The only TV is upstairs in my room. We have a swing set in the back-yard and a playroom. I put on lots of classical music, and I like to sing even if I'm not very good. You won't tell your mom, will you, Sam?" she asks him. He kicks wildly and smiles as though excited. "I think you'll like it here, Sam. You'll make some nice friends." Maureen's voice is so sweet, so exactly how I want Sam's caregiver to sound, that I choke out an involuntary sob. "Oh, it'll be okay, honey. He'll be happy, and frankly, when he's older he won't re-member much of his life before he's in school anyway. I worked when my kids were little, and they don't hate me."

I laugh through a sniffle and ask if she has a tissue. She walks me into the kitchen, and I watch three kids playing in her back-yard. We talk through the logistics, times, cost, qualifications. It all feels very reasonable and stress-free. When I get up to leave, I notice the Walking Man is gone. "Where's Irving?" I ask.

"He must have slipped out when we were talking. He can't stop walking for long, can he?" she asks.

"No," I concur.

Maureen and I set up a day next week to test a half-day run-through with Sam. She hugs me good-bye and kisses Sam lightly on the top of the head. Unlike the pictures of the prince and his nanny, I'm not freaked out.

The Walking Man is nowhere in sight as Sam and I make our way home. I'd like to pretend that I imagined him, as though he were a guardian angel or, yes, even God leading me and Sam to the right place. Or maybe he's just a really nice guy who likes to walk a lot, and I was at the right place at the right time.

Either way, I'm one step closer to going back to work.

150 Days Old

Today was a triple drive-thru kind of day. Sam did not want to take a nap, and I was too sad to be at home. Every empty, sunny spot on the floor reminded me of Doogan. I keep finding catnip pillows tucked between couch cushions, behind doors, under the bed. His hairs continue to appear in my cereal bowls. It's too much, so Sam and I are out for a drive.

After a drive-thru donut breakfast, Sam falls asleep in the car and I get myself lost in the back roads of Northern Illinois. It's hard to believe that this is still considered the suburbs of Chicago, because there is nary a skyscraper in sight, and all roads lead to farmland.

A multitude of turns later, we end up at the Volo Auto Museum. Sam awakens when I shut off the engine, and I nurse him in the front seat without a cover. No one walks by the car, and his head does a nice job of protecting my breast from possible scandal. Even though I'm tired, even though I'm sad, I feel a modicum of pride at this moment. Here we are, mother and son, out on the (small) town, without the need for bottles or packed lunches, just a boy and his trusty boob, a woman and her trusty strawberry-frosted donut with sprinkles. When Sam's through eating, I rest him in the hatchback of our station wagon and adeptly tie the intricate Moby Wrap around and around my body until I have magically created a safe haven for Sam. I feel another twinge of triumph at how natural it has become to tie Sam against me. His head is at exactly the right height for kissing, and I repeatedly partake of inhaling the fuzziest hairs on the top of his head.

We pay our entrance fee to the auto museum, and as I walk I explain cars to Sam. I tell him his grandpa fixed cars for a living, but his dad has never even changed a flat tire. "You and me will learn how to do that together, Sammy. I want you to have all sorts of useful skills."

It dawns on me that Sam will not always be this little log of a person who can't get anywhere or do anything by himself. Someday, Sam will be able to change a tire. Or cook a gourmet meal. Or fly a spaceship. He has a future.

We laugh as we walk through the hall of famous cars: the Batmobile, the Mystery Machine, Ecto One from *Ghostbusters*. "You'll see those movies when you're a little older, Sam," I tell him. Sam will watch movies.

In other buildings stand rows and rows of classic cars, and I imagine myself tooling around in a 1952 pink convertible. "What do you think of this one, Sam? Too pink? How about this yellow one?"

Someday Sam will drive a car.

I buy a grilled cheese and chips at the museum restaurant. The cashier, an older woman with a gap-toothed grin, asks, "How old?"

"He'll be five months tomorrow," I tell her.

"That's a good age. They're all good ages. Enjoy every minute."

For the first time, I am not annoyed by someone telling me to do so. "I'll try," I agree.

"What's his name?" she asks.

"Sam."

"Short for Samuel? My late husband was a Samuel. What's his middle name?" she asks.

"He doesn't have one," I answer, followed by the obligatory explanation: "I don't have one, and his last name is hyphenated, so we thought we'd keep it simple."

She nods, an appeasing sort of nod, as if she's judging my middle-class white-woman hyphenated-naming ways. I will have to get used to it.

"Well, he can always add one later, if he wants. I always wanted my middle name to be Anastasia. I thought it sounded fancy. Better than Wanda, my real middle name."

"I like the name Wanda," I assure her.

"It's not bad. I was named after my aunt who died right before I was born. My mom was very close to her, so she wanted to give me her name as a memory."

"That's a very nice sentiment," I say.

"I suppose it is. I better get this next customer before he goes hungry. Have a nice visit. Bye, Sam-with-no-middle-name."

Sam and I grab a blanket stored in our trunk for winter emergencies and spread it on the lawn outside of the museum. A young couple sits at a nearby picnic table, and two children play at a playground set up on the grass. Sam fiddles contentedly with his toes while I eat my greasy grilled cheese. When I'm finished, I take out my nursing cover and feed Sam, not necessarily because he's hungry but because it keeps him content. The woman of the couple catches my eye and smiles at me. Again, that pride glows inside of me, as though I'm doing something right.

When Sam and I finish our lunch, we stroll across to the antiques mall on the other side of the museum. It boasts six buildings of antiques, and we wind in and out, Sam snug against my chest, happy to look at the sometimes heirloom, sometimes kitschy, items stuffed into every nook and cranny of space. The floor creaks precariously under my feet as I finger a goofy set of *Wizard of Oz* dolls. Maybe Sam will like the film as I always have, or maybe he'll be terrified like Nora was. I buy a set of the Cowardly Lion, the Tin Man, and the Scarecrow for $35. If he doesn't like them, I can always give them to Nora's daughter. I am certain she will have a daughter someday.

As I pay, I have a similar conversation with this clerk as I had with the restaurant cashier. Maybe they are trained to ask women with babies about their kids' names, but all of a sudden Sam-with-no-middle-name doesn't seem like enough. An idea bubbles into my brain, and by the time I'm strapping Sam into his car seat I'm certain I can convince Zach of the change.

Sam falls asleep immediately in the car, and I smile the entire drive home. I even reward myself with a Heath bar Blizzard from a DQ drive-thru. Any excuse for a Blizzard, really.

Later

I tell Zach about our day over dinner, and I almost have to slap the annoying grin off his face.

"What?" I demand.

"You look happy, is all. It's nice to see you enjoying your maternity leave, especially since it's almost over."

"Don't remind me," I say, and I'm not sure if I do it as a reflexive statement or if I mean it.

"Well, make the most of your last few weeks," he says. "Wizard World is next weekend."

"I know. I'm excited! Even though it's hardly about comics anymore, I still love being amongst all of my kindred nerd spirits. I'm thinking of dressing up Sam."

"Oh yeah? Like who?"

"I'm not sure yet. It has to be somewhat easy, since I have to make it in a week. I'm thinking someone classic, like Superman or Batman. Seeing as he can't even walk and most of his costume will be hidden by the Moby Wrap anyway," I consider.

Zach laughs to himself.

"What? Use your words," I demand.

"This is how I pictured it, you know, having a kid? Going to comic conventions, dressing him up like a nerdling, being happy."

"I like that you pictured what having a kid would be like," I admit.

"Like it enough that you want to jump my bones?"

"Like it enough for you to refer to sex in some way other than that of a fifteen-year-old boy."

"Ouch."

"So I was thinking today—"

"About sex?" Zach asks.

"Is that all you think about? Because that wasn't all you thought about before we had a baby."

"It's not all I think about. I thought I was recognizing a subtle segue."

"No. That was me changing the subject. To Sam's middle name."

"Thwarted again. You're not still pushing for Atreyu, are you?

Because I thought we put the kibosh on that in your second trimester."

"No, I was thinking, though, that maybe we could give Sam a middle name. I'm not married to him not having one, and maybe it would be nice to give him a name that has sentimental value instead of merely sci-fi value."

"Samuel was my great-great-grandfather, and the S is for my dad," Zach reminds me.

"Whatever. Since we have a family name from your side"—I pause to dole out a heaping helping of charming eyelash bats—"we give him the middle name from my side. After, you know, Doogan."

"After the cat? Won't that be a little weird?"

"Doogan can be a human name, too. Like that movie *Max Dugan Returns*."

"I never saw that."

"Me neither. But no one has to know why we gave him the middle name Doogan. Maybe they'll think we named the cat after someone, and we're carrying on the tradition by giving our son the same name. They don't have to know that the someone is actually the cat."

Zach ruminates as he shovels pad thai into his mouth.

"He was a good friend. A great pet. You loved him, too. Can we do it?" I press.

Extra pause.

"You realize you're not allowed to say no, since I'm the one that spewed Sam out of my cooch."

"You're going to hold that over me for a while, aren't you?" Zach asks.

"Every damn day until I die," I confirm.

"Okay. Samuel Doogan Schwartz-Jensen it is. But you have to figure out how we get it on his birth certificate and everything." Zach looks over at Sam, batting a frog toy hanging above him in his bouncer. "Sammy D.," he announces. "I like it."

"So do I," I agree. And my heart feels so full, I can barely swallow.

It should be the norm to wait on baby names.

What if you name your kid at the hospital, and they end up not looking or acting like the name you gave them when they were merely a blob of a person? I can already tell Samuel Doogan is the perfect fit.

To: Annie
From: Louise
Dear Annie,

Sorry about my last email. Sometimes I wish I can delete emails I send, not just ones I receive. Make sure you delete all the horrible ones you get from me, ok? I don't want any of that dark shit coming back to me if I ever try to apply for a new job. Speaking of dark shit, how's your belly button looking? I can't believe mine is going to start spreading again. Will it ever go back to its pre-baby cuteness? That was always my favorite body part: my petite belly button. And my right earlobe. The left one has a beauty mark with a hair sticking out of it.

I've slightly warmed up to the idea of another baby, and that's only because Gertie has been extra cute lately. I'm sure it will pass. Or maybe my baby brain will kick into extra high pregnancy gear, and I won't remember all of my misery anyway.

Do you have time for another mommy date before you go back to work, and I become a bloated toad? Let me know—

Lou

151 Days Old

Sam and I may be on better terms, but he's still a buttwad at night.

I am amazed to learn that there are over four hundred people waiting on the QVC phone lines just to order a velveteen table runner. I hope they don't sell out.

152 Days Old

I spend the week constructing a baby Robin costume, à la Batman and Robin circa the television shows of the 1960s. I found a pair of white baby tights, a green diaper cover (both from the girls' section, but I won't tell if Sam won't), and I'm sewing the red tunic out of felt. I also fabricated a black mask that will probably stay on Sam's face for only 1.3 seconds. As long as it's enough time for a picture I can post on Facebook, I'm happy.

153 Days Old

. . . .

After working on Sam's costume and imagining the never-ending stream of cosplay photos people will be taking of him, I realize that the person holding him will be in the photos, too. Me. And my jiggly stomach that stays put only inside the magical waistband of my yoga pants. But I can't wear yoga pants to a comic book convention. I don't want to look like a dork.

Before I try any of my clothes on, I hit the Spanx drawer. Some people bow down at the altar of Spanx, but my relationship has always been less worship and more acquaintance you smile at when you greet them but give them the finger behind their back after they walk away.

I pull out the biker shorts variety, taupe in color and already eyeing me condescendingly. Wearing underwear (I cannot convince myself to go undieless in Spanx, no matter how many people tell me that it is the norm—I know full well what's about to go down in the cotton-stitched crotch area, and I don't think any amount of hand washing can undo the damage), I step each foot into the leg holes. Down around my ankles, things feel promising. Then I yank the waistband upward. That's when the party begins to stall out. My thighs, which have never been my most problematic areas, turn into fat-dappled sausage meat wrestling with their casing. I tug them up as high as they are willing to go, and I have a sickening dividing line between where the Spanx end and my leg begins. It grows whiter by the millisecond. I can see knee fat. My stomach may look smoother and stay relatively in one place when I walk, but the newly formed belly roll that settles over the top, along with its matching thigh Twinkies, is enough to make any woman look for liposuction Groupons.

Did I mention the sweat? Proving me brilliant for wearing underwear, my vagina is already a good fifteen degrees warmer than its average setting.

I look horrid. I feel even worse. The Spanx are so tight that my thumb can barely squeeze its way into the all-powerful waistband.

The juices continue to stew, and I make a mental note never to touch an already opened package of Spanx at a department store. Not that I will ever touch a pair of Spanx again. What sadistic minion of Satan devised these things? Why am I supposed to be keeping my body still anyway? "You will not oppress me any longer!" I yell at the Spanx, and I grab a pair of nail scissors from my nightstand. The tiny blade is no match for the sinister force of the spandex, but I am determined. Plus, I really have to go to the bathroom now. I hack away, little bits of nylon falling willy-nilly until, finally, relief comes as the waistband sags away from my skin and I'm able to roll the beast off of me.

A red mark is etched into my stomach, but I wear it with pride. I fought a battle, and this is my scar. I am the victor. Until we meet again, Spanx. Until we meet again.

154 Days Old

. . . .

Today I managed to wash and dry one load of laundry, fold it, and put away every last piece. This calls for a chocolate cake shake. I need the extra calories and energy because I've started to store up more breastmilk for Sam when I go to work. The timing of everything is beyond complicated: I feed Sam when he wakes up, I feed Sam when he goes down for his nap. So when do I pump? My best bet is to do it while he's sleeping, but if I just fed him, there isn't anything left to pump. If I wait an hour and I start pumping, I'm guaranteed he's going to wake up early. Maybe the melody of the pump motor wakes him up. Sometimes I swear I can hear the grinding breaths of the pump even when I'm not pumping. I better get used to it. Me and Old Pumper are going to be spending a lot of time together in the coming months in a storage closet. I wish that were as sexy as it sounds.

To: Annie

From: Annika

Hey Annie!

What have you been up to? Isn't your maternity leave almost over? I bet you're going to miss all that free time, sitting on the couch, kissing your baby, and working out. You won't have any time to work out when you go back to school. Hope you don't gain back the baby weight!

You look pretty good for someone who just had a baby.
Almost as good as Gwyneth. If you squint, right? If you
have a chance, let's grab brunch before work and you're
too busy to remember your friends.

Xo,

Annika

Dear Annika,

*You think I'm sitting on my ass all day watching "The View" and
eating Thin Mints while toning my abs?*

*I am with this baby all the time. Every second. I spend at least
35 percent of my time trying to get him to sleep, and when he does—
the time you think I must be fanning myself on my chaise lounge—I
have to be so quiet as not to wake him that I can't do 90 percent of the
things I need to do. Not that I have the energy to do them because I am
up with him every three hours during the night. He is sucking all the
nutrients from my body because not only did I grow this human inside
of me, but I am now giving my body to SUSTAIN HIS LIFE. I'm
losing weight because I can't possibly eat enough to regenerate all of
the calories lost to this person who grows an inch every month. And,
oh, maybe I manage to put in a load of laundry here and there, but
then Sam wakes up and I forget about it and by the time tomorrow rolls
around the wet laundry smells so bad I have to rewash it. This week
I washed the same load of laundry four times.*

*And what do you think I'm doing when he's awake? Setting him
on a bed of homemade blankets while I smile at him and read GOOP?
He will not let me put him down for a second. I take shits while he sucks
on my boob. He needs constant feeding, constant connection, and constant entertainment. We played peekaboo for an hour yesterday.*

And you think all I do is sit on my ass? I haven't sat on my ass since this kid was born.

Don't you have a brunch to go to? I'm sure your ass will have a grand ol' time sitting there. My ass has more important things to do.

—Annie

PS: I look a hell of a lot better than Gwyneth because I am REAL, thank you very much.

To: Annika
From: Annie

Hey Annika,

Sorry, but I'm so busy trying to squeeze in every last minute I have with Sam before I go back to work I probably won't have time to get together.

Talk soon—

Annie

That other letter would have gone over her head anyway.

155 Days Old

Sam made a new friend! I suppose babies don't yet have the ability to make friends. Or do anything much more than roll over at this stage. But I did get together with a mom and baby from his music class, and I think that constitutes friend status.

Sam's new friend is one of the Jacksons (the non-x version), and my new friend is named Katie. They live one town over, and

Jackson is her first child, too. After music class, Katie asked me as I gathered up Sam and put on my shoes if we'd like to go to the park just outside the building. Neither of our sons can do anything at a park aside from flail around in a pile of wood chips, so we found a grassy spot nearby.

"Sam was a preemie?" Katie asks.

The jig is up.

"Not really. I go back to work soon, and I wanted to have the chance to take a music class with Sam before I abandon him completely."

"You're not abandoning him. Unless, of course, you actually are and plan to leave him at home, unsupervised."

"I'll set out some bottles for him. Give him a remote. He'll figure it out," I joke.

"I think it's great that you're going back to work. Sam will see that his mom has a life, too, and learn all about responsibility and money and independence. Eventually, I mean. First they've got to learn how to feed themselves."

"Do you work?" I ask, and then realize the faux pas of such a loaded question. "Of course you work, as a mom, but I just meant do you have another job outside of the house, one that pays even though it's probably a hell of a lot easier than the more important job we're expected to do for free?" I hope that covered my ass.

"I was a school librarian for six years, and I applied to have one year of leave for Jackson. Between you and me, I've had a lot of days where I've questioned that decision. It's a lot easier going to work. But I'm afraid if I go back, I'll regret it. If I stay home, I might regret it, but at least I can hold it over Jackson's head when he's older. 'I left my job for you!' " We laugh.

"I've got a whole speech prepared about the pain he caused me during the birth. I'm saving it for when he's a teenager, and slams his door on me."

Both babies start their huge cries, and Katie and I simultaneously reach into our diaper bags. I pull out my nursing cover, she pulls out a bottle.

I want to ask her why she isn't nursing, but I recognize that's completely obnoxious and judgmental. For all I know, there's pumped breastmilk in that bottle. Or she tried nursing, but it wasn't working. Or she never wanted to nurse to begin with. Seeing as we're hanging out for the first time, I keep my opinionated mouth shut on the matter.

"Won't it be nice when they request food instead of scream for it?" Katie asks.

"When *do* they start talking?" I reply.

"Before a year, I think. At least babble and Mama and Dada. It depends on the kid, though. My sister has one that was talking in complete sentences before she turned two but didn't walk until eighteen months. The other walked at thirteen but barely said a word at two. They all catch up eventually. We hope, at least."

The babies finish eating, and we set them down for a few more minutes while we talk about work, husbands, and where to buy the best yoga pants. Naptime for the boys comes soon, so we pack up and say our good-byes.

"What's your number? We should get together after you go back to work. I'm sure Jackson will miss Sam terribly."

"I know. It's like they've bonded for life."

We type each other's numbers into our phones. I enter her under "Katie Jackson," just in case I forget one or both names. I secretly wonder if we'll really ever get in touch, but it feels good to officially have one new mom friend notched into my belt. Or my stretchy waistband.

156 Days Old

Today is the day we do a run-through at Maureen's day care. I pack up three bottles of breastmilk, six baby blankets, six pacifiers, and eight changes of clothes. He will be gone a maximum of three hours, depending on how long he naps. While he's there, I'll finish his Robin costume and tidy up. Or eat a shit ton of ice cream and cry on the couch. I haven't decided.

I wear Sam in the Moby Wrap but push a stroller in front of me with the overstuffed diaper bag balanced precariously in the seat.

Maureen answers her front door, and immediately my heart starts beating triple time. I am really going to leave my Sammy with a stranger. I can't do this.

But I have to.

I don't have a choice.

No. This is my choice.

I have to convince myself I am making the right one. I just need to make it through this morning, three hours, and I will have my baby back with me and he will be okay.

Maureen cautiously approaches Sam as I untwine him from the wrap. I kiss his head fifty or sixty times, and Maureen tells me, "He'll do great today. So will you."

Damn. How does this woman always know what to say to make me cry?

"Best to unassumingly leave now, Mom, so he senses you are relaxed."

"But I'm not—" I start.

"Say bye-bye, Mom," Maureen coos to Sam.

I resist the urge to tackle Maureen and steal back my baby. Instead, I quietly leave her house and don't look back.

I did not anticipate how absolutely painful it would be to walk three blocks with an empty stroller. I can only imagine what people think as they pass the violently sobbing woman pushing a stroller without a baby. One car actually slows down, but I turn my head away in shame.

Pull your shit together, Annie.

Before I sew, I call Louise.

"Lou, I dropped Sam off at day care for the first time." I sniff pathetically.

"Aw, honey, I know how hard that is. The first time Jupiter's sitter came over, I was still home, and she took Jupiter for a walk. The second she left the house I dumped her purse on the counter and read every receipt she left in her wallet."

"Find anything?"

"Just that she likes to shop at T.J. Maxx. Everything is going to be great, and soon you and Sam won't remember what it was like not to be in day care. Wait—that came out wrong. Hold on—" Louise drops the phone, and I hear her retching over the line. "Sorry. Morning sickness."

"Poor Lou," I offer.

"I better go. I'm gonna puke again."

She doesn't give me a chance to say good-bye, and I'm left on my own.

I plunk a Monkees CD into the stereo, and the joyful pop songs bring a little sunshine as I sew the costume for Sam. I take a shower. I have a snack. And before I can do anything else, the three hours are up. I eagerly drive my empty stroller back to Maureen's house.

She's waiting on the front porch with Sam in her arms, two kids drawing with chalk on her driveway.

"He did great. He took one bottle, a two-hour nap, and I thought I'd wait to feed him since he wasn't crying." Maureen hands Sam to me, and it's like I haven't seen him in weeks. His face looks older, different, and I worry that my days away at work will render him unrecognizable. Do I detect some stubble? Then he nuzzles his head into my shoulder, and he's my Sammy once again.

"Thank you, Maureen. We'll be seeing you again in a couple weeks," I say.

"I look forward to it. Bye, Sam." She waves.

"I'm proud of you, Sam," I tell him as we walk home. "Are you proud of me? You should be. I found you a good day care, and I didn't freak out too badly when you were gone. I did miss you, though," I say, and kiss the top of his head. "You better have missed me."

157 Days Old

The buzz of a Comic Con morning is in the air. Zach and I have been going to different comic book conventions since the first year we met. We have both always loved comics and nerd culture, but in different ways. I read the funnies in the Sunday paper religiously while growing up and bought all of the *Calvin and Hobbes*, *Far Side*, and *FoxTrot* compilations as a teen. Zach was more of a *Spider-Man* kind of kid, and we have boxes of comics from his childhood collection in our crawl space. (I like to threaten to sell the collection when we are destitute. He likes to wax lyrical about handing them down to our children someday and how they'll pay for the kids' college tuitions.) As an undergrad I began reading more subversive, independent, and, admittedly, pornographic comics, and Zach discovered works from Drawn and Quarterly and Fantagraphics, personal or odd or quirky stories much different from his Spidey days. Together, along with our love for science-fiction television shows, Zach and I found the perfect partner in each other. Today our progeny will attend his first comic book convention, and we couldn't be more proud.

Later at the Con

We are sitting in a large room, as though several banquet halls have opened their giant, portable doors to make one great space. There are rows and rows of chairs set up, the expectation being that whoever is at the front of the room on the stage will draw such a hefty crowd as to pack the place. Sadly, this is often not the case. Thanks to overlapping programming or lack of interest based on the wrong target audience, these halls may have only ten to twenty people when there are chairs for two hundred. I feel sad for the celebrities who sign on for these events; it must be mortifying to be on a stage and look out at a spotty sea of semiadmirers. Today's victim is one Jason Priestley, with probably zero connection to sci-fi, comics, or fantasy, unless you count the fantasies I had about Brandon Walsh back in 1990 when *Beverly Hills, 90210* began (I quickly moved on to bad boy Dylan, played by Luke Perry, whom Zach and I met two years ago at a different con). The meager audience reflects the disconnect, and Zach and I choose a prime seat in the back row in case Sam decides to be vocal at an inappropriate time. He's already beginning to fuss, so I dig for the nursing cover. "Shit!" I exclaim as I remember I left it in the dryer after a particularly nasty spit-up incident. Sam's complaints grow increasingly louder, so as subtle as I can be, I whip out the ol' boob and stick him on. We're way in the back, so I figure no one will see. But instead of Jason Priestley appearing from a magic door somewhere behind the stage, Mr. Priestley saunters in through the regular, pedestrian door behind us, the very same door through which we entered. I turn around and watch him walking in, surveying the desolate landscape. I can only imagine the dialogue in his head: *Where the fuck is everyone? Thank God I'm getting paid for this. I hope I don't miss my hockey game.*

He walks toward the chairs, down the aisle on which I sit while nursing my baby. As he passes me, he turns his head, and we make eye contact. Mr. Priestley gives a nod of acknowledgment and moves toward the stage. I am giddy at the fact that Jason Priestley, *Brandon Fucking Walsh*, nodded at me. And then I realize that he did so with my boob hanging out in the open. Jason Priestley saw a significant chunk of my breast. This is not exactly how twelve-year-old me imagined my boobs would play out in a scenario with Mr. Priestley.

That Night

We're back home from the con. What a day! I never envisioned myself sitting on a hard convention center floor breastfeeding a baby while three people dressed as the Joker eat lunch on my right side and the Justice League rests to my left. The buxom Wonder Woman was showing more boob than I was.

During Sam's awake period, Zach toted him around face-out so his Robin costume was on full display. We were stopped over and over by people wanting to take his picture. Zach and I loved the attention being on Sam, and I felt like a worthy seamstress. I Google "Baby Robin" in the past twenty-four hours, and I find a close-up of Sam on a cosplay website! (Note to self: Get a manicure the next time you know your hands are going to be widely photographed holding an adorable baby. Has QVC taught you nothing? Also, your stomach doesn't look abnormal. Suck it, Spanx!)

Sam sleeps soundly in his crib, and Zach and I happily climb into bed. "Today was pretty awesome," he enthuses. "Maybe next summer we take him to San Diego for the big Comic-Con."

"By next summer he'll be walking and probably a holy terror," I warn. "Let's just focus on the success of today."

On the bed, cuddling leads to kissing. I try, but I'm still not quite there with the whole "having sex postbaby" thing. However, the day's events, combined with a mental note stored away from a screaming kid-call with Fern, make me propose, "Why don't we try a little role-playing?"

Zach stops kissing my neck and perks up. "Like *Dungeons and Dragons*?" he asks.

"No!" I guffaw. "Like, we pretend to be other people having sex."

"Oooh—a little fantasy fondling. I like it."

"Yes. Especially without the dorky commentary. So who should we be?" I ruminate for a minute. I know whom I've fantasized about when there isn't another actual person involved, but as much as I'd like to, I don't think I can bend time and space enough to envision Zach as Chris Hemsworth as Thor. Plus, if we did that, then I'd have to be the dud Natalie Portman character. Not a turn-on.

"What about Xena and Hercules?" Zach suggests.

I laugh at his antiquated and hilarious reference, which is current again thanks to reruns on MeTV. "Maybe. But wasn't Xena a lesbian?" I ask.

"I think she was bisexual." Zach nods.

"I don't know. I don't think I can make those high-pitched warrior cries that she does. Plus, it's kind of campy."

"Isn't all role-playing campy?" Zach asks. We are most definitely out of our comfort zone with the task at hand.

"No. It could be broody, like vampire role-playing, or violent, which we aren't doing because I'd totally kick your ass—" Zach starts to protest but realizes I'm right and allows me to continue. "Or historical?"

"Historical? Like, you can be Mary Todd Lincoln, and I'll be Honest Abe?"

"Hot stuff, Zach. You really know how to get a gal's vagina blood pumping." Which I realize makes it sound like I'm talking about my period. "How inept are we? At this rate, I'm wondering how we managed to get pregnant in the first place," I say.

"Maybe we're overthinking it. What do we love? Nerd stuff. So let's have nerd sex. You be Cylon Number Six, and I'll be Gaius Baltar."

Zach's *Battlestar Galactica* reference is spot-on, except that Cylon Number Six is a wicked babe and Gaius Baltar is a simpering, traitorous, self-obsessed prat. "You get the way better deal in that scenario. Let's pick a different *Battlestar* couple. How about Starbuck and Apollo?" I've always harbored a secret crush on the actor who plays the pilot Apollo. Zach, however, finds fault with my choice of Starbuck.

"I think she'd be scary to have sex with. Like, maybe she'd hurt me."

"But you'd enjoy that if you were Apollo." I'm definitely warming to the prospect of having sex with Zach as Apollo, but I don't know if I could do the role of Starbuck justice.

"I've got it," Zach announces. "Athena and Helo!"

I realize that anyone listening in on our role-playing sex conversation would think we were two of the dorkiest people alive, so thankfully we get to, as they say, keep it in the bedroom. Helo's a good-looking, moral character, albeit not the brightest, who is in love with Athena, also good-looking and a pilot who just happens to be a human-engineered Cylon. Plus, they have a child together.

"I suppose it could work. Let's try it. Helo and Athena it is. Or, we are, I should say. Do we dress up?" I ask. Most characters spend a large portion of time on *Battlestar Galactica* in tank tops and cargo pants, of which Zach and I both have from years of being *Battlestar* characters at Halloween parties. We could fudge some things together.

"I'd rather we just dress down, if you know what I mean." Zach joggles his eyebrows.

"I'm going to pretend Helo said that, which makes it slightly less dorky."

"Whatever you say, Athena."

The next twenty minutes are spent tweaking *Battlestar Galactica* quotes into ridiculous things like "This is my penis. Actual," and "We have penis contact," then laughing uncontrollably. While it doesn't end up being the sexiest, most passionate lovemaking we've ever had, it certainly does take my out-of-shape Kegel muscles and scabby nipple off the forefront of my mind. And I manage to have an orgasm (or two) in the process. So say we all!

158 Days Old

. . . .

To: Fern

From: Annie

I wanted to let you know that I took your advice and tried role-playing with Zach. It worked! I mean, it made me not so self-conscious.

I'm thinking about you and hope you can write or call soon and let me know how things are going with you and Adam. I'm crossing my fingers for you.

Love,

Annie

159 Days Old

My mom calls to remind me she's returning in one week.

"How can I forget, Ma. I've been scratching away the days onto my headboard."

"I look forward to seeing you, too," she gushes.

"So we'll do a run-through when you get back to see how you'll do with Sam. He's a different person than when you left. You won't even recognize him," I say.

"Are you implying he won't recognize *me*? Are you punishing me for being gone so long? Because I don't feel guilty."

By the sound of her voice, she does, but I don't press the matter. "He'll know it's you by your smell. Maybe. Just come home, Ma."

"See you soon."

Eight days and counting.

160 Days Old

· ·

I am getting better at pumping. I can now hold both suckers in place with my forearm while using my other hand to do useful things like changing the channel and flipping the pages of a book (current read: issue #16 of *Buffy* Season 10 comic). Only once did the maneuver backfire, and I spilled about an ounce of milk on my bedspread. "Motherfucker!" I yelled. "I just lost some liquid gold!" No one was around to hear me except my buddies on QVC. I'm sure they sympathized.

To: Louise
From: Annie
Dear Lou,

How are you feeling? Are you ready to go back to work? Are you going to take any maternity leave with the next one? Maybe you can make it to the end of the school year and have the baby right when school lets out. You can totally mess with the students; pretend you never had the other baby and you've been pregnant for two years! Scare the shit out of them. I think pregnant teachers are the best form of birth control. Remember when you threw up in a garbage can in front of your class? Classic.

I'm a veritable dairy store. We had to ask our next door neighbors if we could use the deep freezer in their garage to store my milk because our kitchen freezer is already full. I hope one of their teenage sons doesn't wake up in the middle of the night craving an ice cream bar and open up a bag of breastmilk by mistake.

See you at Institute Day NEXT WEEK (Holy shit!!!!!)!

♥ Annie

161 Days Old

I have put it off long enough: It is time to try on my work clothes and see if they fit. Yoga pants and summer stretchy shorts easily hid the fact that I may need an entirely new wardrobe. I've already resigned myself to the truth that I will not be wearing any button-down shirts until I stop breastfeeding and my boobs go down to a less bulbous size. I also realize I will need some seriously padded nursing bras; the last thing I want to do is walk into a classroom filled with middle school boys as I sport gigantic boobs and pump-elongated nipples.

I place Sam on a baby blanket inside of my small walk-in closet. Outside, a boombox plays another mix from college, currently on Guided by Voices' "Echos Myron." "You know," I tell Sam, "this closet felt a lot bigger when we first moved in. You should have seen our apartment in Chicago. We had the tiniest closets."

I sift through my rack of clothes and periodically try on a shirt. When it fits, I place it to the left. When it doesn't, it goes on a spot to the right. "We lived on the third floor, it was the top floor, and we had to carry all of our groceries up the stairs and our garbage down the stairs. It was always a little suspenseful—would the garbage bag leak? Would it slip out of our hands and tumble down three flights of stairs?" Sam listens intently. "Doogan lived there with us, and once we had mice in the apartment, which sounds gross but is way better than rats. That happened to Aunt Nora once." Sam exhales noisily. "I know, right? One day I was watching TV on my bed. That was all we could fit into our bedroom: a double bed and a tiny dresser with a TV on top. Doogan had all manner of toys, some that looked like little realistic mice." Sam coos. "You see where I'm going with this. So Doogan is bopping what I thought was a toy mouse all over the place between his paws, and he jumps up onto the bed with his toy mouse. But it wasn't a toy mouse at all. It was a baby mouse! I screamed and whipped my covers up, so the baby mouse flew up into the air and landed somewhere on the floor. Lucky your dad was home. He caught the baby mouse under a bowl and brought him outside. Where he was probably instantly devoured by rats."

I look at Sam, and he smiles at me. I'm encouraged. "Want to hear another mouse story? This one is from college, where I lived in a total dump with two girlfriends. I couldn't sleep one night, so in the dark I got up and started looking for earplugs to help. I threw textbooks around on my floor, went into the bathroom, and finally found a pair. When I went back into my bedroom, I turned on the lights to clean up the books and there, underneath a giant physics volume, were two mouse legs sticking out, feet pointing up to the ceiling. I had thrown a book randomly and killed a mouse!" Sam reacts with a squeal. "Can you believe it? I'm still amazed. My roommate, Annika, I think I may have told you about her—the one that liked canned cheese—she got rid of it for me. College roommates are awesome. You'll see."

For the rest of the hour, I try on clothes and regale my son with college stories. He is a captive audience. It's the first occasion we spend together where I don't feel like I'm alone.

162 Days Old

Sam and I spend the day packing up his newborn-sized clothes into storage bins and listening to the Monkees.

The opening piano notes of "Daydream Believer" tinkle from the stereo. When the dulcet sounds of Davy Jones's voice begin singing, I join in. Sam watches. His eyes are still blue, but I can see they're similar in shape to mine. He looks awfully sweet when he's not torturing me.

The song's chorus swells, "Cheer up, sleepy Jean . . . ," and I lift Sam off the floor. We dance around his bedroom, Sam's head tucked into my neck. Every once in a while he leans out to look at my face. I kiss his nose and laugh, amazed that here I am dancing with Sam—not crying, not wondering what to do, not cursing him with sleeplessness.

"We've got this, Sam," I whisper to him. "We've got this."

163 Days Old

Zach and I had sex again tonight.

"What about Buffy and Angel?" is his initial idea for a role-play.

"What? I don't want to have sex with Angel. If I'm going to be Buffy, you're going to be Spike," I say.

"Really? I always thought Angel was her one true love."

"You're crazy. Spike was funnier. And more passionate. Angel was like a stone statue. Nice guy, but I'd choose Spike over him any day."

"How about any night?" Zach says as he nips at my neck. "I've got a stake for you."

"I'll be the one to dole out the banter, thank you," I tell him, and Buffy and Spike get naked.

164 Days Old

Ack! The company that makes my favorite nursing bra has gone out of business! The bras are now available only on the black market of Canada. I called a Canadian bra store and actually had an employee tell me she couldn't ship to the United States. It's a conspiracy! You'd think all my support of *Degrassi High* lo these many years would count for something.

Trying to find a new bra, I discover something extraordinary: My zit, the one that colonized onto my chest for the last five months, is gone. Packed and moved away to greener pastures. Is it weird that I might miss it a little?

To: Annie

From: Fern

Annie,

So sorry I haven't been in touch. After I talked to you, I confronted Adam about the text. Things got messy, and there was a lot of yelling, then silence, then more yelling. Thankfully we're both committed to trying couples therapy and making things work. Not just for the kids, but for us, too. I'll fill you in more when I get a second.

Good luck when you go back to work! Kick it in the ass! Thanks for listening and for being such a good friend.

Love,

Fern

I don't know if this means Adam cheated or not. Or if that is what matters, if Fern and Adam are willing to work on it. I snuggle Zach a little closer at bedtime and wish on a star for my friend.

165 Days Old

Today I take Sam to my school to see what shape my classroom is in. They're always doing things over the summer that make it look like a poltergeist came in and stacked up the chairs in the most precarious way possible.

I run into my favorite custodian, Stanley, who disinfects my classroom in exchange for freshly baked chocolate-chip cookies whenever I panic when a student coughs. It's a good deal. He helps me take down the mounds of chairs and desks and place them into a U shape for the beginning of the school year. Sam rides calmly in a wrap on my chest as we do this.

"You should wear him on you during the school year. He's so good," Stanley suggests.

"Yeah, I don't know how good he'd be for an entire day."

"You're going to miss him?" Stanley asks.

I lean down and inhale Sam's baby scent. I've spent a lot of time thinking toward the future when I would gain some semblance of myself back, but now I'm definitely feeling, "Yes. I'm going to miss him." I kiss Sam's head several times before returning to furniture moving. Maybe I *could* bring him to work with me. There are those pictures on Tumblr of Licia Ronzulli, a member of the European Parliament, who brings her daughter to work with her, and she looks so good while doing it. I'm guessing the European Parliament is a lot easier to handle than eighty thirteen-year-olds.

166 Days Old

. . . .

I finally found the perfect lullaby for Sam. I remember most of the words, it's sweet, and it's even a little inspirational: "Rainbow Connection" from *The Muppet Movie*. It's like taking a little piece of my childhood and inserting it into Sam's. He loves it. Admittedly, I cried the first time I sang it to him. But I have every night for the rest of his life to perfect it.

167 Days Old

. . . .

Nora and her husband, Eddie, bring over a pizza and some movies. Since I go back to work next week, I get to choose the films. I select a nostalgic double feature of *The Last Unicorn* and *The NeverEnding Story*. Sam is upstairs in bed, and the adults in the house are drinking beer and enjoying watching a boy warrior and his horse named Artax. Nora and I drive the husbands crazy by reciting every line verbatim.

"You should have seen Annie last year at Comic-Con when she got to meet that guy." Zach points to the screen at child actor Noah Hathaway, now a rather lovely, if still diminutive, man covered in tattoos.

"It was thirty years in the making! I'm not supposed to freak out?" I protest. "He was so sweet." I recount the story they've already heard a thousand times. "I asked if we could record him saying, 'Annie, would you hunt the purple buffalo with me?' And he did! He had his arm around me. It was one of the most romantic moments of my life."

"Thanks for that," Zach interjects. "I thought she might go home with the guy," he admits.

"I wouldn't. I don't think. It's not like he asked. Do you think he liked me?" I gush.

We laugh loudly and then shush each other lest we wake up Sam.

In the middle of *The Last Unicorn*, Zach snoring on the couch, Nora elbows Eddie. "I want to tell them."

"I thought we said we'd wait," Eddie whispers unnecessarily. I can hear every word they're saying.

"You two have all the subtlety of a tornado siren. What do you want to tell me?"

"I'm pregnant!" Nora whisper-yells.

"Don't you mean *we're* pregnant?" Eddie asks.

"Who are you kidding? If this thing works, I'm the one getting fat and pushing a human being the size of an American Girl doll out of my cooter." Nora looks at me and reiterates, "I'm pregnant, Annie."

I hug her, and inside I hope and pray this is the one that will stick around to become the daughter or son Nora so deserves.

Zach pops up from his late-night nap on the couch. "Is it over? Are you crying because it's over?" I don't realize I'm crying, but I am. Making babies is magical, mysterious, terrifying, gratifying, and all-encompassing. I can't wait for Nora to experience every bit of it.

Later That Night

Zach and I are in bed when he proposes, "How about we play a little *NeverEnding Story?*"

"Are you talking sexy playing?" I clarify.

"Yes," he answers, stretching the word out like the giant turtle from the film, Morla, the Ancient One.

"Stop. That's creepy. And you do realize there is no romantic plot in that film?"

"You were hot for that kid," he notes.

"When I *was* a kid," I acknowledge.

"Come on. I saw the way you looked at him at Comic-Con last year. I'll be him. And you be . . ." Zach thinks on it.

"Don't you dare say the Childlike Empress. Because we are not going there."

"Yeah. I guess I didn't think this one through," Zach admits. "So who do you want to be tonight?"

I ruminate for a moment and then suggest, "How about Annie and Zach? Or is that too weird?"

"I seem to recall Annie and Zach being way hotter at one point than any fictional couple," Zach butters me up. "Remember that one time on a road trip near Prairie Dog Town—"

"Less talk, Zach. More kissing," I command.

And our imaginary soundtrack swells in the background.

168 Days Old

· ·

My mom is finally home from her trip, and she brings Sam the entire inventory of San Francisco's baby t-shirt line.

"I don't think he'll even be this size for the number of days there are t-shirts," I tell her.

"So I'll change him multiple times a day," she explains. "You won't be here to stop me anyway."

"Ma! What kind of thing is that to say? You know I'm freaked out about going back to work in three days. You don't have to scare me with your psycho grandma threats."

"It was one threat. Hardly a threat. They're just t-shirts. It's not like I'm going to slip chicken soup into his bottles to help him sleep during the night." She smiles slyly.

"You wouldn't," I challenge her.

"I don't think I will. Not consciously, at least," she goads.

"Mom! Please don't make me have to fire you."

"You have to pay someone to fire them," she notes.

"You are being paid in baby kisses and dirty diapers. Besides, you're the one who's always telling me solemn tales of your friends where daughters-in-law never let them spend a single moment alone with their grandbabies. Think of how many moments I'm gifting to you."

"Are you going to keep talking, or are you going to go to work?"

In order to make this a true trial run, and not me just running errands around town and secretly spying on my mom with a pair of never-used binoculars I found in our crawl space, I'm going into my classroom today to set things up, including my pumping closet, which I will also be using for the first time.

My car is packed with folders, papers, snacks, and my pump bag. The fridge is stocked with cold cuts for Mom, along with thawing packets of breastmilk. The kitchen counter is lined with clean bottles, and the refrigerator is covered with neatly typed instructions for everything from feeding to changing to naptime to playtime.

"Call if you have any questions. Really. You won't be bothering me," I remind my mom for the fiftieth time.

"Sam and I are ready, Annie. And so are you. Go have yourself a nice day at work."

I take several starting breaths, searching for one more instruction or warning, but none materialize. I guess it is time to leave.

"I love you," I say to Sam, and kiss his forehead, each cheek, rubberband wrists, and his forehead again.

"Love you, too, honey," my mom says. "Now leave."

"Bye-bye." I wave while backing out the door. Taking deep breaths, I manage not to cry the entire ride to work. In fact, I sometimes manage to enjoy the freedom of driving without having to turn into a contortionist to settle Sam in the backseat.

On the way to my classroom, I run into several colleagues, and we exchange hugs, summer stories, and gossip about who's dating, who's hired, and who left unexpectedly. I barely have time to hang up my bulletin board when it's time to pump.

The first thing I do is tack up a notice I created on the computer and laminated, a smiley clock surrounded by the line

"Privacy needed—Please come back in ten minutes." I don't know if that will encourage too many questions from my students, but even if it inspires a discussion about pumping breastmilk, at least I'm teaching the kids something. Plus, there's this handy slide lock Stanley installed on the inside of the door for me.

I prop up my iPad and play some footage I have of Sam attempting to raise his head during tummy time. Already that seems like so long ago. *My big boy,* I think, and the happy feeling inspires a healthy amount of pumped milk.

When I finish, I snap my nursing bra shut and place the pumped milk into a small cooler bag. I wind up the pump tubes, and I hear a quiet knock resounding through the small closet.

"Annie?" a voice sneaks under the door, and I recognize it as my librarian friend, Devin.

"Can you have lunch?" she asks.

I open the door and shut off the closet light. "Not today. I have to get home. My mom is watching Sam solo for the first time."

"For a second I thought you meant his name was 'Sam Solo.'" Devin chuckles.

"That would have made sense in our house. But actually, it's Sam Doogan."

"Like your cat? Sweet." Devin smiles.

"Yeah. I better get going. I'm afraid I'll get home and find that my mom cut Sam's hair and is feeding him a bagel."

"Good luck," Devin offers.

The morning flies by, and when I get home my mom is knitting on the couch and watching *Out of Africa,* one of her favorites.

"How did it go?" she whispers.

"Fine. How did it go here?" I ask.

"He was perfect. Took the bottle well. He didn't fall asleep right away, but he only fussed for a minute or two. And now he's sleeping."

"Well, okay, then." I nod, partially with relief and just a tiny bit with disappointment. It would be nice if Sam raised a little hell while I was away. Just a drop. But I remember to count my blessings and remind myself that if he is happy, then I should be happy.

I take off my shoes and park myself on the couch next to my mom. I take a moment to relax before I sit up. "You didn't give him any chicken soup, did you?"

Mom winks.

169 Days Old

I planned to spend one of my last days on maternity leave filling out the glaringly blank pages of Sam's baby book. Do I really want to relive his birth? The sleepless nights? The questionable mental health moments? Maybe I'll open it again in a year or two when I've forgotten everything. It's not like Sam is going to care about the first time he held up his head. Or laughed. Or lost his (shudder) belly button crud.

As I ponder whether this will top off my list of parenting flubs, a package arrives. It's small, postmarked from Sweden, and addressed to Sam. Inside is a crocheted R2D2 hat and a note from Annika.

Needed to get away for a bit, so I took off for Sweden. Met a lovely man on the plane. Will tell you all about him when I get home. I knitted this along the way. I miss you.

   Love, Annika

The R2D2 cap is about ten sizes too big for Sam, but I'll save it for when he's older. I'll tell him his wacky aunt Annika made it for him. She'll be the aunt he hears lots of stories about but rarely sees. And she always sends the best gifts.

FACEBOOK STATUS

I go back to work tomorrow! So happy and so sad all at the same time. Definitely a double-dessert kind of day.

I can't believe how many people liked and commented on my Facebook status. All of the high school Facebook friends came out of the woodwork again. It's amazing how many women do this: birth a baby and then go back to work. And they all are so encouraging about it:

You'll be so happy you did.
Best decision I ever made.
The time you have together will be all the more special.

Only one person said, "You'll quit next year." It was some girl I had gym class with who keeps posting bikini selfies of her new boobs. Delete and unfriend.

I read the encouraging comments again. I hope they're right. I hope I made the right choice.

170 Days Old

. . . .

I talked to Sam's doctor today. Even though he is a few weeks shy of six months, she okayed him starting on solids. I wanted to be the one to give him his first taste of rice cereal before I go back to work. I'm afraid of missing out on firsts: first words, first crawling, first steps . . . Zach made the argument that when I experience them, they'll still be firsts for me, but that's not the same thing. Zach doesn't get it. I think there is something very inherently different between the way men and women deal with children. Or maybe it's just me and Zach. But things don't seem as big of a deal to him—the good or the bad. Earlier, Zach didn't understand how I could feel hatred toward Sam. Now, he can't comprehend why I don't want to miss the milestones. Is it different in a house with two Mimis? Am I being overly sentimental?

As I place Sam in his high chair for the first time, a gift from my mom when he was born, I stifle tears at the sight of my big boy sitting up, waiting to be fed. The cereal is liquid mush and doesn't smell very good, but I bought the organic, brown rice kind to start Sam on a road to healthy eating. Maybe the white rice smells better.

I take the tiniest spoonful and place it to Sam's lips, lips that undeniably look like miniature versions of mine: the same small bow on top and full, round bottom lip. He rumples his brow as though trying to make a decision on this new sensation. The food goes in, the food dribbles out, and we repeat for the next ten minutes until Sam gets cranky.

I remove him from his high chair, fumbling with the lock on the sliding tray. "Don't worry, Sammy!" I tell him. "I'll get you out." Eventually I manage to disengage the mechanism, and I lift Sam into my arms. He's too big now to dangle over my shoulder, but he clings to my shirt. I never imagined anything could feel so good.

Today is our last day home together, so I strap him into the Moby Wrap and set out for a long walk. It's a glorious day, with scant humidity, a blue sky freckled with animal-shaped clouds, and a breeze to wick away my hormonal sweat.

Several blocks in, we meet the Walking Man, Irving, and we stop to chat.

"Maureen tells me she's got a new friend." He twiddles Sam's toes.

"Thank you so much for introducing me to her. I think it's going to work out really well."

"Count on it," the retired accountant quips. "Onward!" he announces, finger in the air, and he's off again.

I do enjoy running into the Walking Man, but I'm a tad disappointed that he wasn't some friendly apparition brought to earth to lead me to day care.

I walk and walk until I reach the coffee shop. I'm prepared with an arsenal of witty comebacks for the stay-at-home-mom pusher, but she and her brood are nowhere to be seen. Probably for the better. I wouldn't want to get arrested the day before I go back to work. The judge would side with me, right?

I order an iced coffee, and the woman behind the counter

gushes, "He is so adorable. Oh, my gosh! Jenna, look." She draws over the barista. "Isn't he the cutest little guy you've ever seen?" The two perky coffee purveyors *ooh* and *ahh* over the baby boy strapped to my chest. "He looks just like her, doesn't he?" Jenna asks her coworker. "He looks just like you," she repeats to me.

A customer lines up behind me, and I move aside to wait for my drink. When my name is called, I gather the cool beverage in my hands like a warm drink on a brisk fall day. My body is filled with a new kind of warmth. And I owe it all to this boy I wear over my heart, my son, the one who looks just like me.

Acknowledgments

This book wouldn't exist without the brilliant idea from Jean Feiwel that reawakened my writing joy. Thank you to Liz Szabla, my friend and editor for six (!) novels, and my agent, Rosemary Stimola, for making this happen and riding along for the sleep-deprived journey. Thank you to Brendan Deneen and Nicole Sohl at Macmillan Entertainment, and to everyone at Macmillan, old and new, as we grow up together.

To my mom friends, Lillian Johnston, Tracy Heins Lehman, Ali Kafcas, Emily Keeter, Nina Hess, and Jen Perlis-Glassman, thanks for your invaluable sanity support; and to my non-mom friends, Katie Nelson, Beth Rubin, and Liz Mason, thank you for taking me away from the kids occasionally. And special thanks to my D&D friends—Andrew, Brian, Jake, John, and Mike—for bringing magic and mayhem to my suburban mom existence.

Thank you to all of my Facebook friends, many of whom I barely knew in high school but who offer so much insight and camaraderie in parenthood. To Jim Klise, my writing friend and bagel partner. To Gabrielle Zevin and Mary Hogan, for the excellent advice. To Joyce Buckley, for the best nursing cover ever. To my sister, cousins, aunts, uncles, parents, and in-laws, for the unconditional support.

Thank you to the Warren Newport Public Library and the Round Lake Area Public Library, for providing free and comfortable writing spaces for a mom who needed to get out of the house. Thank you to our veterinarians, Dr. Kathy Berman, who took care of our cat long ago, and Dr. Katie Dymek, for bringing his life to such a humane end. To the Kalinowskis, for being the best neighbors ever. To Laura, Maria, Marta, and Cheli, for the advice and ears and being the only people on the planet who make me feel at all glamorous.

Special thanks to all of the health-care professionals who helped me on my long and complicated road to becoming a mom: Debi Lesnick, Gaye Koconis, and Dr. Pamela Goodwin for the births of my two children, and Dr. Ouyang and Dr. Horton for your unbelievable kindness, compassion, and care. To Dr. Marilyn Zwirn, our most trusted pediatrician. And to Jeanne Cygnus, who changed my life and the lives of my children with her immeasurable and invaluable knowledge of breastfeeding.

And, most important, thank you to Matt, Romy, and Dean. Without you three, I would not hold the most important title on my CV: Mom. I love you more than *Battlestar Galactica*, *Buffy*, and Disney World combined.

Discussion Questions

Maternity Leave is categorized as realistic fiction. What about Annie's situation did you find relatable? Were there any situations or emotions that hit too close to home?

Maternity Leave opens with a graphic and hilarious birth scene. After the physical and emotional roller coaster of giving birth, are there memories that make you laugh?

The paths of Doogan and Sam intersect. Do you see similarities in how Annie dealt with her pet and her son? In what ways do you treat your pets differently/better than your children?

Zach is a somewhat oblivious husband. Why do you think men are often portrayed as less capable in child rearing? Is Zach's level of cluelessness similar or different to your own experiences with partners during child rearing?

Annie struggled with breastfeeding but felt very strongly about persevering. Was there anything you felt you had to do with your children, even if it killed you? Was it worth it?

The grandparent name game can be a source of derision for some families. How do you think it was handled in *Maternity Leave*? Was it a sore spot in your families?

What do you think of the book's cover? Which symbol represents your experience best?

Annie feels a lot of guilt throughout the book, often feeling like a bad mom. Do you think society sets up high expectations for new moms? What way could we help new moms feel successful?

Annie and Zach's sex life becomes far more complicated once baby Sam arrives. What do you think of Annie putting off sex for a while? What do you think of her role-playing solution? Depending on your book group, feel free to discuss how you dealt with the changes and challenges of sex after a baby.

Annie used QVC to help cope with the insanity of middle-of-the-night feedings. What tools did you use to make it through those trying times?

The novel ends somewhat neatly, although life with a baby is never neat. Would you have liked a more realistic, messier ending? Is it okay to have a happy ending in fiction in order to leave the reader on an emotional high?

When Annie's maternity leave nears its end, she finds it harder to leave Sam than she thought. Could you relate to these feelings? How did you make your decision to stay home or return to work?